MW01168839

H. P. Lovecraft

Twayne's United States Authors Series

Warren French, Editor

University of Wales, Swansea

TUSAS 549

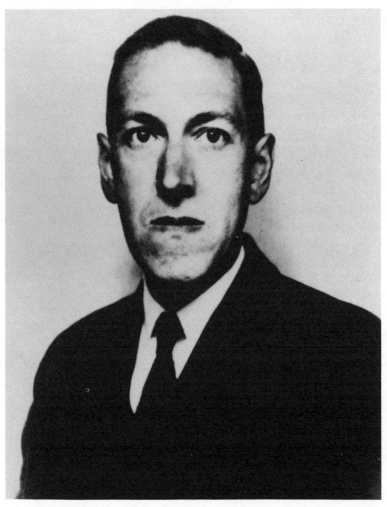

H. P. LOVECRAFT

Photograph courtesy of Lucius B. Truesdell/Arkham House.

H. P. Lovecraft

by Peter Cannon

Twayne Publishers
A Division of G. K. Hall & Co. • *Boston*

H. P. Lovecraft
Peter Cannon

Copyright 1989 by G. K. Hall & Co.
All rights reserved.
Published by Twayne Publishers
A Division of G. K. Hall & Co.
70 Lincoln Street
Boston, Massachusetts 02111

Copyediting supervised by Barbara Sutton
Book production by Gabrielle B. McDonald
Book design by Barbara Anderson

Typeset in 11 pt. Garamond
by Huron Valley Graphics, Inc., Ann Arbor, Michigan

Printed on permanent/durable acid-free paper
and bound in the United States of America

Library of Congress Cataloging-in-Publication Data

Cannon, P. H. (Peter H.)
   H.P. Lovecraft.

   (Twayne's United States authors series ; TUSAS 549)
   Bibliography: p.
   Includes index.
   1. Lovecraft, H. P. (Howard Phillips), 1890–1937—
Criticism and interpretation.   2. Fantastic fiction,
American—History and criticism.   3. Horror tales,
American—History and criticism.   I. Title.   II. Series.
PS3523.0833Z566 1989   813'.52   88-34753
ISBN 0-8057-7539-0 (alk. paper)

Contents

About the Author
Editor's Foreword
Preface
Chronology

Chapter One
Literary Outsider   1

Chapter Two
Dawn   15

Chapter Three
Kingsport and Arkham   35

Chapter Four
Castles, Garrets, and Tombs   45

Chapter Five
New York   55

Chapter Six
Providence and Boston   63

Chapter Seven
New England Dream-Quests   75

Chapter Eight
Cosmic Backwaters   82

Chapter Nine
Beyond New England   97

Chapter Ten
Sunset   112

Chapter Eleven
Critical Reputation   123

Notes and References   127
Selected Bibliography   140
Index   146

About the Author

Introduced at an impressionable age to the horror fiction of H. P. Lovecraft, Peter Cannon has dedicated himself to the study of Lovecraft's life and work since his freshman year at Stanford University. Drawn to Lovecraft's native Providence, Rhode Island, Cannon received his M.A. in English from Brown University. His articles have appeared in such journals as *Lovecraft Studies, Crypt of Cthulhu, Dagon, Nyctalops, Twilight Zone,* and the *Baker Street Journal.* His fiction has been published in *Eldritch Tales, Spectral Tales,* and *Tales of Lovecraftian Horror.* In 1984 Weirdbook Press issued his novella, *Pulptime: Being the Singular Adventure of H. P. Lovecraft, Sherlock Holmes, and the Kalem Club, as if Narrated by Frank Belknap Long, Jr.* For many years he was a member of the Esoteric Order of Dagon amateur press association. A native Californian, he has been living since 1975 in New York City, though he hopes some day to return to New England, where he spent most of his childhood.

Editor's Foreword

One of my earliest literary enthusiasms was for H. P. Lovecraft, whose bizarre tales I discovered in my teens when, bored with the bland romances of the *Saturday Evening Post* of the depression years and having exhausted Poe, I began to search out other American Gothic writers. I first read the reclusive gentleman of Providence, Rhode Island, in *Weird Tales,* one of the luridly illustrated "pulp" magazines of the era, so-called because of the coarse paper on which the supposedly perishable contents were crudely printed. My high school English teachers, who trafficked mostly in inspirational verse, were appalled by my taste. Like many cultural guardians, they considered "Gothic fantasy" (or "supernatural horror," to use the term favored by Lovecraft) a disreputable genre appealing only to the immature and uncultivated. To give them their due, in this respect they resembled our devout early settlers with their puritanical distrust of such time-wasting "lies" of the devil as imaginative fiction. I was fascinated, however, especially by Lovecraft's intricate construction of the myth of Cthulhu—a rare enterprise in American letters—to allegorize his dismay at the degeneration of his beloved New England.

Works that provide a glimpse of the nightmare world beneath the deceptive surface of the American dream have held a prominent place in our literature since Charles Brockden Brown's *Wieland* (1798). The genre would find its most celebrated practitioner in Edgar Allan Poe, who called his first story collection *Tales of the Grotesque and Arabesque* (1840), and today it flourishes unflaggingly in both fiction and film. So, despite establishment disapproval, I remained devoted to Lovecraft through service in World War II and graduate school. When during the 1960s I was asked to take over the reviewing of works about American fiction of the 1920s and 1930s for the new annual *American Literary Scholarship,* I included a survey of Lovecraft scholarship at home and abroad. (Just as the French decadents and symbolists were the first to embrace Poe in the nineteenth century, so have French critics been the first to recognize Lovecraft in our century.) And, when in the mid-1970s the program for the Twayne series was expanded, I urged that it should include an objective study of this neglected author.

In this volume, Peter Cannon's careful analysis of the individual tales shows how Lovecraft's art developed and ultimately transcended the boundaries of the genre. In honor of H. P. Lovecraft's centenary in 1990, we offer this reading in the hope that it will provoke a re-examination of his contribution to American literature and keep alive the question of his rightful place among this nation's great imaginative artists.

Warren French

Swansea, Wales

Preface

I have written this study with two audiences in mind, the believers and the skeptics. Into the first group fall my fellow devotees of Lovecraft, many of them amateur scholars like myself, especially those who balance their obsessive interest in the man and his work with a healthy dose of humor. I trust they will find some fresh insights here, besides coming away with a renewed sense of how ripe the gentleman from Providence remains for analysis. Into the second category I put the nonfans—including most English professors—those who may think of Lovecraft as a second-rate, twentieth-century Poe but are open-minded enough to consider looking past the "pulp" surface of his fiction. I hope this study will help persuade them that Lovecraft is more than a mere horror writer, that at the very least he deserves recognition as one of America's greatest literary eccentrics.

After a biographical sketch in the first chapter I survey Lovecraft's "other" works—the amateur journalism, the travel pieces, the ghost-writing, the letters, the poetry—in order to place in perspective the tales that are necessarily the main focus of any introductory study. In chapter 2 I discuss the apprentice fiction of the late teens and early twenties chronologically by date of composition within six thematic categories. Since setting, in particular Lovecraft's native New England, became of such paramount importance thereafter, I have elected to divide the remaining chapters "geographically," though chapter 4 forms a special case. While this arrangement has its awkwardnesses, I believe it serves to illuminate the stories better than either a rigidly chronological or thematic scheme. At the end of chapter 5, I cover his most significant piece of nonfiction, the long essay *Supernatural Horror in Literature,* while in the conclusion I examine current critical trends in Lovecraft studies.

In preparing this book I have been grateful for the wealth of valuable critical material produced within the last few years. I have had the benefit as well of relying upon S. T. Joshi's new, corrected printings of the Arkham House editions of the tales. These four volumes and three other key collections I have abbreviated in the text as follows:

CP = *Collected Poems* (1963)
D = *Dagon* (1986)

DD = *In Defence of Dagon* (1985)
DH = *The Dunwich Horror* (1984)
HM = *The Horror in the Museum* (1989)
MM = *At the Mountains of Madness* (1985)
QS = *To Quebec and the Stars* (1976)

Quotations from the five volumes of *Selected Letters* also appear paren-
thetically in the text, designated by volume and page number. I have
silently corrected obvious errors.

I wish to thank Arkham House Publishers, Inc., for permission to
quote from their editions of the works of H. P. Lovecraft. Arkham
House's Jim Turner has been especially cooperative. I am also indebted
to S. T. Joshi, Steve Mariconda, and Frank Long for their readings of
this study in manuscript and for their general encouragement and
advice; to Warren French, Liz Traynor, and Barbara Sutton of G. K.
Hall for their collective editorial expertise; and to Alice Layton for her
psychological insights.

Finally, I give loving thanks to my wife, Julie, for her support, both
emotional and editorial.

I dedicate this book to the memory of Mr. Andrew Heyl, history and
current events teacher, who thrilled an entire generation of children at
the Brookwood School by reading aloud—on class time—great tales of
terror and the supernatural. I owe him thanks for introducing me to the
fiction of H. P. Lovecraft.

                                                        Peter Cannon

New York City

Chronology

1890 Howard Phillips Lovecraft born 20 August at his maternal grandparents' house on Angell Street in Providence, Rhode Island, the only child of Winfield Scott and Sarah Susan Phillips Lovecraft; family resides in Boston area.

1893 Father declared insane and committed to Butler Hospital in Providence, where he dies in 1898; mother and son join Phillips household.

1898–1908 Intermittent attendance at Providence public schools, private tutoring; nervous breakdown precludes graduation from high school.

1904 Financial decline following death of grandfather Whipple V. Phillips; mother and son move to apartment on Angell Street.

1906 Astronomy column in the *Pawtuxet Valley Gleaner.*

1908–1913 Period of seclusion at home; undertakes correspondence course in chemistry, later abandoned.

1912 First published verse, "Providence in 2000 A.D.," in *Providence Evening Bulletin.*

1914 Joins United Amateur Press Association.

1917 Volunteers for Rhode Island National Guard, but is rejected as unfit after mother's intervention. "The Tomb" and "Dagon."

1919 Mother institutionalized at Butler Hospital, where she dies in 1921. Hears Lord Dunsany lecture.

1920 Commences correspondence with Frank Belknap Long, whom he meets in 1922.

1921 Meets Sonia Greene at amateur convention in Boston. "The Outsider" and "The Music of Erich Zann."

1922 First visits to New York City and Marblehead. Commences correspondence with Clark Ashton Smith.

1923 Places first story with *Weird Tales* magazine. "The Rats in the Walls."

1924   Marries Sonia Greene in Manhattan; couple settles in Brooklyn. Rejects offer of editorship of *Weird Tales;* starts period of fruitless job-seeking.

1925   Sonia departs for job in Midwest; moves to boarding house near Red Hook district in Brooklyn. Begins research on *Supernatural Horror in Literature* (1927; revised 1933).

1926   Returns to Providence; shares apartment with aunt Lillian D. Clark on Barnes Street. Commences correspondence with August Derleth. "The Call of Cthulhu," "The Silver Key," "Pickman's Model."

1926–1927   *The Dream-Quest of Unknown Kadath.*

1927   *The Case of Charles Dexter Ward* and "The Colour Out of Space." "The Horror at Red Hook" (1925) included in the third volume of the British "Not at Night" series— first anthology appearance.

1928   Brief reunion with Sonia in New York City, though at his request marital relations not resumed. Travels through Vermont and Massachusetts inspire "The Dunwich Horror" and "The Whisperer in Darkness" (1930).

1929   Divorce, on grounds of his desertion, granted by Providence Superior Court; neglects to file final papers.

1929–1930   "The Mound" and *Fungi from Yuggoth.*

1930   Commences correspondence with Robert E. Howard. First trip to Quebec inspires *A Description of the Town of Quebeck,* completed in early 1931.

1931   *At the Mountains of Madness* and "The Shadow over Innsmouth." First trip to Florida.

1932   Visits E. Hoffmann Price in New Orleans. Death of Lillian D. Clark. "The Dreams in the Witch House."

1933   Combines households with younger aunt, Annie E. P. Gamwell, on College Street. "Through the Gates of the Silver Key" and "The Thing on the Doorstep."

1934   Extended summer stay with Robert H. Barlow and family in Florida; repeated in the summer of 1935.

1934–1935   "The Shadow Out of Time" and "The Haunter of the Dark."

1936 Small press publication of "The Shadow over Innsmouth" as a book.

1937 Dies 15 March at Jane Brown Memorial Hospital in Providence of cancer of the intestine.

Chapter One
Literary Outsider

Had Malcolm Cowley in *Exiles Return* extended his list of notable American writers born between 1891 and 1905 to the year 1890, he almost certainly would not have included Howard Phillips Lovecraft. In the age of Fitzgerald and Hemingway "the most important American supernaturalist since Poe,"[1] to borrow E. F. Bleiler's phrase, was operating in an underworld of writing—contributing to amateur journals, composing eighteenth-century verse, revising the works of talentless would-be authors, and on occasion publishing highly original horror fiction in pulp magazines like *Weird Tales*—all far removed from the literary mainstream. Indifferent at best to the major postwar writers of his generation, Lovecraft was content in his own anachronistic way to work in the Gothic tradition—of which he always regarded himself a humble part. "I make no claim to membership in the first rank of weird writers," he once said. "It is enough for me if I can make a good showing amongst the smaller fry represented in the cheap magazines" (3:379).

Such modesty about his fiction was as characteristic of the man as the pride he took in his ancestry. Joseph Lovecraft, his great-grandfather, of "a family of small country gentry in Devonshire" (1:5), had emigrated in 1827 to Canada, but within a few years had settled in Rochester, New York. On his mother's side he was "a complete New-England Yankee" (1:31), the founder of the Phillips line having been, he fancied, "the Rev. George Phillips, who came on the *Arbella* in 1630" (3:363).[2] Thoughts of his genteel heritage, no doubt, provided comfort amid the melancholy circumstances of his immediate family. When he was two his father, Winfield Scott Lovecraft, was declared insane and committed to a sanitarium, where he died five years later of "paresis." As an adult Lovecraft claimed that his father had been "seized with a complete paralytic stroke, due to insomnia and an overstrained nervous system" (1:5), but at some subconscious level he may have suspected that syphilis had brought about his father's breakdown, since a number of his better tales deal with hereditary degeneracy and the coupling of human beings with monsters.

With the onset of her philandering husband's illness, Sarah Susan Phillips Lovecraft left the Boston area, where they had been in residence since their marriage, and returned with her small son to Providence, Rhode Island, where her father, a prosperous businessman, lived with his wife and servants in a large Victorian house on the fringe of fashionable College Hill. In this provincial New England city Lovecraft had been born, his parents' first and only child, and there he would spend the rest of his life except for two years of "exile" in New York City. "A man of culture and extensive travel" (1:33), Whipple V. Phillips became the center of his precocious grandson's universe. From this substitute father and his substantial library Lovecraft gained a love of ancient Rome and an enthusiasm for the English authors of the Augustan Age. As Steven J. Mariconda has demonstrated, his mature prose style "was a product of his avid early reading of eighteenth-century essayists, historians, and scientists."[3] From such models he learned as well to use British spellings, including such archaisms as *shew* for the verb *show*.

By his own account Lovecraft had assimilated the alphabet by age two and was reading at three. Having mastered the rudiments of speech, he became "an inveterate reciter of poesy, delivering such pieces as 'Sheridan's Ride' and selections from 'Mother Goose' with true declamatory finesse."[4] In 1897 he composed "a 'poem' in forty-four lines of internally rhyming iambic heptameter,"[5] "The Poem of Ulysses"—as S. T. Joshi notes, "a phenomenal feat for a lad of seven."[6] Virtually no sign of the future horror fantasist can be detected among the extant juvenilia, though he was already—after reading the *Arabian Nights*—assuming the role of "Abdul Alhazred," to whom one day he would ascribe authorship of the dreaded *Necronomicon,* and dreaming of "nightgaunts," trident-bearing, winged demons probably inspired by Gustave Doré's illustrations in his family's deluxe edition of *Paradise Lost.*

In "The Thing on the Doorstep" Daniel Upton says of the youth of his friend Edward Derby that his coddled seclusion led to "a strange, secretive inner life in the boy, with imagination as his one avenue of freedom" (DH 277). This accurately enough describes Lovecraft's own childhood, with qualifications, as a lengthy, autobiographical letter dating to 1931 reveals: "I was not, like many neurotic and bookish children, essentially solitary by nature. I liked to play war and Indian and policeman and railway man and all that, though I could not abide a mere game which involved no imagination or dramatic unfolding" (3:368). As he grew older he read Sherlock Holmes, whom he adored to the point of organizing his own detective agency, and Edgar Allan Poe, whom he came to regard as his "God of Fiction" (1:20). When not absorbed in books, he rode his bicycle for miles around the countryside, joined the "Slater Avenue Army," a gang "whose wars were waged in the neighboring woods" (1:38), smoked tobacco "behind the stables" though he "always detested the infernal stuff" (1:109), built a club house with his friends, and otherwise behaved like any active, sociable American boy, as normal as Tom Sawyer or Penrod.

As an adult Lovecraft looked back on his childhood with intense nostalgia, an understandable sentiment given that further family misfortune would coincide with his adolescence. In the spring of 1904 the death of Whipple Phillips "brought financial disaster besides its more serious grief," and Lovecraft was "never afterward the same" (1:40). He and his mother were forced to vacate the spacious Angell Street house and move into a modest apartment three blocks away. Having always been prone to nervousness, headaches, and fatigue, he now suffered more acutely from what he presumed were organic ills but whose basis must surely have been psychological. Attending school irregularly, he failed to graduate from high school and abandoned any hope of entering Brown University after his health "completely gave way" (1:41) in 1908. While his boyhood friends were starting to enter the larger life of the world, Lovecraft withdrew from it, rather as Hawthorne did with his retreat home to Salem after college.[7]

Lovecraft's emotional problems stemmed from his relationship with his mother, an anxious woman who had trouble coping with her husband's faithlessness and the family's fall into genteel poverty. Inclined to smother her son with love, to overprotect him, she interfered when he tried to enlist in the Rhode Island National Guard after America's entry into World War I, succeeding through medical connections in getting him reclassified as unfit after a routine physical exam turned up no abnormalities. Writing to his friend Rheinhart Kleiner in June 1917, Lovecraft admitted that he felt disheartened "to be the one non-combatant among a profusion of proud recruits" (1:48). Two months later he regretted that he was not among his peers headed for France: "It would have been an interesting experience, & would have either killed or cured me by this time" (1:49). Because he was a mama's boy, Lovecraft missed the Great War, that proving ground of manhood for so many writers of consequence of his generation.

In 1919, suffering from bouts of hysteria and depression, Mrs. Lovecraft entered the same Providence hospital for the insane that had housed her husband. After her death in 1921, following a gall bladder operation, Lovecraft in his grief described her in a letter as "a person of unusual charm and force of character; accomplished in literature and the fine arts" (1:135). In later years he would on occasion acknowledge indirectly that she had had a deleterious effect on his development. His two Phillips aunts, and for a time his wife, would fill the mother role until his own death in 1937, but in his fiction the closest bonds are, significantly, those between younger and older male relatives. In a figure like Professor Angell, granduncle of the narrator of "The Call of Cthulhu," Lovecraft paid tribute to the memory of his grandfather and also his uncles-in-law, both sympathetic, educated men who had helped foster his intellectual curiosity. Mothers and wives hardly exist. When Charles Dexter Ward's parents begin to see signs of madness in their son in *The Case of Charles Dexter Ward,* his father and Dr. Willett, the avuncular family physician, deal with the situation while Mrs. Ward retires to the seashore, unable to take the strain. "My health improved vastly and rapidly, though without any ascertainable cause, about 1920–21" (3:370), Lovecraft wrote ten years after his mother's death. He may have refrained from openly making the connection, but he was too astute not to realize that his improved health had been in no small part due to her passing.

Amateur Journalist

As an older child Lovecraft produced with the aid of a hectograph a large quantity of scientific writing, including two impressively titled periodicals, the *Scientific Gazette* and the *Rhode Island Journal of Astronomy.* His "affection for the celestial science" (1:7) he owed to his maternal grandmother, "a serene, quiet lady of the old school" (1:33), who died when he was five but left behind an "excellent but somewhat obsolete collection of astronomical books" (1:7). In 1906, soon after his first published piece—a brief critique of astrology—appeared in the *Providence Sunday Journal,* he commenced a monthly astronomy column in the *Providence Tribune.* That same year *Scientific American* printed a letter of his, speculating on the existence of a trans-Neptunian planet— an idea he would employ nearly a quarter-century later in "The Whisperer in Darkness," shortly after the discovery of Pluto. In one of his earlier tales, "The Transition of Juan Romero," he would go so far as to supply an author's note—"a lesson in scientific accuracy for fiction writers" (D 340)—explaining how he had adjusted the date of the action to fit the moon's phase in the story.

In 1899, after absorbing a chemistry book for beginners, Lovecraft persuaded his grandfather to fit him up with a laboratory in the cellar. Between 1909 and 1912, through a correspondence course, he tried to perfect himself as a chemist, "conquering inorganic chemistry and qualitative analysis with ease" (1:30), but abandoned the effort when organic chemistry proved too dull and difficult.

The growth of Lovecraft's passion for the sciences followed from his rejection of the Christian faith he had imbibed at the local Baptist Sunday school. Though he "read much in the Bible from sheer interest," he found that he was "infinitely fonder of the Graeco-Roman mythology" and at eight astounded the family by declaring himself "a Roman pagan" (1:10). As an adult he adhered to the philosophy of mechanistic materialism, which had its basis in the late nineteenth-century physics that was so certain man would soon solve all the mysteries of the universe. With similar smugness Lovecraft liked to pronounce on man's diminished place in such a universe: "The cosmos is simply a perpetual rearrangement of electrons which is constantly seething as it always has been and always will be. Our tiny globe and puny thoughts are but one momentary incident in its eternal mutation; so that the life, aims, and thoughts of mankind are of the utmost triviality and ridiculousness" (1:260). Religion was not the only "superstition" Lovecraft opposed. Through the fall of 1914 he debated an astrologer in the pages of a Providence paper, the *Evening News,* resorting first to logic then to satire in the manner of "Dean Swift's famous attacks on the astrologer Partridge, conducted under the nom de plume of Bickerstaffe" (1:4). Those letters to the editor of the *News,* signed "Isaac Bickerstaffe, Jr.," with their absurdly specific predictions, exhibit Lovecraft at his most amusing.[8]

In the fall of 1913 he had provoked another controversy by writing to the *Argosy,* one of the pulp magazines he had been assiduously reading since age fourteen, to protest the love stories of an author named Fred Jackson. For the next year the pro- and anti-Jackson forces battled in the letters column, Lovecraft contributing such typical displays of wit as "a 44-line satire in the manner of Pope's *Dunciad*" (1:41). This debate led to his recruitment in the spring of 1914 into the United Amateur Press Association, an organization dedicated to the ideal of educating its members in the literary art through the circulation and criticism among themselves of their otherwise unpublishable poetry and prose. "More than just a hobby," as T. E. D. Klein notes, amateur journalism for Lovecraft was "for many years the closest thing he had to a career."⁹ Between 1915 and 1923 he issued thirteen numbers of his journal, the *Conservative,* and was elected to various official positions, including chairman of the Department of Public Criticism, vice-president, and then president of the UAPA.

While much of his energy went into encouraging others in their ephemeral efforts or addressing the fractious politics of amateurdom, Lovecraft also had the pleasure of pontificating on subjects of less parochial interest. As an Anglophile he staunchly supported the Allied cause in the Great War, while as a teetotaler he welcomed Prohibition. In such pieces on language as "The Allowable Rhyme," "Metrical Regularity," and "The Simple Spelling Mania," he advocated traditional forms and usages while deploring modern constructions like *upkeep* and *viewpoint.* He excused Pope for rhyming "line" and "join," not realizing that in Pope's day the vowel sounds of the two were the same. (In his own, New England–accented poetry he freely rhymed such words as "John" and "barn.") Models of clarity and precision themselves, these little essays reveal how naive or uninformed he could be in some of his judgments.

In such other essays as "The Crime of the Century," "A Confession of Unfaith," and "Idealism and Materialism—a Reflection," Lovecraft espoused his conservative political views and his materialist philosophy, asserting the supremacy of the "Teutonic" peoples over other races. If like Dean Swift he held the mass of mankind in contempt, he was in his role as critic, for example, unfailingly kind to individuals. In the encomiums "Helene Hoffman Cole—Litterateur," "Winifred Virginia Jackson: A 'Different' Poetess," and the best of them, "Mrs. Miniter—Estimates and Recollections," written in 1934 during a resurgence of interest in amateur activity, he showed that he could be as gallant as Edgar Allan Poe in singing the praises of mawkish female poets.

Around the time he started to publish fiction professionally, Lovecraft became fed up with amateur journalism. In April 1923 he vowed never again to get involved, "save as an especial favour now and then to some more than ordinarily valued friend. The 1914–1922 chapter of spontaneous activity is closed. I'm now too thoroughly cynical to expect much of amateurdom, or to give many damns about it; save as a perpetually chaotic mess from which a few odd souls can get some impetus toward literary development . . . or at least toward a fairly comfortable literary disillusion" (1:218). Still, he remained motivated by the movement's noncommercial, art-for-art's-sake attitude. When on occasion in later years he did pen an essay on request, the result was invariably more inspired than the bulk of his earlier prose. In late 1926, for example, for a meeting of some of his New York literary friends, he composed "Cats and Dogs," a learned, if at times long-winded, tongue-in-cheek dissertation arguing the superiority of cats to dogs. Lightly edited and retitled "Something About Cats" by August Derleth for the posthumous collection of miscellany *Something About Cats* (1949), it is an appealing piece that Lovecraft could have easily sold had it occurred to him to try.

Traveler

In 1915 Lovecraft informed a correspondent, "I have never been outside the three states of Rhode Island, Massachusetts, and Connecticut!" (1:10). This geographical isolation was not to last. In February 1919 he attended his first amateur convention in Boston, a city he would visit regularly over the next five years as an active member of the local Hub Club. Starting in the early twenties he made journeys farther afield—to New Hampshire, Cleveland, and New York City, in order to meet such fellow amateurs as Samuel Loveman and Frank Belknap Long—as well as antiquarian excursions to the towns along the Massachusetts North Shore. Having grown up among if not actually in one of the grand old Georgian houses of his native Providence, he sought out examples of colonial architecture with all the enthusiasm of a connoisseur.

In March 1924 he moved to New York City to marry Sonia Greene, an older Jewish woman of great charm and presence, who had been pursuing him romantically since soon after their meeting at a Hub Club gathering in the summer of 1921. After his return to Providence in April 1926 to resume the bachelor life that his venture into matrimony led him to realize he preferred, Lovecraft continued to travel as often as his limited funds allowed. Frugal by nature, he usually rode the bus, ate cheap packaged foods like bread, cheese, and beans, cut his own hair, washed and pressed his own clothes, and stayed at YMCAs or with friends. As a free-lance writer with no family other than his aunts to worry about, he could devote weeks to summer trips that now encompassed the eastern half of North America, from Portsmouth, Newburyport, Marblehead, and Newport in New England, to Charleston, Saint Augustine, and New Orleans in the South. Jumping off the coast by boat, he reached such scenic outposts as Provincetown, Nantucket, and Key West.

An infrequent trip inland—in August 1930 to the Canadian city of

Quebec—prompted his longest work, *A Description of the Town of Quebeck, in New-France, Lately Added to His Majesty's Dominions*. Divided
into two books, the first a history, the second a walking-tour of the
city, it took him nearly five months that following fall and winter to
write—in the style of an eighteenth-century Tory gentleman, namely
"H. Lovecraft, Armiger, of Providence, in New-England" (QS 111).
Siding with the British in the Revolution, he speculates that the break
of the thirteen colonies from the mother country "may in times to come
bring about their tragicall ingulphment in a new & alien barbarism of
mongrel & autochthonous origin, in which all the standards of
civilisation will be lost in a brainless worship of size, speed, wealth,
success, & luxury, sad chapter to record!" (QS 196). In the act of
composing this quaint 75,000-word travelogue solely for his own pleasure, Lovecraft thumbed his nose at the commercial dictates of an
American society in which he felt a couple of centuries out of place. The
handwritten manuscript remained unpublished until L. Sprague de
Camp, his biographer, went to the trouble to transcribe it more than
forty-five years later as the centerpiece for a collection of Lovecraft
miscellany, *To Quebec and the Stars*.

In his last decade he produced a number of shorter travel essays of
note for his friends' delectation. Among these are "A Descent to
Avernus," an account with horrific undertones of the Endless Caverns
in Virginia's Shenandoah Valley; "Vermont—A First Impression," a
celebration of that state's escape from the industrial plague of southern
New England; "Charleston," his most ambitious guide next to *Quebeck*
(it exists in several states, including an "eighteenth-century" version);
and "The Unknown City in the Ocean," a tribute to the island of
Nantucket, which has "lingered in the past, almost untouched by the
changes and confusions of today" (QS 107).

Ghostwriter

Since Lovecraft's dwindling private income did not supply enough
for him to live on, he began through amateur contacts to take on free-
lance "revision" jobs, ranging from light editing to occasional ghost-
writing. This hack work included poetry more dismal than his own,
material for a slick self-help promoter named David V. Bush, a history
of Dartmouth College, a European travelogue for his ex-wife, an obsolete guide to good English entitled *Well-Bred Speech,* and—though the
final count may never be known—more than two dozen weird tales.

Among forgettable early examples in the genre are the collaborations "The Green Meadow" and "The Crawling Chaos" with Winifred V. Jackson, "Poetry and the Gods" with Anna Helen Crofts, and the four extant tales that he patched up for Clifford M. Eddy. Better are those stories containing pure or near-pure Lovecraft prose, such as the ghost-written "Under the Pyramids" for Harry Houdini, "The Mound" for Zealia Bishop, "Through the Gates of the Silver Key" with E. Hoffmann Price, and "Out of the Aeons" for Hazel Heald, all of which can be regarded as his own work. For this reason I will cover them in appropriate sequence in later chapters.

Where a manuscript does not survive or where evidence in the letters is missing or equivocal, caution must be used in gauging the extent of Lovecraft's role in any given tale. In recent years, based on a misleading remark in a letter, some have hailed Robert Barlow's "The Night Ocean," first published in 1936 in an amateur journal called the *Californian,* as Lovecraft's last masterpiece. I suspect that at most he edited this sluggish tale, with its nebulous similes and metaphors. While a credit to a promising but inexperienced writer like the teenage Barlow, "The Night Ocean" has little more grounds for inclusion in the Lovecraft canon than August Derleth's posthumous "collaborations."[10] Certainly it possesses none of the careful plotting and vivid imagery of the science-fiction yarn, "In the Walls of Eryx," that Lovecraft produced for Kenneth Sterling earlier in 1936. S. T. Joshi speculates that "Lovecraft and Barlow contributed equally"[11] to "The Night Ocean," but my guess is that Lovecraft could have had only a slight share in a tale about the sea from which the smell of the sea is absent.

Epistolarian

In December 1917 Lovecraft wrote to Rheinhart Kleiner: "As to letters, my case is peculiar. I write such things exactly as easily and as rapidly as I would utter the same topics in conversation; indeed, epistolary expression is with me largely replacing conversation" (1:52). Since most of his amateur friends like Kleiner lived far from Providence, a city virtually bereft of soul mates after his youth, he naturally turned to letter-writing as a substitute for ordinary human companionship. Over the years he developed into the Horace Walpole of this century, a compulsive communicator who generated in his abbreviated lifetime tens of thousands of missives, ranging from postcards to treatises forty, fifty, sixty, even seventy, closely handwritten pages long. The five volumes of the *Selected Letters* contain a mere 930 letters, many abridged. Were the surviving correspondence all collected it would occupy hundreds of volumes, dwarfing the rest of his output and forming an almost daily record of the observations and opinions of "the man who lived to write and wrote to live,"[12] as S. T. Joshi so aptly concludes his essay on Lovecraft's epistolary art.

In his letters he raved about such subjects dear to him as the architecture and history of colonial New England, ancient Rome, tiny kittens, sunsets, and coffee ice cream. He also railed against non–Anglo-Saxons—Negroes, Jews, Mediterraneans, Orientals—most venomously in letters to his aunts after everything had gone sour for him in New York. While he never wholly abandoned his ethnic prejudices, his tolerance increased as he became more liberal in his political and economic views. In a letter dating to July 1936 he explained his shift from conservative elitist to New Deal Democrat:

> I used to be a hide-bound Tory simply for traditional and antiquarian reasons—and because I had never done any real *thinking* on civics and industry and the future. The depression—and its concomitant publicisation of industrial, financial, and governmental problems—jolted me out of my lethary and led me to reëxamine the facts of history in the light of unsentimental scientific analysis; and it was not long before I realised what an ass I had been. The liberals at whom I used to laugh were the ones who were right—for they were living in the present while I had been living in the past. They had been using science whilst I had been using romantic antiquarianism. . . . Well—I was converted at last, and in the spring of 1931 took the left-wing side of social and political arguments for the first time in a long life. Nor has there been any retreat. Instead, I have gone even farther toward the left—although totally rejecting the special dogmatisms of pure Marxism, which are certainly founded on definite scientific and philosophical fallacies.(5:279–80)

Shortly before the presidential election of 1936 Lovecraft attended a New Deal rally, "with the eminent Rabbi Wise of New York as principal speaker." The man who could imagine "the Wall Street Nazis of Hoover and Ogden Mills" cursing Stephen Wise as "a dangerous non-Aryan intellectual" (5:426) was no longer the hate-filled bigot he once had been.

At the end of his life Lovecraft was acutely aware of his earlier failings. To Willis Conover, a young correspondent who had surprised him in January 1937 with a copy of an autobiographical letter dated 3 February 1924 to Edwin Baird, then editor of *Weird Tales,* he replied:

"I gape with mortification at its egotistical smugness, florid purple passages, ostentatious exhibitionism, ponderous jauntiness, and general callowness. It wouldn't be so bad if I had written it at thirteen or twenty-three—but at *thirty-three!* What a complacent, self-assured, egocentric jackass I was in those days! All that gabble about the shaping and development of—the world's most perfect cipher!"[13] Within weeks after making this brutal self-assessment Lovecraft would be dead of intestinal cancer, the cause of "the grippe" that he had been complaining about off and on for a year. Unlike Horace Walpole, he had not written his letters with his eye on posterity. Only at the eleventh hour, to his embarrassment, did it occur to him that they might gain a wider audience.

Lovecraft's erudition often awed his correspondents, many of whom, like Willis Conover, were adolescent horror-fiction fans who lacked the learning to challenge his more wrong-headed beliefs. His more intellectual letters tend to be addressed to such fellow *Weird Tales* contributors as Frank Belknap Long, Clark Ashton Smith, and Robert E. Howard, themselves largely autodidacts. While in his letters from the mid-twenties on he frequently discussed his own tastes and theories of supernatural horror in literature, his diffidence kept him from writing to his real peers in the genre, his distinguished British contemporaries M. R. James, Algernon Blackwood, Arthur Machen, and Lord Dunsany.

That Lovecraft was an outstanding thinker and original philosopher, as some claim, has yet to be confirmed, in part because he exchanged ideas with none of the eminent minds of his era. Also, as he himself observed in February 1934 to J. Vernon Shea, who had complimented him on the potential essays embedded in his epistles, "They are, after all, only the random thoughts of a rank layman—not the well-considered utterances of a qualified student of the subjects involved" (4:351). The greatest legacy of his letters to date lies in the devotion that they inspired in his friends, many of whom never met him face to face. Had Lovecraft not been such a kind, scrupulous correspondent, August Derleth would probably not have founded Arkham House to preserve his fiction in hardcover, nor would Willis Conover have put together that magnificent tribute to his memory, *Lovecraft at Last.* Far from wasting his time on letter-writing, which must have filled most of his adult waking hours, Lovecraft helped assure the survival of his fiction, besides establishing himself as, in the words of Vincent Starrett, "his own most fantastic creation."[14]

Poet

Winfield Townley Scott has fairly said of Lovecraft that "at one time or another he thought of himself as primarily a poet."[15] For the amateur press he wrote a great deal of poetry, the bulk of it in heroic couplets. Typical specimens include pastorals like "To Templeton and Mount Monadnock" and occasional verse like "The Members of the Men's Club of the First Universalist Church of Providence, R.I., to Its President, About to Leave for Florida on Account of His Health." As Scott observed of such poems, "They are completely out of touch with Lovecraft's actual time as no vital poetry can ever be."[16] In a letter of March 1929 Lovecraft himself acknowledged this fault: "In my metrical novitiate I was, alas, a chronic & inveterate mimic; allowing my antiquarian tendencies to get the better of my abstract poetic feeling. As a result, the whole purpose of my writing soon became distorted—till at length I wrote only as a means of re-creating around me the atmosphere of my 18th century favourites. Self-expression as such sank out of sight, & my sole test of excellence was the degree with which I approached the style of Mr. Pope, Dr. Young, Mr. Thomson, Mr. Addison, Mr. Tickell, Mr. Parnell, Dr. Goldsmith, Dr. Johnson, & so on" (2:314–15).

At times in his poetry, in keeping with its outdated form, Lovecraft comes across as a crotchety opponent of change. In his first published poem, "Providence in 2000 A.D.," which appeared in the *Providence Evening Bulletin* of 4 March 1912, he derided the proposal that Atwells Avenue, the main thoroughfare of the city's Italian district, be renamed Columbus Avenue. In 1922–23, having no sympathy for the modernist poetry of the day, he wrote a 134-line parody of T. S. Eliot's *The Waste Land* entitled *Waste Paper: A Poem of Profound Insignificance.* As Barton St. Armand and John H. Stanley have pointed out, this satirical exercise happens to share some affinities with *The Waste Land* before Eliot made the cuts recommended by Ezra Pound.[17] Less strident are such whimsical efforts as "My Favourite Character," on his reading preferences, and "A Year Off," an armchair traveler's reverie, both dating to 1925.

In the teens and early twenties Lovecraft also produced a quantity of horror verse, including *Psychopompos,* an unexceptional werewolf narrative that he would later list among his fiction as a tale in rhyme, and some shorter poems—"Despair," "Nemesis," "The Eidolon"— modeled after Poe at his most mechanical. More successful are such related but less imitative pieces as "The Ancient Track," "The Outpost," and "The Wood," all dating to 1929, his most fruitful year for poetry.

In November 1929 Lovecraft penned two horrific sonnets, "Recapture" and "The Messenger," the latter dedicated to Bertrand K. Hart, who had been conducting a discussion of weird fiction in his *Providence Journal* column "The Sideshow" and had taken mock umbrage at Lovecraft's use of his former residence, 7 Thomas Street, as the home of one of the characters in "The Call of Cthulhu." "The Messenger" was Lovecraft's playful response to Hart's threat to send him a ghostly late-night visitor in retaliation. These two sonnets, together with the eloquent "East India Brick Row," written in early December to protest the demolition of a row of old Providence warehouses "in the name of aesthetic 'progress' " (CP 89), proved to be the preludes to his extraordinary sonnet cycle, *Fungi from Yuggoth*. Between 27 December 1929 and 4 January 1930, he turned out thirty-five sonnets, to which he would later add "Recapture," number 34 in the series, for a total of thirty-six. The coherence of the whole has been a matter of debate—R. Boerem has argued that they form "a unified sequence,"[18] while S. T. Joshi has cited their "utter randomness of tone, mood, and import"[19]—but no one disputes their status as Lovecraft's finest poetical endeavor.

Finally casting off the artificial diction of the past, Lovecraft demonstrated in the *Fungi* that he could express himself within exacting poetic strictures in bold, almost vernacular language. As Boerem notes, "The reader who dislikes the content of these verses will at least have to admit to their skill."[20] At their best the sonnets embody in miniature the same themes as the fiction of his last decade. "Background," one of the more philosophical in the series, can be considered representative, a paradigm of Lovecraft's personal faith:

> I never can be tied to raw, new things,
> For I first saw the light in an old town,
> Where from my window huddled roofs sloped down
> To a quaint harbour rich with visionings.
> Streets with carved doorways where the sunset beams
> Flooded old fanlights and small window-panes,
> And Georgian steeples topped with gilded vanes—
> These were the sights that shaped my childhood dreams.
>
> Such treasures, left from times of cautious leaven,
> Cannot but loose the hold of flimsier wraiths
> That flit with shifting ways and muddled faiths

Across the changeless walls of earth and heaven.
They cut the moment's thongs and leave me free
To stand alone before eternity.

(CP 130)

Through contemplation of traditional scenes—colonial architectural detail, supplemented by sunsets and childhood dreams—the speaker feels a kind of cosmic rapture before the unknown, what Lovecraft elsewhere calls a sense of "adventurous expectancy." As he asserts in sonnet number 28, "Expectancy," "its lure alone makes life worth living" (CP 129).

In 1936 Lovecraft wrote two final sonnets, tributes to his friends Virgil Finlay, an illustrator, and Clark Ashton Smith. Both are as well wrought and as redolent of horror, notwithstanding their sentiment, as any of the *Fungi*. Almost as good is the acrostic poem of the same year, "In a Sequester'd Providence Churchyard Where Once Poe Walk'd," which would have been a sonnet had the name Edgar Allan Poe contained one more letter. Letters aside, these represent his last creative work before his untimely death.

Chapter Two

Dawn

In 1917, prompted by W. Paul Cook and other amateurs who had been impressed by two youthful efforts, "The Beast in the Cave" (1905) and "The Alchemist" (1908), Lovecraft wrote "The Tomb" and "Dagon," the tales that mark the start of his career as an author of horror fiction. Over the next several years he circulated in the amateur press some three dozen stories, the average one no longer than a few thousand words. *Weird Tales* later reprinted nearly all of them, starting with "Dagon" in 1923. Ranging from Poe-esque narratives of madness and obsession to dreamlike fantasies in the manner of Lord Dunsany, they show Lovecraft, like any neophyte writer, imitating certain favorite authors on his way to finding his own voice. In "The Thing on the Doorstep" Upton says of Edward Derby that "his lack of contacts and responsibilities had slowed down his literary growth by making his products derivative and overbookish" (DH 279). Such a statement applies aptly enough to Lovecraft's own apprentice fiction.

Despite their derivative nature, even the crudest of these early stories exhibit themes that are distinctly Lovecraft's own, reflecting the ideas and issues, chiefly aesthetic, that concerned him as a reclusive, unworldly young man from the time of America's entry into the Great War on into the Jazz Age. Under the six categories that follow I discuss the major areas where Lovecraft located his horrors, since place or setting or background is generally more important than either character or plot. Where two or more elements could be considered significant in a story, I have grouped it according to which is dominant. Later, longer tales typically weave several of these elements into a complex web. Indeed, in "The Dunwich Horror" Lovecraft characterizes the dying cries of the horror in terms of what I call "below," "beyond," and "the past" within a single sentence: "From what black wells of Acherontic fear or feeling, from what unplumbed gulfs of extra-cosmic consciousness or obscure, long-latent heredity, were those half-articulate thunder-croakings drawn?" (DH 196). Through such concentrated adjectival and alliterative bursts does Lovecraft attempt to invoke the awesomeness of time and space.

The Past

In his fiction Lovecraft, as a keen antiquarian, preferred more often than not to hark back to the past. While "The Tomb" (1917) is a contemporary tale, set in the vicinity of Boston, the narrator seems scarcely to exist in the modern world. "My name is Jervas Dudley, and from earliest childhood I have been a dreamer and a visionary," he declares, having already admitted that his story is open to doubt owing to his "confinement within this refuge for the demented" (D 3). Again, as befits an aristocratic aesthete in the Poe tradition, Dudley has none of the financial worries that plagued Lovecraft throughout adulthood: "Wealthy beyond the necessity of a commercial life, and temperamentally unfitted for the formal studies and social recreations of my acquaintances, I have dwelt ever in realms apart from the visible world; spending my youth and adolescence in ancient and little-known books, and roaming the fields and groves of the region near my ancestral home" (D 3–4). Despite the trace of self-portraiture here and the evident relish with which Lovecraft chronicles his hero's morbid preoccupation with the family tomb, Dudley never emerges beyond stock type. Of the climactic ghostly gathering at the family mansion that burned down a century earlier, Dudley asserts: "Amidst a wild and reckless throng I was the wildest and most abandoned. Gay blasphemies poured in torrents from my lips, and in my shocking sallies I heeded no law of God, Man, or Nature" (D 11). But without further elaboration Dudley's excesses remain no more than Gothic rhetoric. In the larger context of Lovecraft's fiction, he takes on significance mainly as a foreshadowing of Charles Dexter Ward, just as Sir Geoffrey Hyde, founder of the line in America of which Dudley is the last descendant, looks forward to Joseph Curwen.

For all its shortcomings "The Tomb" does contain plenty of lively detail. Under the influence of nightly visits to the tomb, Dudley—oddly perhaps for a crazed romantic—begins to assume the speech and manners of the Augustan Age: "My formerly silent tongue waxed voluble with the easy grace of a Chesterfield or the godless cynicism of a Rochester" (D 9). Furthermore, at breakfast one morning Dudley spontaneously recites "an effusion of eighteenth-century Bacchanalian mirth" (D 9), which T. O. Mabbott cites for "the magnificent line" "Better under the table than under the ground!" (D 10).[1] Such touches as this drinking song elevate "The Tomb" above mere pastiche.

Lovecraft put his eighteenth-century erudition to more impressive use in "A Reminiscence of Dr. Samuel Johnson" (1917). In this playful fantasy the narrator, Lovecraft himself, professes to have consorted as a minor man of letters with the likes of Dryden, Addison, Swift, and Dr. Johnson:

> Tho' many of my readers have at times observ'd and remark'd a Sort of Antique Flow in my Stile of Writing, it hath pleased me to pass amongst the Members of this Generation as a young Man, giving out the Fiction that I was born in 1890, in America. I am now, however, resolv'd to unburthen myself of a secret which I have hitherto kept thro' Dread of Incredulity; and to impart to the Publick a true knowledge of my long years, in order to gratifie their taste for authentick Information of an Age with whose famous Personages I was on familiar Terms. Be it then known that I was born on the family Estate in Devonshire, of the 10th day of August, 1690, (or in the new Gregorian Stile of Reckoning, the 20th of August) being therefore now in my 228th year. (QS 52)

In effect Lovecraft emulates Boswell, whom he alludes to as "a young Scotchman of excellent Family and great Learning, but small Wit, whose metrical Effusions I had sometimes revis'd" (QS 52). At the same time this preternaturally aged narrator anticipates other, less benign characters of eighteenth-century origin, such as the garrulous old cannibal in "The Picture in the House," the gentleman in "He," and, most menacing of all, Joseph Curwen.

If the *Life of Johnson* was his immediate inspiration, Lovecraft may have derived the idea for the sketch's conceit from Hawthorne's "P's Correspondence," wherein the protagonist reports on his meetings with such literary giants as Byron, Shelley, and Keats, whom he imagines have survived into his own day. In his encounter with Byron he undergoes the same sort of comic deflation that the fatuous Lovecraft character repeatedly receives at Johnson's hands. Says Lovecraft of one exchange: "When, to agree with him, I said I was distrustful of the Authenticity of Ossian's Poems, Mr. Johnson said: 'That, Sir, does not do your Understanding particular Credit; for what all the Town is sensible of, is no great Discovery for a Grub-Street Critick to make. You might as well say, you have a strong Suspicion that Milton wrote *Paradise Lost!*' " (QS 53). Able to poke fun at his own pretensions, Lovecraft in "A Reminiscence of Dr. Samuel Johnson" displays a wit worthy of the venerable sage himself.

In contrast to Jervas Dudley, who may go mad but turns up no unpleasant ancestral secrets, the protagonist of "Facts Concerning the Late Arthur Jermyn and His Family"[2] (1920) gets a nasty surprise when he investigates his family's past. Arthur Jermyn, "poet and scholar" (D 73), last of his line, incinerates himself after discovering that the wife brought back from Africa by his great-great-great-grandfather, Sir Wade Jermyn, "one of the earliest explorers of the Congo region" (D 74), had been a "white ape."[3] Here for the first time appears Lovecraft's pet theme of hereditary degeneracy, albeit in rather unsubtle form.

Lovecraft thought well of "Arthur Jermyn," referring to it in a 1934 letter to the editor of *Weird Tales,* regarding its reprint, as "always one of my favourites" (4:406), a puzzling assessment given the inferiority of "Arthur Jermyn" to such later efforts in this atavistic vein as "The Rats in the Walls" and "The Shadow over Innsmouth." The tale's first half consists of an extended flashback that summarizes the salient events in the life of each Jermyn scion. Since they all tend to be apelike in build and to marry gypsies or music-hall girls or to join the circus, the point becomes obvious very quickly. Such a repetitive approach, giving equal weight to every generation, is inherently less dramatic than restricting the focus to a single ancestor. Perhaps the most notable feature of the tale is its sententious beginning: "Life is a hideous thing, and from the background behind what we know of it peer daemoniacal hints of truth which make it sometimes a thousandfold more hideous. Science, already oppressive with its shocking revelations, will perhaps be the ultimate exterminator of our human species—if separate species we be—for its reserve of unguessed horrors could never be borne by mortal brains if loosed upon the world" (D 73). Here is a glimmer of the memorable opening paragraph of "The Call of Cthulhu," which puts forth the same idea more quietly.

Denys Barry, protagonist of "The Moon-Bog" (1921), comes from America to Ireland to restore the old family castle. Preparations to drain the bog surrounding the castle disturb the bog-wraiths there who, presumably resenting the intrusion, turn Barry and his workmen into frogs. The narrator has had dreams of classical antiquity, "of piping flutes and marble peristyles" (D 121), but Lovecraft never makes clear the connection between these visions and the ghostly denouement. Written for a gathering of amateurs on Saint Patrick's Day, "The Moon-Bog" amounts to a relatively tame handling of a piece of Irish folklore, though again it contains elements that will appear to better advantage elsewhere. The flight of the narrator from the castle, for example, foreshadows such far more dramatic nighttime escapes as those of Albert Wilmarth in "The Whisperer in Darkness" and the narrator of "The Shadow over Innsmouth" in that tale.

"The Lurking Fear" (1922), the second, after "Herbert West—Reanimator," of his serial stories for the short-lived magazine *Home Brew*, features the first of Lovecraft's decadent rural communities. News of an inexplicable massacre brings the anonymous narrator, whose "love of the grotesque and the terrible" has made his career "a series of quests for strange horrors in literature and in life" (D 179), to Tempest Mountain in a "part of the Catskills where Dutch civilisation once feebly and transiently penetrated, leaving behind as it receded only a few ruined mansions and a degenerate squatter population inhabiting pitiful hamlets on isolated slopes" (D 180). Like Joe Slater, "the Catskill degenerate" (D 30) of "Beyond the Wall of Sleep," these folk are scarcely human: "Simple animals they were, gently descending the evolutionary scale because of their unfortunate ancestry and stultifying isolation" (D 186). Basically harmless, they anticipate the natives of Dunwich, who also suffer on account of one family in the region with an especially malignant hereditary streak.

In the tale's four segments Lovecraft avoids the plot recapitulations of "Herbert West," but he seems to care far less about providing plausible motivation or coherent story line. To the horrible deaths of his various companions who help him investigate the ancient Martense family and their deserted, tempest-wracked mansion, the narrator reacts with a callousness comparable to that of the decadents in "The Hound," written a couple of months earlier, which also contains a Dutch background and a monster that tears its victims apart. Too often summary serves in place of dramatization, as in the narrator's cursory description of the initial scene of mayhem: "Of a possible 75 natives who had inhabited this spot, not one living specimen was visible" (D 181). This particular line could well have been what prompted T. O. Mabbott to accuse Lovecraft of "a tendency to melodrama, to kill off a dozen victims where one would have served better."[4]

At the climax the narrator finally sees one of the creatures who have been mauling the local citizenry—which happens to look like Arthur Jermyn's great-great-great-grandmother: "The object was naseous; a filthy whitish gorilla thing with sharp yellow fangs and matted fur. It was the ultimate product of mammalian degeneration; the frightful outcome of isolated spawning, multiplication, and cannibal nutrition above and below the ground; the embodiment of all the snarling chaos and grinning fear that lurk behind life" (D 199). While the narrator reels at the implications for humankind of the existence of such a beast, he has by this point put the reader off by spouting too many fevered clichés. The closing words of "The Lurking Fear"—"the terrible and thunder-crazed house of Martense" (D 199), echoing the end of "The Fall of the House of Usher"—arrive as only the last of such overwrought turns.

The Sea

As Ralph E. Vaughan has noted, "The sea played a very important part both in H. P. Lovecraft's prose and in his life."[5] As a native of Providence, Rhode Island, with its maritime heritage, Lovecraft could not help having some affinity for the sea, despite his lifelong aversion to the odor and taste of fish. Two slight stories of nautical adventure, "The Little Glass Bottle" (1897) and "The Mysterious Ship" (1902), survive from his childhood. As an adult, perhaps because he never ventured far from shore, he did not attempt to make a ship the focus for a realistic tale of the supernatural as did William Hope Hodgson, a former sailor.[6] He did, however, employ the sea as a setting in a number of major tales. Ocean voyages figure in the fantasies "The White Ship" and *The Dream-Quest of Unknown Kadath,* while in "The Call of Cthulhu" and "Out of the Aeons" horrors dwell in the South Pacific, on islands that suddenly rise above the surface then just as quickly sink—a geological anomaly introduced in "Dagon."

Whereas Jervas Dudley at the start of "The Tomb" confesses that he is of questionable sanity, the anonymous narrator of "Dagon" (1917) in his opening assertion admits that he is on the brink of suicide: "I am writing this under an appreciable mental strain, since by tonight I shall be no more. Penniless, and at the end of my supply of the drug which alone makes life endurable, I can bear the torture no longer; and shall cast myself from this garret window into the squalid street below" (D 14). An account of how he came to reach such a predicament, "Dagon" in its flashback structure establishes the pattern, along with "The Tomb," for the majority of Lovecraft's narratives.

Although scarcely less melodramatic than "The Tomb," "Dagon" has a topical basis. The second paragraph of the story begins: "It was in one of the most open and least frequented parts of the broad Pacific that the packet of which I was supercargo fell a victim to the German sea-raider" (D 14). Familiar with *Paradise Lost,*[7] Doré's illustrations, the fiction of Poe and Bulwer-Lytton, the narrator is evidently another character with romantic inclinations, yet in his description of the newly risen island he lands on he seems reliable enough. The weakness of the tale lies in its brevity. "Vast, Polyphemus-like, and loathsome" (D 18), Dagon rises from the waters too abruptly, despite the foreshadowing of the bas-reliefs of the fish-men—elements that recur on a grander scale in *At the Mountains of Madness* and "The Shadow over Innsmouth." The narrator claims he is awestruck by the glimpse he gets "into a past beyond the conception of the most daring anthropologist" (D 18), but because Dagon's background remains a mystery, other than the implied connection with the actual Phoenician god of that name, his horrific impact is minimal. Not until "The Call of Cthulhu," which "Dagon" so resembles in outline, will Lovecraft place one of his monsters, another Cyclops-like creature, in a situation where its emergence is truly affecting.

In "The Temple" (1920) the sinking of a merchant ship by a German war vessel likewise sets the plot in motion, although this time the tale is told from the viewpoint of the aggressor, "Karl Heinrich, Graf von Altberg-Ehrenstein, Lieutenant-Commander in the Imperial German Navy and in charge of the submarine U-29" (D 59). However much the stereotypically fanatical Prussian, cold and iron-willed, Heinrich nonetheless has a profession—unlike the mad, wealthy aesthetes of other early tales. From the discovery of the "very odd bit of ivory carved to represent a youth's head crowned with laurel" (D 60), through the progressive madness of the entire crew, to his final decision to don his diving suit and "walk boldly up the steps into that primal shrine" (D 72), he records all the eerie yet related events with a clarity and consistency foreign to the narrators of, say, "The Tomb" or "The Lurking Fear." His story is all the more compelling in that he comes to accept the existence of the supernatural only after exhausting every natural explanation. If Lovecraft teases the reader by leaving his protagonist on the verge of learning the secrets behind the weird phenomena associated with the temple, he also takes care to suggest that what Heinrich happens upon is no less than the Atlantis of classical myth.

"The Temple" shows traces of the Poe influence as well. The note below the title, "(Manuscript found on the coast of Yucatan.)" (D 59), evokes "MS. Found in a Bottle," while the uncontrolled drifting of the disabled U-boat to the south echoes the final voyage in *Arthur Gordon Pym*. Most significant, the image of the light in the window of the temple would seem to have a source in "The City in the Sea," where "light from out the lurid sea / Streams up the turrets silently." Within the context of his own work, Lovecraft's unnamed Atlantis anticipates the underwater realm of the Old Ones that Dyer and Danforth seek toward the end of *At the Mountains of Madness,* and Y'ha-nthlei, the city beyond and below the reef in "The Shadow over Innsmouth."

Below

Just as Lovecraft's aquatic horrors tend naturally to reside beneath the waves, so too do many of his "land" horrors lurk below the earth—in a variety of burrows, tunnels, caverns, caves, crypts, and grottoes. Some of his more human characters, like Herbert West and Joseph Curwen, maintain secret underground laboratories. In "The Transition of Juan Romero" (1919), set in "the drear expanses of the Cactus Mountains" of the American West, a dynamite blast "at the celebrated Norton Mine"—where the narrator has been working as "a common labourer" (D 337)—has an unexpected result: "a new abyss yawned indefinitely below the seat of the blast; an abyss so monstrous that no handy line could fathom it, nor any lamp illuminate it" (D 339). The remoteness of this pit in the earth reminds the narrator of Poe's quotation from Joseph Glanvill regarding the well of Democritus, which Lovecraft identifies in a footnote as the motto of "A Descent into the Maelstrom." Wells, bottomless and otherwise—a motif of especial potency for Lovecraft—serve as gateways to horror in such later tales as "Pickman's Model" and "The Colour Out of Space" and in the *Fungi* sonnet "The Well," where "a black hole deeper than we could say" proves "too deep for any line to sound" (CP 117).

"One of a large herd of unkempt Mexicans" (D 337–38) employed at the mine, Juan Romero falls victim to whatever force lies below the ground. Peering into the chasm the narrator cries: "*I dare not tell you what I saw!*" (D 342). As in "The Temple" Lovecraft means to be subtly suggestive through such obscurity, but here the effect is less satisfying. The narrator's "Hindoo" ring and Romero's recognition of it, Romero's appearing to be of noble Aztec blood, the narrator's cryptic, Poe-esque reticence about his past—"My name and origin need not be related to posterity" (D 337)—tantalize without adding up to a coherent whole. The narrator recalls Juan Romero's "transition" years afterward out of a "sense of duty to science" (D 337), but unlike the scientifically inclined protagonists of later tales he comes across as pure Gothic stereotype. His presence in a western, even a supernatural one, borders on absurdity.

In "The Statement of Randolph Carter" (1919) the eponymous narrator and his friend, Harley Warren, open a grave in an ancient cemetery one night, uncovering a flight of stone steps that Warren descends while Carter waits above, connected by a portable telephone line. Below he finds that, like the narrator of "The Transition of Juan Romero," he cannot express what he sees: " *'I can't tell you, Carter! It's too utterly beyond thought—I dare not tell you—no man could know it and live—Great God! I never dreamed of THIS!'* " (MM 303). In a climax more imaginatively conceived than that in "Juan Romero," Carter learns of his companion's fate from a highly uncanny source. " *'YOU FOOL, HARLEY WARREN IS DEAD!'* " (MM 305) he hears a strange voice assert over the phone in the story's final sentence. As he will do in the next "Carter" story, "The Unnamable," Lovecraft here contrives a demonstration of the weird theory of one of two friends—to wit, Warren's speculation on *"why certain corpses never decay, but rest firm and fat in their tombs for a thousand years"* (MM 300), a concept he will reuse in "The Festival." Presumably such a corpse is what speaks to Carter in that shocking punch line, an altogether fitting close to surely one of Lovecraft's most egregious exercises in overwriting. At the time he seems not to have recognized how near he had come to self-parody in his heavy reliance on italics and capitals and in a phrase like "the unbelievable, unthinkable, almost unmentionable thing" (MM 304), for in a letter dated 8 February 1922 he could state with pride that the tale "has the most hideous suspense and surging terror of anything I have evolved" (1:166).

Based quite literally on a dream involving himself and his friend Sam Loveman, poet and protégé of Hart Crane, "The Statement of Randolph Carter" is mainly significant for the debut of Lovecraft's Randolph Carter persona. While the majority of his protagonists can be regarded in varying degree as autobiographical, only Carter stands as a conscious self-portrait. In this early tale, however, to the reader ignorant of its dream origin, Carter could be any erudite seeker after forbidden knowledge. Significant as well is Harley Warren's "fiend-inspired book" (MM 300) as a prototype for "the forbidden *Necronomicon* of the mad Arab Abdul Alhazred" (D 174), whose celebrated couplet will be quoted in "The Nameless City," though the *Necronomicon* itself will not receive mention by name until "The Hound."

Where Harley Warren encounters *"legions"* (MM 304) in the course of his underground excursion, the narrator of "The Nameless City" (1921), another tale with a dream basis, finds the remains of an entire civilization below some ruins in the remote Arabian desert. For once a character dares to describe in full the monsters he sees, here the reptilian creatures depicted in mural paintings and present as mummies that in the unsurprising denouement prove neither allegorical nor dead: "To nothing can such things be well compared—in one flash I thought of comparisons as varied as the cat, the bulldog, the mythic Satyr, and the human being. Not Jove himself had so colossal and protuberant a forehead, yet the horns and the noselessness and the alligator-like jaw placed the things outside all established categories" (D 104). In this shotgun approach Lovecraft risks more smiles than shudders. His monsters in *At the Mountains of Madness* and "The Shadow Out of Time," later tales that expand this notion of man's discovery of great, prehuman races to epic proportions, will be no less outlandish, but they will be far more convincingly portrayed—in part because viewed through the eyes of ordinary men. The fevered account of a character prone to reciting the mad poet Abdul Alhazred's "unexplainable couplet: 'That is not dead which can eternal lie / And with strange aeons even death may die' " (D 109), besides quoting from Lord Dunsany and Thomas Moore, cannot be taken as seriously.

Shortly before his marriage Lovecraft produced another Middle Eastern tale with an underground setting, "Under the Pyramids" (1924), published in *Weird Tales* as "Imprisoned with the Pharaohs."[8] Ghost-written for Harry Houdini, whom he considered "supremely egotistical" (1:312), this extended story depends to an unusual degree on character. That the famed magician and escape artist should come off in the course of the narrative as a somewhat ridiculous hero is entirely in keeping with Lovecraft's perception of him.

Vanity sets the plot in motion. Traveling incognito aboard ship to Port Said en route to Australia, Houdini reveals his identity in order to show up a rival magician. The advance publicity alerts those in Cairo who would wish to put his powers to a severe test. Whereas the first half of the tale amounts to an urbane travelogue, filled with all the Egyptian local color Lovecraft had gleaned from his researches, the second part, set in a vast vault below the pyramid into which sinister Arabs lower the gullible showman bound and gagged, consists of a series of Poe-like horrors. In particular, such details as his finding himself tied up in the dark, his repeated faintings and awakenings, and his lost time sense call to mind "The Pit and the Pendulum." When Lovecraft wrote to a friend that here "I let myself loose and coughed up some of the most nameless, slithering, unmentionable HORROR that ever stalked cloven-hooved through the tenebrous and necrophagous abysses of elder night" (1:326), he was not exaggerating. With scant regard for credibility, he exposes Houdini to one extravagance after another—the rope that falls for miles, the columns higher than the Eiffel Tower, the "hybrid blasphemies" (D 241) like the animal mummies in "The Nameless City," the "five-headed monster as large as a hippopotamus" (D 243) that lunges for him at the climax. "I tacked on the 'it-was-all-a-dream' bromide" (1:326), reported Lovecraft, soon after completing the tale, but the possibility is also implicit that Houdini's adventures are all one giant Munchausen, as would befit his boastful character. In either event, while "Under the Pyramids" contains many features of interest, its horrors remain subordinate to Lovecraft's purpose of having some fun at his client's expense.

Beyond

While most of Lovecraft's early horrors dwell beneath the ground or the sea, a few lie in the opposite direction—in the heavens that so fascinated him as an adolescent astronomer. Eschewing the clumsy rocketships of science fiction, Lovecraft hit upon telepathic means to bring his protagonist into contact with an extraterrestrial mind in "Beyond the Wall of Sleep" (1919), which opens on a characteristically ruminative, philosophical note:

I have frequently wondered if the majority of mankind ever pause to reflect upon the occasionally titanic significance of dreams, and of the obscure world to which they belong. Whilst the greater number of our nocturnal visions are perhaps no more than faint and fantastic reflections of our waking experiences—Freud to the contrary with his puerile symbolism—there are still a certain remainder whose immundane and ethereal character permits of no ordinary interpretation, and whose vaguely exciting and disquieting effect suggests possible minute glimpses into a sphere of mental existence no less important than physical life, yet separated from that life by an all but impassable barrier. (D 25)

For Lovecraft dreams are valuable not for the insights they give into the human psyche, as Freud would have it, but as imaginative windows through which the mysteries of time and space may be spied. In his fiction man finds emotional satisfaction not in any inward psychological examination but in outward contemplation of the universe.

The nameless narrator, with the aid of a special "radio," penetrates the consciousness of Joe Slater, "one of those strange, repellent scions of a primitive colonial peasant stock whose isolation for nearly three centuries in the hilly fastnesses of a little-travelled countryside has caused them to sink to a kind of barbaric degeneracy" (D 26). In keeping with Lovecraft's elitism, Slater proves "unfit to bear the active intellect of cosmic entity," according to "the soul-petrifying voice or agency from beyond the wall of sleep," who further informs the narrator: "I am your brother of light, and have floated with you in the effulgent valleys. It is not permitted me to tell your waking earth-self of your real self, but we are all roamers of vast spaces and travellers in many ages" (D 34). Here the voice no more than blandly hints at the cosmic marvels available to the brighter, more sensitive members of the human race. Such later tales as "The Call of Cthulhu" and "The Shadow Out of Time"[9] will expand on this theme of psychic alien possession, exploring the implications of such marvels at a more profound level.

In "From Beyond" (1920), using an electrical machine no less preposterous than the device in "Beyond the Wall of Sleep," Crawford Tillinghast, another belittler of Freud—"I laugh at the shallow endocrinologist, fellow-dupe and fellow-parvenu of the Freudian" (D 93)—succeeds in transcending the limits of the five senses and plugging into "whole worlds of alien, unknown entities." His friend the narrator does not hesitate to describe the fantastic behavior of the "great inky, jellyish monstrosities" (D 95) he observes, but the sight of such creatures evokes very little fear in the context of a trite tale. "I have seen beyond the bounds of infinity and drawn down daemons from the stars" (D 96), Tillinghast declares, but he is too much the conventional mad scientist to be persuasive. Yet beneath the clichés—the not so mysterious disappearance of the servants, Tillinghast's falling victim at the last second to the monsters he had stirred up to sic on the narrator—"From Beyond," as S. T. Joshi has demonstrated, does have a philosophical basis in Hugh Elliot's *Modern Science and Materialism* (1919).[10] And again the supernatural concept—malignant beings existing undetected in another dimension—will find more powerful expression in a later tale, "The Dunwich Horror," where Old Whateley will even refer to "them from beyont" (DH 167).

Dreamland

In the fall of 1919 Lovecraft read *A Dreamer's Tales* by the Anglo-Irish author Lord Dunsany.[11] Ten years later he would say of the opening story of this collection of ornate fantasies: "The first paragraph arrested me as with an electric shock, & I had not read two pages before I became a Dunsany devotee for life" (2:328). While in his day the prolific Dunsany cut a considerable literary swath as a poet, playwright, and novelist, his reputation since his death in 1957 has declined to the extent that he is now chiefly remembered for his influence on his disciple. "Truly," Lovecraft wrote in 1923, "Dunsany has influenced me more than anyone else except Poe—his rich language, his cosmic point of view, his remote dream-world, & his exquisite sense of the fantastic, all appeal to me more than anything else in modern literature" (1:243). In a number of early tales, set in exotic lands with queer names presided over by strange gods, he attempts to capture the same feelings of beauty and wonder as his mentor.

Lovecraft had anticipated by a year the Dunsanian manner in "Polaris" (1918), a tale unmistakably Lovecraftian in its astronomical basis, confusion between the dream and the real worlds, and racial bias. In this brief story of prehistoric cultures in collision near the North Pole, the Inutos, "squat, hellish, yellow fiends," threaten "the marble city of Olathoë that lies betwixt the peaks of Noton and Kadiphonek," home of the "tall, gray-eyed men of Lomar," who are too honorable to engage in the "ruthless conquest" (D 22) favored by their foes. Chosen because of his keen eyesight to act as watchman, the narrator lets down his compatriots by falling asleep at his post, a calamity anticipated by his admission that "I was feeble and given to strange faintings" (D 22). He also tends to personify natural objects, describing the Pole Star as "winking hideously like an insane watching eye" (D 24), an eye far more dependable than his own though it cannot save the men of Lomar. As silly as the narrator sometimes sounds, he tells his poignant tale relatively simply and directly, making "Polaris" one of Lovecraft's more engaging early efforts.

"The White Ship" (1919), Lovecraft's first deliberately Dunsanian tale, possesses the poetic language, the alliteration and repetition, characteristic of the mode. Proclaims the narrator, Basil Elton, "keeper of the North Point light" (D 36):

Out of the South it was that the White Ship used to come when the moon was full and high in the heavens. Out of the South it would glide very smoothly and silently over the sea. And whether the sea was rough or calm, and whether the wind was friendly or adverse, it would glide smoothly and silently, its sails distent and its long strange tiers of oars moving rhythmically. One night I espied upon the deck a man, bearded and robed, and he seemed to beckon me to embark for fair unknown shores. Many times afterward I saw him under the full moon, and ever did he beckon me. (D 37)

Dirk W. Mosig has called "The White Ship" "perhaps the most openly allegorical"[12] of Lovecraft's tales. Taking a Jungian approach, Mosig interprets the narrator's dream voyage as a search for the Self, though more broadly the voyage illustrates how hope inevitably leads to disappointment. As Donald R. Burleson has pointed out, the weakness of "The White Ship" lies in its being *"mere* allegory."[13] Unlike, for example, Hawthorne's "Celestial Railroad," it has no reality on a literal level, and in the final analysis is just as boring in its modest way as the bulk of Melville's *Mardi.*

If, as Darrell Schweitzer has noted, "The White Ship" parallels Dunsany's "Idle Days on the Yann,"[14] a trace of Poe's *Arthur Gordon Pym* is also discernible, particularly in the reference in the penultimate sentence to "a strange dead bird whose hue was as of the azure sky, and a single shattered spar, of a whiteness greater than that of the wave-tips or of the mountain snow" (D 42). The dead bird, the words *hue, whiteness,* and *snow,* the "of" prepositional phrases—all come straight from the ending of *Pym.* Even in his loftiest fantasies Lovecraft could not help but echo the man he deemed "the one real literary figure of America" (1:174).

As in other dreamland stories the style of "The Doom That Came to Sarnath" (1919) is evocative of the King James Bible, but the plot as well has about it a decidedly Old Testament air. Like Belshazzar and his lords, who ignore the handwriting on the wall, the men of Sarnath fail to heed "the sign of DOOM" (D 45) that the dying high-priest Taran-ish has scrawled upon the altar of chyrsolite. Ages later, after a feast to rival Belshazzar's, King Nargis-Hei and his nobles along with the entire city of Sarnath are destroyed by the rightful heirs of the land of Mnar, the voiceless, green-hued beings of Ib, who with their "bulging eyes, pouting, flabby lips, and curious ears" (D 43) anticipate the natives of Innsmouth. Jahweh has no place in Lovecraft's pagan world, of course, divine justice being meted out through the agency of "a sea-green stone idol chiselled in the likeness of Bokrug, the great water-lizard" (D 43). The bog-wraiths of "The Moon-Bog" will turn Denys Barry into a frog for trying to drain their swamp, while the sly, lizardlike creatures of "In the Walls of Eryx" will trap and kill the arrogant earthlings out to take over their territory. In Lovecraft, retribution comes surely to any outsider, whether human or reptile, who dares disrupt the established culture.

Of the plot of "The Tree" (1920) Lovecraft reported at the time that "it was the result of some rather cynical reflection on the possible real motives which may underlie even the most splendid-appearing acts of mankind" (1:121). His selection of ancient Greece as a setting would seem appropriate for this otherwise Dunsanian trifle, given the focus on the bond between "the two sculptors Kalos and Musides" (D 50), of whom men marvel "that no shadow of artistic jealousy cooled the warmth of their brotherly friendship" (D 51). Apart from Lovecraft's naive portrayal of what some would perceive as a homosexual relationship, one other element of interest in this moralistic tale of betrayal is the "unnaturally large olive tree of oddly repellent shape; so like to some grotesque man, or death-distorted body of a man" (D 50), which may have a source in "the apple-tree root which enter'd Roger Williams' coffin and is said to have follow'd the lines of the skeleton" (5:126).

In "The Cats of Ulthar" (1920), with the aid of that feline tribe of which Lovecraft was so fond, Menes, "a little boy with no father or mother, but only a tiny black kitten to cherish" (D 56), gets revenge on the old couple who murder his kitten. Springing, unlike "The Tree," from genuine emotion, "The Cats of Ulthar" stands as Lovecraft's most personal dreamland fantasy. In keeping with his usual preference for the company of cats to people, his favorite animals here play a more prominent role than the humans. Menes, while he may be one of Lovecraft's few child characters of consequence, could be any orphan boy of folklore.

If children are "almost non-existent"[15] in the fiction, as J. Vernon Shea has observed, certain older characters try desperately to revert to their childhood. In "Celephaïs" (1920) Kuranes, fallen English aristocrat and failed writer, seeks "beauty alone" (D 83), which he finds "on his very doorstep, amid the nebulous memories of childhood tales and dreams" (D 84). Here the dreamworld—"Ooth-Nargai, beyond the Tanarian Hills" (D 86)—appears for the first time to be an alternative dimension distinct from the actual earth, the creation of the dreamer himself, as Kuranes discovers when he meets "the cortege of knights come from Celephaïs to bear him thither forever" (D 88). Reinforcing this fairy-tale quality, the narrative voice asserts that Kuranes reigns over the city of Celephaïs after his bodily death "and will reign happily forever" (D 89). To escape from reality into some vague dreamworld is happiness enough for him in "Celephaïs," but in *The Dream-Quest of Unknown Kadath,* the culmination of Lovecraft's dreamland phase, Kuranes will learn that such a fate has its drawbacks.

In "The Quest of Iranon" (1921) the "vine-crowned" youth Iranon, "a singer of songs," tells the men of Teloth that "my calling is to make beauty with the things remembered of childhood" (D 111). Like Kuranes (and Lovecraft himself) he is another misunderstood artist. Temperamentally unsuited to earning a practical living, he has "no heart for the cobbler's trade" (D 113). "Aira, city of marble and beryl" (D 112), which he spends a lifetime seeking, proves in contrast to "the granite city of Teloth" (D 111) to have belonged to an ideal dream-world of his own imagining. But unlike Kuranes he cannot escape into his dreamworld. Disillusioned, his dreams no longer able to prevent him from aging, Iranon walks into "the lethal quicksands a very old man in tattered purple . . . That night something of youth and beauty died in the elder world." (D 117) In this pathos-laden tale Lovecraft suggests that dreams, however powerful, do not always lead to a happy ending, at least not for a dreamer in dreamland.

In "The Other Gods" (1921) "the gods of earth" dwell atop "the tallest of earth's peaks," including "unknown Kadath in the cold waste" (D 127). On occasion they descend to "the summit of high and rocky Hatheg-Kla" (D 128), which Barzai the Wise and Atal, the innkeeper's son from "The Cats of Ulthar," set out to climb in an act of hubris comparable to Randolph Carter's in *The Dream-Quest of Unknown Kadath*. Like Carter in "The Statement of Randolph Carter," only Atal survives to tell the tale. Disappearing into the clouds, Barzai meets "the *other* gods" (D 131) of which the tame gods of earth are afraid. So too in *At the Mountains of Madness* will Dyer and Danforth encounter other horrors far worse than those previously faced in the course of their exploration of Kadath in its Antarctic incarnation. As is the case with "Celephaïs," "The Other Gods" has value largely for its intimations of thematic concerns in the later fiction.

The last story of Lovecraft's initial Dunsanian phase, "The Other Gods" includes references to people, places, and things from previous tales. Barzai, for example, consults "the Pnakotic Manuscripts of distant and frozen Lomar" (D 128), first alluded to in "Polaris." By creating such links Lovecraft leaves it ambiguous whether the dream-world exists in some imaginary past on earth, in the minds of solipsistic dreamers like Basil Elton or Kuranes, or in some paradoxical combination of both. As S. T. Joshi has shown in his attempt to reconcile Lovecraft's dreamworld with his "real" world, contradictions arise that render any conclusions "tentative and confused."[16] The precise relation between dreams and reality, however, matters less perhaps than that Lovecraft was beginning to grow disenchanted with the pure Dunsanian mode. By 1930, long after he had completely embraced his special brand of realism, he could dismiss "The White Ship," the tale that epitomizes the manner, as "artificial & namby-pamby" (3:192). When in 1926 he returned to dreamland for a second and final round, he would root it firmly in that New England world that he had come to realize was essential to his happiness and his art.

Decadence

During his amateur phase Lovecraft tried his hand at the prose poem, a form perfected by Poe and the French decadents. These brief, somber mood pieces include "Memory" (1919), an ironic, "Ozymandias"-like projection of man's extinction; "Nyarlathotep" (1920), an apocalyptic vision based on a dream of a menacing figure out of Egypt (later to be expressed more succinctly in the *Fungi* sonnet of the same title); "Ex Oblivione" (1920/21), a statement of the appeal of escape into dreams and finally into oblivion; and "What the Moon Brings" (1922), the most gruesome of the four, in which a malignant moon and an object revealed by the receding sea combine to drive the narrator to join the dead underwater. Akin to the dreamland tales in their language and tone, and in such particulars as their moon imagery and quasi-Arcadian settings, the prose poems propound his view of life at its bleakest.

Barton St. Armand has assessed Lovecraft as "an artist of the after-glow of Decadence," noting that "while he often gloried in being (like the Oliver Alden of Santayana's novel) a 'Last Puritan,' Lovecraft also played the role of a solitary American Aesthete, a Rhode Island Oscar Wilde or a provincial Algernon Swinburne."[17] Following the meeting in April 1922 of his young protégé Frank Belknap Long, Jr., "a sincere and intelligent disciple of Poe, Baudelaire, and the French decadents" (1:175), Lovecraft looked closely at that school and acknowledged his own place in it, but only up to a point. In a letter dated 13 May 1923 he admitted to Long that he agreed with a friend's opinion that he was "no true decadent, for much that decadents love seems to me either absurd or merely disgusting" (1:228–29). Furthermore, he saw a crucial aesthetic difference between decadent practitioners and himself: "I am not so much thrilled by a visible charnel house or conclave of daemons, as I am by the *suspicion* that a charnel vault exists below an immemorially ancient castle, or that a certain very old man has taken part in a daemoniac conclave fifty years ago" (1:228). If he was too much of a Victorian ever to consider personally violating propriety,

Lovecraft found the decadent tradition sufficiently fascinating to write a couple of tales in homage.

In his memoir *Dreamer on the Nightside* Long reports that during a visit to the Poe Cottage in Fordham Lovecraft dedicated "Hypnos" (1922), with its epigraph from Baudelaire, to Edgar Allan Poe.[18] Indeed, Lovecraft makes the tribute explicit in the description of the unfortunate whom the narrator picks up at a London railway station: "I think he was then approaching forty years of age, for there were deep lines in the face, wan and hollow-cheeked, but oval and actually beautiful; and touches of grey in the thick, waving hair and small full beard which had once been of the deepest raven black. His brow was white as the marble of Pentelicus, and of a height and breadth almost godlike" (D 164–65). In this portrait of Roderick Usher–like grandeur, disguised by a beard that had once been "raven" black, undoubtedly lies Lovecraft's favorite author, though he remains as anonymous as a similar figure in Melville's *The Confidence Man*.

Together, "Poe" and the narrator lead a life of decadent indulgence. With exotic drugs they court "terrible and forbidden dreams in the tower studio chamber of the old manorhouse in hoary Kent" (D 166), seeking not sensual pleasures but cosmic thrills. As in "Beyond the Wall of Sleep," dreams provide access to the outside, though as usual the narrator has trouble describing their adventures: "What I learned and saw in those hours of impious exploration can never be told—for want of symbols or suggestions in any language" (D 166). Later in the same paragraph, however, he does make the attempt: "Human utterance can best convey the general character of our experiences by calling them plungings or soarings, for in every period of revelation some part of our minds broke boldly away from all that is real and present, rushing aerially along shocking, unlighted, and fear-haunted abysses, and occasionally tearing through certain well-marked and typical obstacles describable only as viscous, uncouth clouds of vapours" (D 166). Without a coherent plot to support them, such abstractions neither frighten nor enlighten. Familiar too is the ending where the narrator realizes that like Iranon he has been deluded by his own imagination, that his companion has never existed, that in truth the "godlike head" (D 170) he has sculpted of him resembles his own younger visage. Despite a promising "what if" premise, Lovecraft never really gets beyond tenderly describing Poe's head.

In "The Hound" (1922), written a few months after "Hypnos," the narrator declares that only "the sombre philosophy of the Decadents"

(D 171) could hold him and his friend St. John. After the dreamy voyagings of "Hypnos" this exuberant tale marks a return to the ghoulish boys' realm of "Herbert West—Reanimator," complete with underground hideaway:

Our museum was a blasphemous, unthinkable place, where with the satanic taste of neurotic virtuosi we had assembled an universe of terror and decay to excite our jaded sensibilities. It was a secret room, far, far underground; where huge winged daemons carven of basalt and onyx vomited from wide grinning mouths weird green and orange light, and hidden pneumatic pipes ruffled into kaleidoscopic dances of death the lines of red charnel things hand in hand woven in voluminous black hangings. Through these pipes came at will the odours our moods most craved; sometimes the scent of pale funeral lilies, sometimes the narcotic incense of imagined Eastern shrines of the kingly dead, and sometimes—how I shudder to recall it!—the frightful, soul-upheaving stenches of the uncovered grave. (D 172)

Steven J. Mariconda has observed that such a florid passage is "very much in the style of Huysmans,"[19] while pointing out the general thematic influence of *A Rebours* on the tale.

Shuttling between England and Holland in the year "19—" (though the date could as well be Poe's "18—") in pursuit of their preferred pastime of grave-robbing, the two decadents eventually retreat like the characters in "Hypnos" to "an ancient manor-house on a bleak and unfrequented moor" (D 175). There the horrors they have unearthed, predictably, catch up with them. In an almost nonchalant manner the narrator refers to the death of St. John, "seized by some frightful carnivorous thing and torn to ribbons" (D 176).[20] In such excess Lovecraft flirts with parody, a fact he seems to have forgotten eight years later when in a humorless mood he dismisses "The Hound" as a "piece of junk" (3:192). Embarrassingly overwritten the tale may be, but it deserves better than this low estimation by virtue of its vivacity alone.

While characters with decadent proclivities will crop up in "Medusa's Coil" and "The Thing on the Doorstep," accounts of their wild activities will be confined to rumor or hints. More significant, the decadent example lent support to Lovecraft's impulse to appeal frequently in his fiction to the senses other than sight, especially smell. Many of his Cthulhoid monsters will exude "foetid" or "noisome" odors, but never will grossness intrude for its own sake, only as a suggestive means toward heightening the horror. In his mature fiction Lovecraft will be far more concerned with decadence in the broader sense of social decline. Such New England tales as "The Dunwich Horror" and "The Shadow over Innsmouth" put him in the company of the Eugene O'Neill of *Mourning Becomes Electra*.

Chapter Three
Kingsport and Arkham

Perhaps in part because of his great fondness for his native New England, its natural landscape and colonial architecture in particular, Lovecraft did not immediately recognize its suitability as a setting for supernatural horror. Not until 1920 did it occur to him to look beyond the Gothicism of Poe and the otherworldly fantasy of Dunsany and take inspiration, as had Hawthorne, from the distant past of the region that had fostered them both. Drawing more upon his experiences of life than upon his book reading, Lovecraft began to place New England increasingly at the heart of his fiction. Over the next fifteen years he would succeed in transforming portions of Essex County, Massachusetts, and environs into a territory as mythically potent as Faulkner's Yoknapatawpha County or the London of Sherlock Holmes. Granted, Lovecraft's Arkham landscape has little of the dark, psychological complexity of Faulkner's Mississippi, nor can it claim the same nostalgic appeal as the detective's late Victorian England, yet it too has an enduring allure, at any rate for those few blessed with minds of the "requisite sensitiveness," as he phrases it in *Supernatural Horror in Literature*.

In these earliest New England tales Lovecraft introduces Kingsport and Arkham, Massachusetts, that pair of fictitious towns of somewhat uncertain provenance. "Vaguely, 'Arkham' corresponds to Salem (though Salem has no college)," he wrote in 1931, "while 'Kingsport' corresponds to Marblehead" (3:432). *Vaguely* is the key word in this assertion, for as Will Murray has shown, Lovecraft did not consistently identify Arkham as a seaport, and in several cases he seems actually to have located it well inland.[1] Where Kingsport becomes fixed as a constant as early as "The Festival," Arkham remains a variable, developing over the course of some dozen tales into Lovecraft's quintessential, cosmically haunted New England town. As befits such status, Arkham transcends any one spot on the map.

"The Terrible Old Man"

Admirers might wish it otherwise, but Lovecraft's bigotry pervades
his first tale with a distinct New England setting, "The Terrible Old
Man" (1920). Within its brief, tidy, ironic span it shows the same
disdain exhibited in the poem "Providence in 2000 A.D." for "that new
and heterogeneous alien stock which lies outside the charmed circle of
New England life and traditions" (DH 273). By selecting a diverse
national mix for his thieves, "Angelo Ricci and Joe Czanek and Manuel
Silva" (DH 272)—Italian, Slav, and Portuguese—Lovecraft at least
comes across as impartial in his prejudice. The three robbers, of course,
prove no match for the Terrible Old Man, a "tottering, almost helpless
greybeard" (DH 273), for he acts as heroic defender of those "New
England traditions" that Lovecraft was so keen to preserve. Supernatural horror, at the service of the Yankee establishment, brutally puts the
ethnic upstarts in their place. To set it in perspective, if not to excuse
it, such resentment recurs throughout our literature, from the "yellow
peril" writings of Frank Norris to the more snobbish poetry of T. S.
Eliot.

If "The Terrible Old Man" suffers as heavy-handed polemic, it nonetheless reveals Lovecraft beginning to use realistic New England elements. The title character, "believed to have been a captain of East
India clipper ships in his day" (DH 272), sets the pattern for later sea
captains like Obed Marsh who engage in dubious traffic in the Pacific
and the Far East. He also anticipates in outline a character like old
Wizard Whateley, with whom he would appear to share an appreciation of large standing stones: "Among the gnarled trees in the front
yard of his aged and neglected place he maintains a strange collection of
large stones, oddly grouped and painted so that they resemble the idols
in some obscure Eastern temple"[2] (DH 272). But where in "The
Dunwich Horror" such stones help to call down Yog-Sothoth, here they
function as no more than suggestive ornaments. Likewise Kingsport,
not yet inspired by any particular New England site, is simply a generic
coastal town with street names like "Ship" and "Water."

Even less to Lovecraft's credit is "The Street" (1920), a quasipoetic
attack on "foreign" subversion of Anglo-Saxon America, probably composed within a few months of "The Terrible Old Man," to which it
forms a kind of thematic footnote. In this petulant sketch, filled with
paraphrastic locutions in place of characters, a sole reference to "grave
men in conical hats" (D 344) specifically evokes New England, while

the street of the title is an idealized conglomeration of Lovecraft's beloved old houses. These buildings, "with their forgotten lore of nobler, departed centuries; of sturdy colonial tenants and dewy rose-gardens in the moonlight," have degenerated by the present into such establishments as "Petrovitch's Bakery, the squalid Rifkin School of Modern Economics, the Circle Social Club, and the Liberty Café," patronized by "alien makers of discord" (D 347), upon whom at the climax they collapse—in a ludicrous display of architecture animated by Lovecraft's own intolerance. Of negligible literary value, "The Street" is of interest chiefly as it reflects its author's conservative reaction to the Red Scare of the period.

"The Picture in the House"

"The Picture in the House" (1920), after the false starts of "The Terrible Old Man" and "The Street," stands as Lovecraft's first tale effectively to employ local New England color. Here Arkham makes its debut, though the action occurs outside the town, in the general region of the "Miskatonic Valley," where the anonymous narrator, the first of Lovecraft's sober-minded scholars, is "in quest of certain genealogical data" (DH 117). The time for the tale's action—November 1896—may not be as irrelevantly specific as April 11 for the thieves' call upon the Terrible Old Man, since such precision would be in keeping with the protagonist's pedantry.

The opening paragraph, an outstanding example of Lovecraftian bombast, sets forth what amounts to a declaration of aesthetic independence:

Searchers after horror haunt strange, far places. For them are the catacombs of Ptolemais, and the carven mausolea of the nightmare countries. They climb to the moonlit towers of ruined Rhine castles, and falter down black cobwebbed steps beneath the scattered stones of forgotten cities in Asia. The haunted wood and the desolate mountain are their shrines, and they linger around the sinister monoliths on uninhabited islands. But the true epicure in the terrible, to whom a new thrill of unutterable ghastliness is the chief end and justification, esteems most of all the ancient, lonely farmhouses of backwoods New England; for there the dark elements of strength, solitude, grotesqueness, and ignorance combine to form the perfection of the hideous. (DH 116)

With this manifesto Lovecraft serves notice that he will rely less upon stock Gothic backgrounds and turn more and more to his own New England as a source for horror.[3]

From this rhetorical height the narrative voice shifts smoothly to a broad view of these backwoods houses and their degenerate inhabitants, who "cowered in an appalling slavery to the dismal phantasms of their own minds" (DH 117), thus rooting the story proper in authentic Puritan psychohistory. In contrast to "The Street," the sentient quality of these houses keeps within credible bounds. When the narrator says of the "antique and repellent wooden building" in which he takes refuge, "Honest, wholesome structures do not stare at travellers so slyly and hauntingly" (DH 117), he is revealing not the objectivity of his judgment but the sensitivity of his imagination. Like Lovecraft, he can be at once the rationalist and the romantic.

From fanciful impression the narrator goes on to give an exact and naturalistic description of the exterior and interior of the house. Such finely observed details as the contents of the library shelf—"an eighteenth-century Bible, a *Pilgrim's Progress* of like period, illustrated with grotesque woodcuts and printed by the almanack-maker Isaiah Thomas, the rotting bulk of Cotton Mather's *Magnalia Christi Americana*" (DH 119)—vividly contribute to the mood of sinister antiquity. The character of the narrator, through such erudite particulars as his recognition of Pigafetta's *Regnum Congo*,[4] "written in Latin from the notes of the sailor Lopez and printed at Frankfort in 1598" (DH 119), emerges just enough to be convincing. His host, another menacing, preternaturally aged individual like the Terrible Old Man (though robust in physique, thanks to his diet of human flesh), speaks in an exaggerated, archaic dialect—" 'Ketched in the rain, be ye?' he greeted" (DH 120)—that contrasts nicely with the civilized diction of the narrator. Their exchange is an early instance of Lovecraft's habit of restricting quoted speech to a monologue: typically, to a rustic's account of strange goings-on given to a learned narrator who never records his side of the conversation. If this technique allowed Lovecraft to avoid the dialogue for which he felt he had no talent, it also helped him to tell his tales with considerable economy. Here, as in all of his better first-person narratives, dialogue never intrudes upon that intimate mental contact the narrator establishes with the reader.

At the climax, with a finesse unknown to those present-day horror writers who delight in graphic violence, Lovecraft suggests the worst through "a very simple though somewhat unusual happening" (DH 123): the tiny spattering of blood onto the open book page that causes the narrator to look up to the ceiling and see "a large irregular spot of wet crimson which seemed to spread even as I viewed it" (DH 124).

Unlike narrators of later tales, he has no time for philosophical rumina-
tions in face of such gruesome evidence, as fate intervenes in the next
moment in the form of "the titanic thunderbolt of thunderbolts; blast-
ing that accursed house of unutterable secrets and bringing the oblivion
that alone saved my mind" (DH 124). This deus ex machina ending,
trite though it may be, in effect reduces the tale to a nightmare from
which the narrator suddenly awakens when the danger becomes too
much to bear. His survival unhurt amid the blackened ruins of the
house is nothing miraculous for one in a dream. After the careful
realism and subtle plot development leading up to this denouement,
Lovecraft wisely refrains from any overt dream explanation. Such restraint helps make "The Picture in the House," however conventional
its cannibal theme, the strongest of Lovecraft's early New England
tales.

"Herbert West—Reanimator"

"I am become a Grub-Street hack," declared Lovecraft in announcing
his first professional story project. "My sole inducement is the mone-
tary reward" (1:157). When George Houtain, the editor of *Home Brew*
magazine, made him the offer, the hitherto amateur gentleman gamely
enough set aside his ideals and produced the six self-contained episodes
that together constitute "Herbert West—Reanimator" (1921–22). As
perhaps his most contrived work of fiction, it adds up to an awkward
and repetitious whole. No doubt length restrictions put a strain on his
invention. For example, the account of the thing that had been Dr.
Allan Halsey, "public benefactor and dean of the medical school of
Miskatonic University" (D 143), running amok for three days and
killing a total of nineteen Arkham residents, might have been less
grotesquely comic had it not been so compressed. That Lovecraft later
condemned "Herbert West" as "my poorest work—stuff done to order
for a vulgar magazine, & written down to the herd's level" (1:201),
however, should not obscure the fact that the plot, which builds in
neat, logical increments from one section to the next, took some skill to
construct. Within an artificial framework lies an ingenious tale, as
lurid and lively as any of Robert E. Howard's pulp action yarns that
would so excite *Weird Tales* readers later in the decade.

As monomaniacally as Captain Ahab seeks the white whale, Herbert
West strives to perfect his corpse-reanimating techniques, assisted by
the compliant, Ishmael-like narrator, until undone by his unholy cre-

ations. Of course, on the scale of Faustian fiction "Herbert West" is closer in value to *Frankenstein* than to *Moby-Dick,* yet by selecting a pseudoscientific premise in accord with his own philosophical views— West's theories "hinged on the essentially mechanistic nature of life" (D 134)—Lovecraft betrays some degree of seriousness. Says the narrator: "Holding with Haeckel that all life is a chemical and physical process, and that the so-called 'soul' is a myth, my friend believed that artificial reanimation of the dead can depend only on the condition of the tissues; and that unless actual decomposition has set in, a corpse fully equipped with organs may with suitable measures be set going again in the peculiar fashion known as life" (D 134). In a letter to Frank Belknap Long from the fall of 1921 describing his progress on the serial, Lovecraft advised him to read Ernst Haeckel's *Riddle of the Universe* "before placing too much credence in any vague and unexplainable force of 'life' beyond the ordinarily known mechanical forms" (1:158).

Emphasizing action over atmosphere, Lovecraft provides little local color. The first two sections, stocked with references to such new Arkham sites as Meadow Hill and Christchurch Cemetery, contain none of the architectural and historical detail that enriches "The Picture in the House." Only Miskatonic University, in its initial appearance, assumes any character—primarily as the institution where Herbert West and the narrator get started in their profane medical researches. Parts 3 and 4 transpire in nearby Bolton, an inexplicable use of an actual Massachusetts town northeast of Worcester, though again it might be any mill town of the region.[5] Only in the sixth and concluding section, after a grisly interlude behind the front in Flanders in part 5, does Lovecraft make a passing attempt to particularize place. Having finally settled "in a venerable house of much elegance, overlooking one of the oldest burying-grounds in Boston" (D 160), West is back on familiar ground—that is, below it. In the process of having a subcellar dug out for his laboratory, he discovers some "exceedingly ancient masonry" that he calculates must form a "secret chamber beneath the tomb of the Averills, where the last interment had been made in 1768" (D 160). Even in his hackwork Lovecraft could not resist slipping in an antiquarian touch or two.

Such incidental features redeem a tale like "Herbert West," as is true of his weaker efforts in general, imbuing it with a certain naive charm. Only in a Lovecraft story could two young men not pursue attractive female specimens for their experiments, remaining bachelors for seventeen years, all without a hint of deviant sexual behavior. (In 1985

Hollywood would supply the missing sex element in its gory if good-natured film version, *Re-Animator*.) If "Herbert West—Reanimator" represents an unnatural detour from Lovecraft's own development, it nonetheless shows how entertainingly he could write when compelled to satisfy someone else's story requirements.

"The Unnamable"

With "The Unnamable" (1923) Lovecraft returned to the vein begun in "The Picture in the House," adapting a bit of New England folklore out of Cotton Mather's "chaotic *Magnalia Christi Americana*" (D 203), of which he possessed an ancestral copy. The narrator, Lovecraft's persona Randolph Carter (referred to only as "Carter"), is, in a touch of self-parody, an author of weird fiction. With his friend "Joel Manton,"[6] "principal of the East High School, born and bred in Boston and sharing New England's self-satisfied deafness to the delicate overtones of life" (D 201), Carter conducts a stilted debate over the existence of the "unnamable," while "sitting on a dilapidated seventeenth-century tomb in the late afternoon of an autumn day at the old burying-ground in Arkham" (D 200). In a letter answering some small matters about the tale's obscure plot, Lovecraft noted that there was "actually an ancient slab half engulfed by a giant willow tree in the middle of the Charter St. Burying Ground in Salem" (2:139). References to the Salem witchcraft in the tale itself also connect Arkham to the venerable Essex County seaport.

As in "The Picture in the House," the narrator hints at horrors in colonial Massachusetts far worse than any known to the history books:

> It had been an eldritch thing—no wonder sensitive students shudder at the Puritan age in Massachusetts. So little is known of what went on beneath the surface—so little, yet such a ghastly festering as it bubbles up putrescently in occasional ghoulish glimpses. The witchcraft terror is a horrible ray of light on what was stewing in men's crushed brains, but even that is a trifle. There was no beauty; no freedom—we can see that from the architectural and household remains, and the poisonous sermons of the cramped divines. And inside that rusted iron strait-jacket lurked gibbering hideousness, perversion, and diabolism. Here, truly, was the apotheosis of the unnamable. (D 203)

Unlike "The Picture in the House," however, "The Unnamable" fails to deliver the horrors such an assertion promises, being nearly as stagey and static as that poorest of Sherlock Holmes stories, "The Adventure of the Mazarin Stone."[7] Carter may boast that his tale "The Attic Window" led to the removal of the magazine it appeared in from the stands in many places "at the complaints of silly milksops" (D 202), but, judging from his smug, inappropriately offhand manner, his "lowly standing as an author" (D 200) is not undeserved. Indeed, the uncharacteristic use of dialogue suggests that on some parodic level Lovecraft may have conceived the tale as more Carter's than his own.

Manton's impressionistic description of the monster that shows up from nowhere at the climax to gore them like a bull, "a gelatin—a slime . . . the pit—the maelstrom" (D 207), incongruously mixes the viscous and the literary, as it confirms rather too patly Carter's belief in the impossibility of naming the unnamable. Lovecraft will link shoggoths and Poe less crudely in *At the Mountains of Madness*.

"The Festival"

More than seven years after his initial visit to Marblehead, Massachusetts, Lovecraft wrote: "God! Shall I ever forget my first stupefying glimpse of MARBLEHEAD'S huddled and archaick roofs under the snow in the delirious sunset glory of four p.m., Dec. 17, 1922!!! I did not know until an hour before that I should ever behold such a place as Marblehead, and I did not know *until that moment itself* the full extent of the wonder I was to behold. I account that instant—about 4:05 to 4:10 p.m., Dec. 17, 1922—the most powerful single emotional climax during my nearly forty years of existence" (3:126). Such a declaration, while it should not be taken wholly at face value, can be considered an honest expression of Lovecraft's preference for emotions of purely aesthetic origin to those generated by human relationships. In particular, it indicates, as none of his direct comments on the matter do, why his marriage in the interval was doomed.

"The Festival" (1923) marks Lovecraft's first and most literal attempt to recapture in fiction the ecstasy prompted by the sight of a well-preserved New England town of colonial vintage. The unnamed narrator, as he nears Kingsport by foot at "Yuletide," experiences architectural rapture of an intensity far beyond any felt by the narrator of "The Picture in the House":

Then beyond the hill's crest I saw Kingsport outspread frostily in the gloaming; snowy Kingsport with its ancient vanes and steeples, ridgepoles and

chimney-pots, wharves and small bridges, willow-trees and graveyards; endless labyrinths of steep, narrow, crooked streets, and dizzy church-crowned
central peak that time durst not touch; ceaseless mazes of colonial houses piled
and scattered at all angles and levels like a child's disordered blocks; antiquity
hovering on grey wings over winter-whitened gables and gambrel roofs;
fanlights and small-paned windows one by one gleaming out in the cold dusk
to join Orion and the archaic stars. (D 209)

Lovecraft used such similar phrases as "small buildings heap'd about at
all angles and all levels like an infant's blocks" (1:204) to describe
Marblehead in a letter to Rheinhart Kleiner dated 11 January 1923,
suggesting a common set of notes for both the letter and the tale that
was to follow later in the year.

As in "The Lurking Fear," something is odd about an entire community: "they were strange, because they had come as dark furtive folk
from opiate southern gardens of orchids, and spoken another tongue
before they learnt the tongue of the blue-eyed fishers" (D 209). Here
Lovecraft resorts to the flowery language of dreamland, but for no other
purpose than to distinguish the inhabitants of Kingsport from more
traditional Puritan settlers. Their background and motives remain
vague. Unlike the ghouls of "Pickman's Model," these "dark furtive
folk" have no real stake in the scene set out so lovingly in the first part
of the story. After all the effort put into the creation of the mood
picture of the antique town, Lovecraft seems to have been too exhausted
to devise a horrific premise of equal power.

In this perhaps most Hawthornesque of Lovecraft tales, the narrator
has been called, like the title character of Hawthorne's "Young Goodman Brown," to attend a Sabbath rendezvous.[8] There he experiences a
hideous revelation, discovering not that he belongs to a fallen brotherhood of man but that his own ancestors are evil, reanimated corpses—a
far less profound insight, to say the least, than that gained by Goodman
Brown. Faced with conventional monsters he reacts with conventional
fear, his responses bordering on the illogical. While in the cavern
below the church he regards with comparative calm the "tame, trained,
hybrid winged things" that are "not altogether crows, nor moles, nor
buzzards, nor ants, nor vampire bats, nor decomposed human beings,"
yet he flings himself into the oily underground river only after the mask
of the old man who has guided him slips and he glimpses "what should
have been his head" (D 215), an arguably less frightening vision.

"The Festival," overwritten and melodramatic though it may be,

especially at its climax, does have value as more than just an atmo-
spheric study. In "Herbert West" an artificial head had allowed a
reanimated corpse missing the genuine item to pass among the living,
while in "The Festival," a bit more plausibly, a waxen mask and gloves
serve to hide the decay of what had once been human. This face-hands
deception motif will reappear as a vital plot feature in "The Whisperer
in Darkness" and "Through the Gates of the Silver Key," and less
centrally in "The Dunwich Horror," where the relatively normal face
and hands of Wilbur Whateley disguise his fundamentally alien nature.
The colonial house in "The Festival," like that in "The Picture in the
House," holds a library of ancient books but of a plainly sinister import: "I saw that the books were hoary and mouldy, and that they
included old Morryster's wild *Marvells of Science,* the terrible *Saducismus
Triumphatus* of Joseph Glanvill, published in 1681, the shocking
Daemonolatreia of Remigius, printed in 1595 at Lyons, and worst of all,
the unmentionable *Necronomicon* of the mad Arab Abdul Alhazred, in
Olaus Wormius's forbidden Latin translation; a book which I had never
seen, but of which I had heard monstrous things whispered" (D 211).
In this surely conscious echo of the catalogue of books in "The Fall of
the House of Usher," Lovecraft establishes the *Necronomicon* as the acme
of all such dreaded volumes. As with Kingsport and Arkham, each new
appearance makes Alhazred's wondrous tome seem that much more
convincing. Defined only through guarded mentions and rare quoted
passages, it will come to seem more real than any actual book.[9] There is
nothing comparable in Poe.

Chapter Four
Castles, Garrets, and Tombs

Lovecraft first began to formulate his aesthetics of the weird tale in a series of essay-letters to the Transatlantic Circulator, a loose organization of amateurs in the United States and England to which in the early twenties he contributed a number of his stories and poems. While mainly concerned with pointing out the logical contradictions in the Christian concepts of the soul and immortality, he prefaces each of the three pieces with a justification of his horror fiction. "In replying to the adverse criticism of my weird tale 'Dagon', I must begin by conceding that all such work is necessarily directed to a very limited section of the public," he says at the start of "The Defence Reopens!", dated January 1921. After dividing fiction into three major divisions, "romantic, realistic, and imaginative," he goes on to argue the superiority of the imaginative writer, who "devotes himself to art in its most essential sense. It is not his business to fashion a pretty trifle to please the children, to point a useful moral, to concoct superficial 'uplift' stuff for the mid-Victorian hold-over, or to rehash insolvable human problems didactically. He is the painter of moods and mind-pictures—a capturer and amplifier of elusive dreams and fancies—a voyager into those unheard-of lands which are glimpsed through the veil of actuality but rarely, and only by the most sensitive" (DD 11–12). Lovecraft would repeat these sentiments in much the same language a few years later in *Supernatural Horror in Literature.*

In the second essay, "The Defence Remains Open!", dated April 1921, he states that "tales of ordinary characters would appeal to a larger class, but I have no wish to make such an appeal. The opinions of the masses are of no interest to me, for praise can truly gratify only when it comes from a mind sharing the author's perspective. There are probably seven persons, in all, who really like my work; and they are enough. I should write even if I were the only patient reader, for my aim is merely self-expression. I could not write about 'ordinary people' because I am not in the least interested in them. Without interest there can be no art. Man's relations to man do not captivate my fancy. It is man's relations to the cosmos—to the unknown—which alone arouses in me the spark of creative imagination" (DD 21). The inherently small audience for his work would not always be such a matter of indifference once he started to publish professionally, but time would only confirm his faith that man's relations to the "cosmos" were his proper subject.

In the third essay, "Final Words," dated September 1921, he continues to affect the same benignly arrogant tone, but acknowledges his shortcomings: "For the endorsement and interest of the public I care not at all, writing solely for my own satisfaction. Writing for any other motive could not possibly be art—the professional author is the ultimate antithesis of the artist. My own failure to be an artist results from limited genius rather than mischosen object" (DD 34). In support of his artistic ideal he quotes at length from Oscar Wilde's preface to *The Picture of Dorian Gray*. Repulsed by Wilde's sexual degeneracy, Lovecraft would say in January 1927 that he "was never in any basic sense what one likes to call a *gentleman*" and generally belittle his accomplishment, but here he is unpriggish enough to align himself with the "Prince of Dandies" (2:98) against "bourgeois critics" (DD 34).

Lovecraft's involvement in the Transatlantic Circulator coincided with the most prolific phase of the first half of his career, extending from the end of 1919 into 1922. The quality of his output would remain uneven up to 1926, but in the best of these early tales, starting in 1921 with "The Outsider" and "The Music of Erich Zann," he demonstrated that he was capable of greatness in the genre. If rooted in comparatively traditional ghostly concepts, they nonetheless achieve heights equal to any in the later fiction.

"The Outsider"

"My principal fault with beginnings is to make them too Poesque & sententious," Lovecraft wrote Clark Ashton Smith in 1930. "Since Poe affected me most of all horror-writers, I can never feel that a tale starts out right unless it has something of his manner" (3:219). In "The Outsider" (1921) he managed to capture the Poe manner not only in the opening—"Unhappy is he to whom the memories of childhood bring only fear and sadness" (DH 46)—but to maintain it, with nary a false note, through the italicized closing.

Colin Wilson observes that "The Outsider" "owes something to 'William Wilson' and perhaps Wilde's 'Birthday of the Infanta.' "[1] L. Sprague de Camp cites as influences "The Masque of the Red Death" and possibly Hawthorne's "Fragments from the Journal of a Solitary Man."[2] Such echoes, rather than reflecting a dependence on the ideas of others, underline the tale's archetypal richness. As Dirk W. Mosig and Robert M. Price have shown, this parable of the plight of the individual who feels alienated from the rest of mankind readily lends itself to allegorical analysis.[3]

Neither based on a dream nor set in a dreamworld, "The Outsider" *is* a dream, "riddled with illogic and absurdity,"[4] as William Fulwiler has suggested, taking his cue from the Keats epigraph whose first line reads: "That night the Baron dreamt of many a woe" (DH 46). The narrator, the "outsider" of the title, can get no definite fix on either space or time: "I know not where I was born, save that the castle was infinitely old and infinitely horrible" (DH 46); "I must have lived years in this place, but I cannot measure the time" (DH 47). Despite such tenuousness the story abounds with specifics. Certainly the outsider's abode, the dimly lit castle surrounded by a forest so thick that only a partially ruined tower pushes above the treetops "into the unknown outer sky" (DH 47), rivals Poe's House of Usher as a symbolically potent image. The castle contains "maddening rows of antique books" (DH 46). "From such books I learned all that I know," asserts the outsider, though they mislead him in the impression he gains of his own identity: "I merely regarded myself by instinct as akin to the youthful figures I saw drawn and painted in the books" (DH 47). Here Lovecraft makes a rare admission of the limitations of book learning.

The outsider remains ignorant of his real nature until, like some character out of classical myth, he climbs up the ruined tower, emerges from his underworld into the land of the living, and enters a familiar-looking castle, where he sees beyond an "arch" "the ghoulish shade of decay, antiquity, and desolation; the putrid, dripping eidolon of unwholesome revelation; the awful baring of that which the merciful earth should always hide" ·(DH 51). In the course of his identity crisis the outsider successively evinces bewilderment, discontent, elation, bafflement, horror, despair, and finally resignation and acceptance. Seeking forgetfulness and finding balm in "nepenthe," he elects to "ride with the mocking and friendly ghouls on the night-wind, and play by day amongst the catacombs of Nephren-Ka in the sealed and unknown valley of Hadoth by the Nile" (DH 52), an appropriate fate for one who has been imprisoned like a pharaoh, as Price notes, with his personal "possessions and effects."[5] Working on both a literal and an allegorical level, "The Outsider" is the most dramatically compelling of Lovecraft's early tales—only the climax of "The Rats in the Walls" surpasses it in emotional intensity.

In a letter of June 1931 to J. Vernon Shea, Lovecraft condemned "The Outsider" as "too glibly *mechanical* in its elimination effect" (3:379), the postponing to the final sentence the foregone revelation that the outsider has stumbled against a mirror, "*a cold and unyielding surface of polished glass*" (DH 52). Yet since Lovecraft employed this gimmick of saving the confirming piece of evidence to the end in subsequent tales and would resort to it again in his last extended narrative, "The Shadow Out of Time," such criticism perhaps masks a subconscious urge to reject a tale veiling disturbing autobiographical truths, like his need for love. In the same letter to Shea he conceded that "The Outsider" "has the single merit of an original point of view" (3:379)—a point of view fundamentally human. Despite the appeal for him of writing a weird tale from a wholly alien perspective (like that of Wilbur Whateley's twin brother), Lovecraft never made the attempt. He may have realized that even he was incapable of such total detachment.

"The Music of Erich Zann"

"The Music of Erich Zann" (1921), in contrast to "The Outsider," opens calmly, in a wistful key: "I have examined maps of the city with the greatest care, yet have never again found the Rue d'Auseil" (DH 83). With as much care as the anonymous narrator examines the maps of this French city that appears to be Paris, Lovecraft lays out the scene of the story, a steep, narrow street lined with archaic buildings: "The houses were tall, peaked-roofed, incredibly old, and crazily leaning backward, forward, and sidewise" (DH 84). Here the architectural description is neither so obscure as in "The Street" nor so precise as in "The Picture in the House," but serves to define an unrecapturable realm that would seem to exist somewhere between the dream landscape of "The Outsider" and the realistic settings of the New England fiction. The narrator shares some of the outsider's disorientation—"I do not know how I came to live on such a street, but I was not myself when I moved there" (DH 84)—but he never forgets who he is.

References to his "impoverished life as a student of metaphysics at the university" (DH 83) and to his poor physical and mental health stamp the narrator as a character solidly in the Gothic tradition. Like Washington Irving's protagonist in "The Adventure of the German Student," he has a supernatural encounter in Paris. Instead of going to bed with a beautiful girl who turns out to have been guillotined, however, he gets involved with "an old German viol-player, a strange dumb man who signed his name Erich Zann," who has the garret above his room in the place they board at in the Rue d'Auseil, "the third house from the top of the street, and by far the tallest of them all" (DH 84). Where Irving explores sexual guilt in his tale, Lovecraft concerns himself, typically, with cosmic mystery in his.

Just what propels Herr Zann to play his wild, unearthly tunes remains unknown. During the old man's final recital, amidst "the shrieking and whining of that desperate viol" (DH 89), the narrator looks out the high garret window: "I saw no city spread below, and no friendly lights gleamed from remembered streets, but only the blackness of space illimitable; unimagined space alive with motion and music, and having no semblance of anything on earth" (DH 90). Such abstractions, so disappointing after a portentous buildup, cast no light on the contents of Zann's tantalizing manuscript swept out the window by the wind, "a full account in German of all the marvels and terrors which beset him" (DH 90). As Lovecraft observed in 1930 to Robert E. Howard regarding "excessive indefiniteness" in weird fiction, "Drawing the line between concrete description and trans-dimensional suggestion is a very ticklish job" (3:174).

If he did not quite strike the right balance in "The Music of Erich Zann," Lovecraft was sufficiently satisfied in later years to rate it second among his own work after "The Colour Out of Space," another tale of ineffable, unexplained horror. While this high ranking may represent an overreaction to the charge of overexplicitness in much of his better fiction, Lovecraft was in this judgment not too far off the critical mark. "The Music of Erich Zann" is one of his strongest pre-1926 tales, with a denouement more subtle than, say, that of "The Outsider." At the climax the narrator, like the outsider, reaches out with his hand and touches "death," here Zann's "still face; the ice-cold, stiffened, unbreathing face whose glassy eyes bulged uselessly into the void" (DH 91). Instead of coming in the last sentence, however, this shattering, unitalicized revelation occurs in the third paragraph from the end. The story closes symmetrically on the same plaintive note sounded in the opening: "Despite my most careful searches and investigations, I have never since been able to find the Rue d'Auseil." By asserting that he is "not wholly sorry" (DH 91) for this fact, the narrator looks ahead to the ambivalent heroes of later, more profoundly cosmic tales who feel both attracted and repelled by the horrors they happen upon.

Psychological undercurrents run deep in "The Music of Erich Zann." The narrator, who states that "my metaphysical studies had taught me kindness" (DH 87), evinces the sympathy, if not quite the respect and affection, that younger men often feel for much older men in the fiction. Breaking down Zann's reserve indeed constitutes the dramatic core of the story. Coming to the musician's rescue at a crucial juncture, the narrator notices that his "distorted face gleamed with relief while he clutched at my coat as a child clutches at its mother's skirts" (DH 88). Like "The Outsider," if on a more muted scale, "The Music of Erich Zann" concerns the misery of loneliness and the need to connect, however futile the effort, with other human beings.

"The Rats in the Walls"

"The Rats in the Walls" (1923) stands as Lovecraft's single most brilliant Gothic exercise, his equivalent of "The Fall of the House of Usher." Despite its being his longest to date, this tale exhibits, more strongly than any before it, Lovecraft's grasp of Poe's unity of effect principle. This story of a castle haunted by spectral rats also invites comparison with such classic novels of the genre as *The Castle of Otranto* and *Dracula,* as Barton St. Armand has pointed out in his penetrating study, *The Roots of Horror in the Fiction of H. P. Lovecraft.* By referring to the local citizenry as "peasants" and making such remarks as "I had not been a day in Anchester before I knew I came of an accursed house" (DH 27), the narrator shows his kinship with the doomed, aristocratic heroes of moldy romance. Yet "The Rats in the Walls" is unmistakably the work of a twentieth-century consciousness (or subconsciousness), a realistic tale whose opening sentence immediately fixes the scene in the contemporary world: "On July 16, 1923, I moved into Exham Priory after the last workman had finished his labours" (DH 26). Here there is no coy disguising of dates as in "The Hound," nor does the narrator launch into an anguished lament as in "The Outsider."

Delapore, who like the protagonist of Hawthorne's *The Ancestral Footstep* has come to England from America to claim an old family estate, relates the tragic history behind this event with the composure and dignity befitting "a retired manufacturer no longer young" whose career began with his merging into "the greyness of Massachusetts business life" (DH 28). His account of past generations forms no awkward digression, like that of the narrator in "Arthur Jermyn," but serves naturally as background to the priory's restoration. While he may be repressed, Delapore is no narcissistic loner, judging from the grief he evinces at the death of his only son, who returns from the Great War "a maimed invalid": "During the two years that he lived I thought of nothing but his care, having even placed my business under the direction of partners" (DH 28). This glimpse of the sadness behind the stoic mask, perhaps obliquely revealing in its role reversal of Lovecraft's feelings over the loss of his father, prepares the psychological ground for Delapore's fall. The old man pridefully looks forward "to redeeming at last the local fame of the line which ended in me" and to proving "that a de la Poer (for I had adopted again the original spelling of the name) need not be a fiend" (DH 32), but in the end he cannot escape the curse of his heredity.

In Exham Priory Lovecraft finally conceived of an edifice with a profound symbolic function. Where the forbidding House of Usher outwardly expresses Roderick Usher's gloomy mental state, Exham Priory, with its "peculiarly composite architecture" of "Gothic towers resting on a Saxon or Romanesque substructure, whose foundation in turn was of a still earlier order or blend of orders—Roman, and even Druidic or native Cymric, if legends speak truly" (DH 27), represents Delapore's mind with all its layers of consciousness. Here Lovecraft has clearly entered Jungian territory. Indeed, as Barton St. Armand was the first to remark, he has coincidentally fleshed out in fiction a dream Jung recounts in *Man and His Symbols*—a dream of going down through a house, each level older than the one above, until coming across some human bones in a cave below the cellar. Of this extraordinary parallel St. Armand notes that "if it were not for the fact that it was nearly impossible for Lovecraft to have known of Jung's dream, its similarity to the symbolic action of the story might lead one (on purely internal evidence) to cite it as a source."[6]

In this, indisputably Lovecraft's most subtle and suspenseful tale, the plot consists of a series of small, portentous episodes, starting with de la Poer's favorite cat sniffing at the walls, an incident "so simple as to be almost negligible" (DH 33). The agitated behavior of all the cats, the stirring of the arras, the sprung traps, de la Poer's frightful dream of "a twilit grotto, knee-deep in filth, where a white-bearded swineherd drove about with his staff a flock of fungous, flabby beasts" (DH 35)—these and other details generate an acute sense of dread, anticipating and yet giving nothing away of the shocking denouement. The twilit grotto that the team of savants uncovers below the altar in the subcellar holds anthropological remains that spectacularly realize de la Poer's nightmares. Commencing with the observation that the passage they descend "must have been chiselled *from beneath*" (DH 41) and the view of the "insane tangle of human bones" that stretches before them like "a foamy sea" (DH 42), he must face terrible truths about his family's past and by extension the past of all mankind. Occultism, according to Lovecraft, has no better explanation than science for the revelations of that "subterraneous world of limitless mystery and horrible suggestion" (DH 41–42), for the psychic among the party, Thornton, is if anything less prepared for them than his rational companions.

In the course of exploring the grotto, after wondering ironically "that any man among us lived and kept his sanity through that hideous day of discovery" (DH 42), de la Poer does in fact go mad, as his progressively hysterical language so dramatically demonstrates. At first, in an echo of the end of "The Outsider," he invokes the evil antiquity of Egypt. His old black cat darts past him like "a winged Egyptian god" in pursuit of "the eldritch scurrying of those fiend-born rats" that would lead them "even unto those grinning caverns of earth's centre where Nyarlathotep, the mad faceless god, howls blindly in the darkness to the piping of two amorphous idiot flute-players" (DH 44). Lovecraft will repeat with variation this image embodying the universe's essential meaningless in later tales until it becomes almost commonplace, but here, original and unexpected, it has a devastating impact, extending the implications of traditional mythology as represented by those sinister gods worshipped by the Romans, the Magna Mater and Atys.

At the climax, no longer able to suppress his emotions, de la Poer gives in to his atavistic urges and turns on the "plump" Capt. Norrys, his late son's friend, with cannibalistic intent. Through a sequence of ever more archaic exclamations Lovecraft masterfully renders de la Poer's cathartic devolution:

Who says I am a de la Poer? He lived, but my boy died! . . . Shall a Norrys hold the lands of a de la Poer? . . . It's voodoo, I tell you . . . that spotted snake . . . Curse you, Thornton, I'll teach you to faint at what my family do! . . . 'Sblood, thou stinkard, I'll learn ye how to gust . . . wolde ye swynke me thilke wys? . . . *Magna Mater! Magna Mater! . . . Atys . . . Dia ad aghaidh 's ad aodann . . . agus bas dunach ort! Dhonas 's dholas ort, agus leat-sa! . . . Ungl . . . ungl . . . rrlh . . . chchch . . .* (DH 44–45)

At the end, shut up in "this barred room at Hanwell" (DH 45), de la Poer lets on that all along his has been the tale of a madman. Unlike the narrator of "The Tomb," he has not made the mistake of blurting out this information at the beginning, but has properly set the stage for it by making passing mention early on that "this week the workmen have blown up Exham Priory, and are busy obliterating the traces of its foundations" (DH 27).

If "The Rats in the Walls" lends itself readily to Jungian interpretation, its message would seem to run contrary to Jung's belief in man's ability to cure his psychic ills through analysis. De la Poer's psychic digging leads, after all, to an outcome that would seem grimly to support the Freudian notion that man can do little to change his basic nature. In terms of the disciplines metaphorically associated with the two great psychological schools of our century, "The Rats in the Walls" may be ultimately more archaeologically Freudian than alchemically Jungian. Lovecraft, of course, would probably not have been comfortable with either view. His extant remarks on "Rats" are curiously neutral, pertaining chiefly to its anthropological and linguistic background. In the most probing of his pre-1926 tales he had achieved a far better balance between suggestion and explicitness than in, say, "The Music of Erich Zann," but his gentlemanly reserve (appropriately for a story about the breakdown of gentlemanly reserve) likely kept him from regarding it as highly.

"In the Vault"

"In the Vault" (1925), while it lacks the psychological complexity of the best of the earlier fiction, has a structure as tight as either "The Outsider" or "The Rats in the Walls." In this homely story of "a bungling and thick-fibred village undertaker" (DH 3), Lovecraft is as thrifty with words as his protagonist is with coffins, even though the anonymous narrator, "no practiced teller of tales," does tend to overstate the salient traits of the principals—George Birch, "thoughtless, careless, and liquorish" (DH 4), and the corpse of the late Asaph Sawyer, "not a lovable man" of whom "many stories were told of his almost inhuman vindictiveness and tenacious memory for wrongs real or fancied" (DH 5). Dedicated to C. W. Smith, a bucolic, old amateur colleague from Massachusetts, "from whose suggestion the central situation is taken" (DH 3), "In the Vault" stays true to Yankee character type, even while the locale could be anywhere in the rural Northeast.

After getting accidentally locked in the receiving tomb of the "Peck Valley Cemetery" (DH 3), George Birch resorts to piling up coffins awaiting the spring thaw for burial in order to reach the narrow transom above the door, thereby effecting an escape as thrilling and as unexpected in its consequences as the climb of the outsider up the ruined tower of his castle. Birch's "miniature Tower of Babel" (DH 7) proves no more stable than the Old Testament original. As he prepares to heave himself through the opening that he has spent hours enlarging, the rotting lid of the topmost coffin gives way, "jouncing him two feet down on a surface which even he did not care to imagine" (DH 8). Lovecraft knows better than to go into bloody detail, letting suggestion convey the sardonic grisliness that is the keynote of the story. As in "The Outsider," the clinching bit of information arrives in the last sentence, here delivered by the doctor who has visited the tomb after examining the undertaker's strangely wounded feet. Of the state of Asaph Sawyer's body, knocked out of its coffin in Birch's struggle, Dr. Davis says, "The skull turned my stomach, but the other was worse—*those ankles cut neatly off to fit Matt Fenner's cast-aside coffin!*" (DH 11). However gruesome this ending, it is restrained by contemporary standards, more the stuff of Poe and Bierce than of Stephen King and Clive Barker.

Like Joseph Curwen in *The Case of Charles Dexter Ward,* Asaph Sawyer returns to life (if only for the moment) on Good Friday, an example perhaps of what Donald R. Burleson has called the "overbearingly ironic"[7] quality of "In the Vault." This date, however, like Sawyer's "eye-for-an-eye fury" (DH 11), does by association nicely support the moralistic tone of this tale of revenge from the grave. Despite his antireligious fervor, Lovecraft was not above drawing upon biblical tradition when on occasion it suited his horrific purposes.

Chapter Five

New York

At the time Lovecraft moved to New York to marry Sonia Greene in 1924, he was optimistic about his chances of earning a living from his fiction. Edwin Baird, editor of *Weird Tales,* had accepted every story he had submitted. Immediately after settling in with Sonia at her fashionable Parkside address in Brooklyn, however, he learned that *Weird Tales* was on the verge of bankruptcy and undergoing reorganization. Offered the editorship of "The Unique Magazine," Lovecraft turned it down, in part because, as he informed Frank Belknap Long three weeks after the wedding, it would have meant moving to Chicago, a city far from the "Colonial atmosphere which supplies my very breath of life" (1:332).

In the following months all efforts to find work in New York making use of his writing and editing skills came to naught, employers being understandably reluctant to hire a thirty-four-year-old man who had never before held a regular job. Meanwhile, Sonia, who had been supporting them both, suffered setbacks in her millinery business and had to accept a position in the Midwest. With her departure at New Year's 1925, Lovecraft moved to a boardinghouse near the seedy Red Hook district in Brooklyn. Although Sonia would return for visits whenever she could, the marriage was effectively at an end. Founded on fragile bonds in the first place, it could not stand the test of financial hardship. Only the company of Frank Long, Sam Loveman, and others of his literary "gang" called the Kalem Club provided any distraction from cares. Presented with the opportunity on separate occasions of meeting Theodore Dreiser and Edna St. Vincent Millay, Lovecraft declined in each instance. According to his friend Vrest Orton, he avoided Dreiser because he "was not a good wielder of the English tongue" and Millay because "he said he did not have the proper clothes."[1]

Before he gave up and went home to Providence in the spring of 1926, Lovecraft wrote three stories with New York City settings. All reflect the misery of this period.

"The Horror at Red Hook"

Soon after composing "The Horror at Red Hook" (1925) Lovecraft wrote to Clark Ashton Smith: "The idea that black magic exists in secret today, or that hellish antique rites still survive in obscurity, is one that I have used & shall use again. When you see my new tale 'The Horror at Red Hook', you will see what use I make of the idea in connexion with the gangs of young loafers & herds of evil-looking foreigners that one sees everywhere in New York"[2] (2:27). The epigraph from Arthur Machen, whose works Lovecraft had been reading keenly since 1923, reinforces this survival of evil theme, but in the tale that follows the horrors lack that "incomparable substance and realistic acuteness" (D 421) that they attain in the fiction of the Welsh mystic he so admired.[3]

Critics since have noted the tale's lapses in logic and confusion of plot. The nerve-shattered protagonist, Thomas F. Malone, finds refuge from New York squalor in Chepachet, Rhode Island, only because Lovecraft happened to have visited this out-of-the-way hamlet in September 1923. At the time he called it "a veritable bucolic poem—a study in ancient New-England village atmosphere, with its deep, grass-bordered gorge, its venerable bridge, and its picturesque, centuried houses" (1:251). This pastoral rhapsody, had he thought to adapt it for the tale, might have made Malone's escape there more meaningful.

Malone, "a Dublin university man born in a Georgian villa near Phoenix Park," with "many poignant things to his credit in the *Dublin Review*" (D 246), fits the familiar sensitive aesthete pattern. A poet in his youth, brought low by "poverty and sorrow and exile" (D 247), he has become "a New York police detective" (D 245), an occupation so improbable for such a character (Irish though he may be) that Lovecraft can but lamely ask: "was not his very act of plunging into the polyglot abyss of New York's underworld a freak beyond sensible explanation?" (D 246). Clearly with this plethora of biographical data Lovecraft meant to set up Malone in counterpoint to the dubious Robert Suydam, "a lettered recluse of ancient Dutch family" (D 249), whose career in outline anticipates that of Charles Dexter Ward (Suydam likewise studies black magic abroad and associates with unsavory types who do him in when he gets cold feet), but such details remain inert.[4] Since Malone does little more than passively observe Suydam's activities, despite the claim that "he felt poised upon the brink of nameless terrors, with the

shabby, unkempt figure of Robert Suydam as arch-fiend and adversary"
(D 252), the two never really come into conflict.

At the climax in the cellar below Suydam's mansion, the wedding
between Suydam's reanimated corpse and "the naked, tittering, phos-
phorescent thing" (D 262), Malone voyeuristically watches the proces-
sion of demons—Lilith, Gorgo, Mormo, the incubi and succubi—
whose incantations Lovecraft admits he lifted, without any imaginative
transformation, from the article on "Magic" in the ninth edition of the
Encyclopedia Britannica (2:28). Malone reacts to this frightful scene with
conventional shock, showing no concern for his physical safety, let
alone any worry about his sanity. After the reluctant bridegroom spurns
his bride at the altar and topples the golden pedestal, the buildings
above collapse with scarcely more cause than do those in "The Street."

Near the tale's beginning Lovecraft invokes Poe's "German authority, '*es lässt sich nicht lesen*—it does not permit itself to be read' " (D
246) from "The Man of the Crowd." Toward the end he states that "at
one place under the Suydam house the canal was observed to sink into a
well too deep for dredging" (D 264), which leads to the observation
that "the cults of darkness are rooted in blasphemies deeper than the
well of Democritus" (D 265). Such literary allusions, however, like the
Machen epigraph, sound hollow in a story as poorly executed as "The
Horror at Red Hook." For once Lovecraft was not being overly harsh
when he said, "The tale is rather long and rambling, and I don't think
it is very good" (2:20).

"He"

If in "The Horror at Red Hook" Lovecraft's discontent with New
York only simmers, in "He" (1925) it boils over in the extended
autobiographical lament—"My coming to New York had been a mistake" (D 266)—that forms the preamble to the tale proper. Such a
passage as the following quite literally constitutes a confession of his
own feelings of disillusion and failure:

But success and happiness were not to be. Garish daylight shewed only
squalor and alienage and the noxious elephantiasis of climbing, spreading
stone where the moon had hinted of loveliness and elder magic; and the
throngs of people that seethed through the flume-like streets were squat,
swarthy strangers with hardened faces and narrow eyes, shrewd strangers
without dreams and without kinship to the scenes about them, who could

never mean aught to a blue-eyed man of the old folk, with the love of fair green lanes and white New England steeples in his heart. (D 267)

The narrator adds that he "refrained from going home to my people lest I seem to crawl back ignobly in defeat" (D 267), of which W. Paul Cook has said, "There is the cry of a soul in torment."[5] At the end the narrator does escape, returning to the "pure New England lanes up which fragrant sea-winds sweep at evening" (D 276), an image slightly less perfunctory than that of Chepachet in "The Horror at Red Hook." Here again Lovecraft could not bring himself to detail the paradise from which pride and despair still held him back.

The unnamed narrator, in typical Lovecraftian fashion, seeks solace in the past, in the remnants of eighteenth-century Greenwich Village, whose present-day denizens he disdains: "I found the poets and artists to be loud-voiced pretenders" (D 267). Only among the buildings and alleys that "could not be on any map of today" (D 268), a district like the Paris neighborhood in "The Music of Erich Zann," can he find satisfaction: "in those dreary days my quest for antique beauty and mystery was all that I had to keep my soul alive" (D 269). For this most transparent of autobiographical heroes, disappointing to say, Lovecraft was unable to devise more than a fairly stock supernatural encounter with one of his evil survivors from the eighteenth century, the "he" of the title, who poses as his own descendant, a practice Joseph Curwen will pursue with greater subtlety in *The Case of Charles Dexter Ward*.

This gentleman, who "bore the marks of a lineage and refinement unusual for the age and place" (D 269) and who says "sartain" for "certain" and otherwise affects the speech of the colonial era, grants the narrator a peek through a cosmic window similar to that in "Erich Zann." The narrator sees Greenwich Village at various points in time, including a future vision of "a hellish black city of giant stone terraces with impious pyramids flung savagely to the moon" inhabited by "yellow, squint-eyed people" (D 273). While more concrete than the music and motion glimpsed in the earlier tale, this picture of Manhattan overrun by orientals is no more than a variation on the tired "yellow peril" theme first expressed in "Polaris." At the climax, with a detachment equal to Thomas Malone's, the narrator witnesses the villain swept up by the ghosts of the Indians he has let on that he poisoned long ago. In his flight, in yet another instance of Lovecraft relying on trite formula, the narrator barely avoids being trapped in the literal fall of the rotting house of "He." The penultimate sentence of the story

points to the ultimately arbitrary relationship between these supernatural events and the narrator's attitude toward New York: "Of who or
what that ancient creature was, I have no idea; but I repeat that the city
is dead and full of unsuspected horrors" (D 276). In sum, the "ancient
creature" of "He" would seem to have even less claim to kinship to the
scenes around him than the "squat, swarthy strangers" of Lovecraft's
bigoted nightmares.

"Cool Air"

In "Cool Air" (1926), composed shortly before his joyful return to
Providence, Lovecraft was able to avoid the rage and self-pity that mar
"The Horror at Red Hook" and "He." Although the action could have
taken place in any sordid city neighborhood, touches of New York local
color—from the Spanish-speaking landlady to the "seedy-looking
loafer" (DH 206) whom the unnamed narrator hires on the corner of
Eighth Avenue to supply him with ice—stand out distinctly. Lovecraft's own aversion to cold temperatures contributes as well to the
sense of conviction that underlies "Cool Air."

The narrator, like the narrator of "The Picture in the House," asserts
that the greatest fear is to be found in the relatively mundane: "It is a
mistake to fancy that horror is associated inextricably with darkness,
silence, and solitude. I found it in the glare of mid-afternoon, in the
clangour of a metropolis, and in the teeming midst of a shabby and
commonplace rooming-house with a prosaic landlady and two stalwart
men by my side" (DH 199). Where in the earlier tale it took a paragraph of lofty rhetoric to get this idea across, here two straightforward,
naturalistic sentences suffice. The narrator continues: "In the spring of
1923 I had secured some dreary and unprofitable magazine work in the
city of New York; and being unable to pay any substantial rent, began
drifting from one cheap boarding establishment to another in search of
a room which might combine the qualities of decent cleanliness, endurable furnishings, and very reasonable price. It soon developed that I had
only a choice between evils, but after a time I came upon a house in
West Fourteenth Street which disgusted me much less than the others I
had sampled" (DH 199–200). Neither mystic nor romantic, this narrator exists as a character alive in the modern world, even as he retains
autobiographical vestiges in his guise of poor, if fastidious, writer.

Like the narrator of "The Music of Erich Zann," the narrator of "Cool
Air" gives an account of the strange fellow lodger he befriends. In a

gradual, credible manner, he describes the odd doings of Dr. Hector
Muñoz, "a man of birth, cultivation, and discrimination" (DH 201),
who maintains a well-chilled apartment laboratory full of bottles and
machines. Like that other eccentric doctor, Herbert West, Muñoz
strives to defy death, but in a solitary effort with himself as subject.
Like Herr Zann he knows many mysteries and even imparts them to
paper: "He acquired a habit of writing long documents of some sort,
which he carefully sealed and filled with injunctions that I transmit
them after his death to certain persons whom he named—for the most
part lettered East Indians, but including a once celebrated French
physician now generally thought dead, and about whom the most
inconceivable things had been whispered" (DH 205). As will Joseph
Curwen, he evidently keeps in touch with sympathetic souls around the
world. But as with similar communications in "The Music of Erich
Zann," "The Rats in the Walls," and later *The Case of Charles Dexter
Ward,* Muñoz's letters never reach their intended recipients. Admits
the narrator: "As it happened, I burned all these papers undelivered and
unopened" (DH 205). Such testaments will have a higher survival rate
in later, longer tales, where Lovecraft has the room to expand on the
cosmic implications inherent in their contents. Since the narrator recounts only the external circumstances of Muñoz's last days, the success
of the tale depends primarily on the skill with which the immediate
action unfolds.

Critics have cited as the chief fault of "Cool Air" its close resemblance to "Facts in the Case of M. Valdemar." In effect, Lovecraft, ever
the materialist, substitutes a mechanical apparatus for Poe's mesmerism
in order to hold his hero together. Muñoz's final dissolution, however,
has a more direct source in Machen's "The Novel of the White Powder," as J. Vernon Shea has suggested and Donald R. Burleson has
elaborated upon.[6] The climaxes of the two other New York stories also
show this influence. In "The Horror at Red Hook" Suydam collapses
"to a muddy blotch of corruption" (D 262), while in "He" the old man
shrivels and blackens, then sinks to the floor where he is engulfed by "a
colossal, shapeless influx of inky substance" (D 275), only his eyes
staying whole, as do the victim's in Machen's tale. In contrast to these
labored effects, Muñoz's no less ghastly fate at the climax of "Cool Air"
comes after careful and suitable build-up. The narrator, upon breaking
into the doctor's apartment, finds that the "dark, slimy trail" leads to
the couch where it ends "unutterably" (DH 206–7). In keeping with
the general restraint of the story, Lovecraft leaves it at that.

Supernatural Horror in Literature

Late in 1925 Lovecraft agreed to prepare a critical survey of supernatural literature for his friend and fellow amateur W. Paul Cook, proprietor of the Driftwind Press in Vermont. The product of months of research in which he read and reread many of the classics in the genre, *Supernatural Horror in Literature* was published in 1927 in what proved to be a one-shot amateur journal, the *Recluse*. In the thirties Lovecraft slightly revised and expanded it for serialization in yet another amateur magazine, the *Fantasy Fan,* but not until its appearance in 1939 in the initial Arkham House volume, *The Outsider,* then as a separate booklet put out by Ben Abramson in 1945, did the essay attract attention beyond a small circle. T. O. Mabbott commented that "it contains discussions of Poe, Hawthorne, and Bierce, so penetrating, sympathetic, and imaginatively keen that scholars will not want to miss them,"[7] while Fred Lewis Pattee called it "a brilliant piece of criticism."[8] As E. F. Bleiler remarks in his introduction to the Dover edition of 1973, "Even after nearly fifty years it remains the finest historical discussion of supernatural fiction."[9]

Beyond its value as a reading guide, *Supernatural Horror in Literature* stands as Lovecraft's "Philosophy of Composition," a manifesto of his aesthetic theory. In the opening paragraph he asserts the validity of the weird tale while granting that its "appeal, if not always universal, must necessarily be poignant and permanent to minds of the requisite sensitiveness" (D 365). "Atmosphere is the all-important thing" he states a few paragraphs later, "for the final criterion of authenticity is not the dovetailing of a plot but the creation of a given sensation." Furthermore, "The one test of the really weird is simply this—whether or not there be excited in the reader a profound sense of dread, and of contact with unknown spheres and powers; a subtle attitude of awed listening, as if for the beating of black wings or the scratching of outside shapes and entities on the known universe's utmost rim" (D 368–69). Here Lovecraft with characteristic hyperbole makes a case for effect as an end in itself, as he had earlier in the Transatlantic Circulator.

His discussions of Poe and Hawthorne, as illuminating as they may be of those authors, serve to support his own breed of horror fiction. Of the works of Poe, "indisputably the one great literary figure of the United States" (1:137), he singles out "MS. Found in a Bottle," "Facts in the Case of M. Valdemar," the polar portion of *The Narrative of Arthur Gordon Pym,* and "Metzengerstein"—tales of supernatural horror whose protagonists appear to be more at the mercy of forces outside themselves than prey to inner psychological terrors. While he ranks "Ligeia" second only to "The Fall of the House of Usher," his silence on the matter implies his indifference to Poe's claim in "The Philosophy of Composition" that the death of a beautiful woman is the "most poetical topic in the world." He simply ignores the passion in Poe.

Lovecraft is even more selective in his treatment of Hawthorne, as he himself admits: "The heritage of American weirdness was his to a most intense degree, and he saw a dismal throng of vague spectres behind the common phenomena of life; but he was not disinterested enough to value impressions, sensations, and beauties of narration for their own sake. He must needs weave his phantasy into some quietly melancholy fabric of didactic or allegorical cast, in which his meekly resigned cynicism may display with naive moral appraisal the perfidy of a human race which he cannot cease to cherish and mourn despite his insight into its hypocrisy" (D 402). After chiding Hawthorne for not sharing his own cosmic indifferentism, Lovecraft proceeds to dwell on *The House of the Seven Gables*, with its congenial theme of the working out of a family curse over the generations. In *The Case of Charles Dexter Ward*, written the same year he completed *Supernatural Horror in Literature*, Joseph Curwen casts as dark a shadow from the past over his descendant as his Salem contemporary Colonel Pyncheon does over the characters in Hawthorne's novel. The telling difference, of course, is that the colonel leaves behind a legacy of moral evil while Curwen rises from the dead to visit supernatural horror upon the present. [10]

In terms of quality Lovecraft's stories divide broadly into two periods: the nine years from 1917 to 1926 that include the apprentice fiction, and the nine years after his return to Providence that encompass all the longer narratives, the tales of cosmic horror that in their aggregate form his most enduring literary achievement. If Lovecraft assesses his illustrious predecessors narrowly, he reveals in *Supernatural Horror in Literature*, composed largely during that creative surge from the summer of 1926 to the spring of 1927, that he had assimilated their influence and was with confidence starting to extend the boundaries of the genre in work distinctively his own. [11]

Chapter Six
Providence and Boston

Lovecraft's earlier tales contain scant references to real places. In "From Beyond," for example, Crawford Tillinghast lives in an "ancient, lonely house set back from Benevolent Street" (D 91), while the narrator has carried a revolver since the night he was "held up in East Providence" (D 93). In "The Tomb" the narrator resides near Boston. All these, however, are passing mentions. Not until he was undergoing exile in New York did Lovecraft think to use the architectural and historical heritage of an actual New England city, undisguised, as background. In several tales he would transform Providence and, to a lesser extent, Boston into bastions of horror to rival Kingsport and Arkham. As in his fictional towns, the supernatural threats tend to lie just below the surface, irrupting in isolated pockets, typically within the confines of an individual house.

"The Shunned House"

During a visit to Elizabeth, New Jersey, his first fall in New York, Lovecraft saw "a terrible old house" (2:357) that in its decay reminded him of one on Benefit Street in Providence. Soon after, largely because "he was homesick,"[1] as David E. Schultz has pointed out, he wrote "The Shunned House" (1924), his first tale to pay homage to his native city. One of his lengthier early stories, it opens with a leisurely description of the house at 135 Benefit Street, which Poe, "the world's greatest master of the terrible and the bizarre," often passed on his way to court the "gifted poetess" (MM 235) Sarah Helen Whitman in the late 1840s. Lovecraft's own courtship and marriage must have been much on his mind at the time, but the text reflects none of his domestic turmoil. Indeed, in its special emphasis on the affectionate bond between the anonymous narrator and his aged, antiquarian uncle, Dr. Elihu Whipple, "a sane, conservative physician of the old school" (MM 239), the tale evokes Lovecraft's only truly satisfying family relationships—those with his uncles and grandfather. "I am lonely without that gentle soul whose long years were filled only with honour, virtue, good taste, benevolence, and learning" (MM 240), the narrator says in retrospect, a declaration of grief rather less moving than that of de la Poer at the death of his son in "The Rats in the Walls" in light of the weaknesses of "The Shunned House."

Like de la Poer, the narrator investigates an old house with something odd about the cellar, but here the background is not so skillfully integrated into the main action. A plethora of genealogical data—the names, birth and death dates of successive tenants of the shunned house—clogs up the story line. The narrator eventually figures out that the evil essence that has been plaguing the house can be traced back via Huguenot descendants buried at the site to "*Jacques Roulet, of Caude,*" evidently a werewolf, "who in 1598 was condemned to death as a daemoniac but afterward saved from the stake by the Paris parliament and shut in a madhouse" (MM 249). In the early nineteenth century a servant alleges "that there must lie buried beneath the house one of those vampires—the dead who retain their bodily form and live on the blood or breath of the living" (MM 245). At the climax in the cellar the narrator unearths an object "like a mammoth soft blue-white stovepipe doubled in two" that he shortly recognizes as "a titan *elbow*" (MM 261).[2] In his attempt to avoid the triteness of the traditional by making his monster a werewolf, a vampire, a giant, and a ghost, Lovecraft overloads the horror to the point of absurdity, just as he had earlier in the year in "Under the Pyramids." The "rugose insect-like head" (MM 257) of the creature, however, does anticipate the later, more original concept of the rugose, cone-shaped Great Race of "The Shadow Out of Time."

With a bow toward "the theories of relativity and intra-atomic action" (MM 252), the narrator considers using such weapons of pulp science fiction as "a large and specially fitted Crookes tube operated by powerful storage batteries and provided with peculiar screens and reflectors" and "a pair of military flame-throwers" (MM 253). In the end, by means of "great carboys of acid" (MM 260), he dispatches "the unthinkable abnormality" (MM 261) with an ease and finality that most future Lovecraft protagonists would envy. Conventional and sentimental, "The Shunned House" lacks the cosmic quality that distinguishes Lovecraft's next story with a Providence setting.

"The Call of Cthulhu"

Like the narrator of "The Shunned House," the narrator of "The Call of Cthulhu" (1926) uncovers horror in Providence—a horror, however, that transcends local boundaries. The first of several major works that Lovecraft completed in the year following his return home from New York,[3] "The Call of Cthulhu" is the tale that epitomizes the "Cthulhu Mythos," the term that August Derleth originally imposed along with the preconceptions born of his Catholic upbringing upon Lovecraft's stories of cosmic scope and that has since gained popular currency despite efforts of recent scholars to come up with a substitute of broader application.[4] Here it is, as Fritz Leiber puts it in "A Literary Copernicus," that Lovecraft first truly "shifted the focus of supernatural dread from man and his little world and his gods, to the stars and the black and unplumbed gulfs of intergalactic space."[5]

The opening paragraph, the first sentence of which has been enshrined in the fifteenth edition (1980) of *Bartlett's Familiar Quotations,* sets forth the theme that underlies Lovecraft's mature fiction:

The most merciful thing in the world, I think, is the inability of the human mind to correlate all its contents. We live on a placid island of ignorance in the midst of black seas of infinity, and it was not meant that we should voyage far. The sciences, each straining in its own direction, have hitherto harmed us little; but some day the piecing together of dissociated knowledge will open up such terrifying vistas of reality, and of our frightful position therein, that we shall either go mad from the revelation or flee from the deadly light into the peace and safety of a new dark age. (DH 125)

Compared to similar such openings in "Beyond the Wall of Sleep," "Arthur Jermyn," and "The Picture in the House," this passage rings with almost Churchillian eloquence.

The tale, which itself purports to be a manuscript, "(Found Among the Papers of the Late Francis Wayland Thurston, of Boston)" (DH 125), according to the note below the title, consists of three distinct narratives that in turn incorporate other accounts, a structure more complex than any hitherto in the fiction.[6] In a parallel to the reader's own experience of the story, Thurston finds among the papers of his late granduncle, "George Gammell Angell, Professor Emeritus of Semitic Languages in Brown University, Providence, Rhode Island" (DH 126), a character analogous to the scholarly Dr. Whipple in "The Shunned House" but who remains unobtrusively off-stage, a document headed "CTHULHU CULT" together with a "queer clay bas-relief" depicting "a sort of monster, or symbol representing a monster, of a form only a diseased fancy could conceive" (DH 127). A closer description of this creature follows: "A pulpy, tentacled head surmounted a grotesque and scaly body with rudimentary wings; but it was the *general outline* of the whole which made it most shockingly frightful. Behind the figure was a vague suggestion of a Cyclopean architectural background" (DH 127). Thus Cthulhu, one of the principal entities of the Lovecraft pantheon, makes its debut, a small figure in clay.[7]

After an account of the student artist who had sculpted the bas-relief from a dream, "a precocious youth of known genius but great eccentricity" (DH 128) named Henry Wilcox, Thurston relates the tale of Inspector Legrasse, who at the annual meeting of the American Archaeological Society seventeen years before had presented an "apparently very ancient stone statuette" that had been captured "in the wooded swamps south of New Orleans during a raid on a supposed voodoo meeting" (DH 133). The statuette has a familiar cast: "It represented a monster of vaguely anthropoid outline, but with octopus-like head whose face was a mass of feelers, a scaly, rubbery-looking body, prodigious claws on hind and fore feet, and long, narrow wings behind" (DH 134). By twice presenting him at a remove on a graspable scale, Lovecraft prepares for Cthulhu's rise from his sunken island city in the Pacific, as witnessed by second-mate Johansen and his crew.

In his synopsis of Johansen's manuscript, Thurston abandons any pretence of objectivity and calm: "The Thing cannot be described— there is no language for such abysms of shrieking and immemorial lunacy, such eldritch contradictions of all matter, force, and cosmic order" (DH 152). In fact, he does find the language to do Cthulhu justice, invoking classical myth and modern painting. Johansen and his men land "at a sloping mud-bank on this monstrous Acropolis" (DH 151), while "the Titan thing from the stars," which slavers and gibbers "like Polytheme cursing the fleeing ship of Odysseus," proves "bolder than the storied Cyclops" (DH 153) by pursuing the humans into the sea. "Without knowing what futurism is like," Johansen speaks of the island city in terms of "broad impressions of vast angles and stone surfaces" rather than "any definite structure or building" (DH 150). Earlier Thurston had called Henry Wilcox's home in Providence "a hideous Victorian imitation of seventeenth-century Breton architecture which flaunts its stuccoed front amidst the lovely colonial houses on the ancient hill, and under the very shadow of the finest Georgian steeple in America" (DH 142). In this incidental remark Lovecraft, more than simply airing his architectural prejudices, sets up a subtle parallel: the Fleur-de-Lys Building in its modest way is as frightfully out of place on

College Hill as "the nightmare corpse-city of R'lyeh" (DH 150) is on the globe at large.

Professor Angell's manuscript papers also include "comments on long-surviving secret societies and hidden cults, with references to passages in such mythological and anthropological source-books as Frazer's *Golden Bough* and Miss Murray's *Witch-Cult in Western Europe*" (DH 128). In "Dagon" and "The Temple" traditional myth had lain behind the supernatural phenomena, but in "The Call of Cthulhu" the reverse is true. The cultists arrested in Inspector Legrasse's raid assert a "reality" far more disturbing than any cloaked by familiar myth:

> They worshipped, so they said, the Great Old Ones who lived ages before there were any men, and who came to the young world out of the sky. Those Old Ones were gone now, inside the earth and under the sea; but their dead bodies had told their secrets in dreams to the first men, who formed a cult which had never died. This was that cult, and the prisoners said it had always existed and always would exist, hidden in distant wastes and dark places all over the world until the time when the great priest Cthulhu, from his dark house in the mighty city of R'lyeh under the waters, should rise and bring the earth again beneath his sway. Some day he would call, when the stars were ready, and the secret cult would always be waiting to liberate him. (DH 139)

Such a cosmic scheme clearly lends itself to religious and hence psychological interpretation, but for Lovecraft it serves only to affirm man's insignificance. Thurston, whose attitude is one of "absolute materialism" (DH 144), can find no consolation in such a universe, and resigns himself to death: "As my uncle went, as poor Johansen went, so I shall go. I know too much, and the cult still lives" (DH 154).

Assessing it in a letter dated 10 November 1936 in relation to other stories of his, Lovecraft rated "The Call of Cthulhu" as "rather middling—not as bad as the worst, but full of cheap and cumbrous touches" (5:348). While Lovecraft is again too hard on his work, the disjointed structure, effective though it may be as a distancing technique, coupled with a paucity of action in the immediate present, makes for a narrative less compelling in the aggregate than those of other longer tales where a single narrative line predominates. Thurston interviews Wilcox and travels to New Zealand and Norway, but he comes across as an armchair investigator, a dilettante. Like Randolph Carter, he seemingly possesses unlimited wealth with a minimum of job and family responsibilities. Still, he has his appealing quirks, mainly to the degree that he incidentally resembles Lovecraft himself. He happens upon the final bit of information in the chain of evidence, the newspaper cutting headed "Mystery Derelict Found at Sea," while "visiting a learned friend in Paterson, New Jersey; the curator of a local museum and a mineralogist of note" (DH 145): to wit, Lovecraft's friend James F. Morton. Moreover, he gives Wilcox's sculpture his highest praise: "He will, I believe, some time be heard from as one of the great decadents; for he has crystallised in clay and will one day mirror in marble those nightmares and phantasies which Arthur Machen evokes in prose, and Clark Ashton Smith makes visible in verse and in painting" (DH 143). Even as he aimed at total detachment in his fiction, Lovecraft could not help but humanize his cosmic perspective by letting slip, as here, the value he placed on his friends (and admired writers). For him this was what made life worth living.

"Pickman's Model"

Thomas Malone at the beginning of "The Horror at Red Hook" cannot abide the sight of tall buildings, while the narrator of "Cool Air" is afraid of "a draught of cool air" (DH 199). These phobias pale, however, when measured against that of the narrator of "Pickman's Model" (1926), Thurber, who "can't use the subway or . . . go down into cellars any more" (DH 13). Like Thurston, Thurber encounters an artist whose morbid work impresses him with its genius—"Boston never had a greater painter than Richard Upton Pickman" (DH 13)—and likewise he discovers a monstrous reality behind it.

As in "Cool Air," the narrator addresses an audience, a "you" to whom he tells his tale in a manner as colloquially conversational as that of the narrator of "In the Vault." "Why the third degree? You didn't used to be so inquisitive," he says to "Eliot" (DH 12) at the start of his monologue, evidently within the civilized confines of a Beacon Hill study, where they can reach for the decanter or ring for coffee. Thus Lovecraft takes more than usual care in this shorter tale to frame the narrative, establishing the coziness of the immediate scene, the better to heighten the contrast with Thurber's account of his claustrophobic visit to Pickman's cellar studio in a less proper part of town.

As in "The Music of Erich Zann," the narrator ventures into a neigh-borhood of exaggerated antiquity. Unlike the dream Paris of the earlier story, however, the Boston of "Pickman's Model" closely corresponds to a real place on the map. Thurber notes the major landmarks—the South

Station, Battery Street, Constitution Wharf—en route to the North End, until he and Pickman reach the crucial transition point: "I didn't keep track of the cross streets, and can't tell you yet which it was we turned up, but I know it wasn't Greenough Lane" (DH 17). From here on he names no streets, but his eye for architectural detail remains acute:

> When we did turn, it was to climb through the deserted length of the oldest and dirtiest alley I ever saw in my life, with crumbling-looking gables, broken small-paned windows, and archaic chimneys that stood out half-disintegrated against the moonlit sky. I don't believe there were three houses in sight that hadn't been standing in Cotton Mather's time—certainly I glimpsed at least two with an overhang, and once I thought I saw a peaked roof-line of the almost forgotten pre-gambrel type, though antiquarians tell us there are none left in Boston. (DH 17–18)

In effect, they have entered the sinister seventeenth-century city evoked by Pickman in his harangue before setting out, a realm where Cotton Mather "knew things he didn't dare put into that stupid *Magnalia* or that puerile *Wonders of the Invisible World*" (DH 16).

Thurber "never swerved an inch" (DH 13) when Pickman showed him the representatively titled "Ghoul Feeding," but in describing the subjects of the pictures that Pickman "couldn't paint or even shew in Newbury Street" (DH 18) he has trouble maintaining his composure: "These figures were seldom completely human, but often approached humanity in varying degree. Most of the bodies, while roughly bi-pedal, had a forward slumping, and a vaguely canine cast. The texture of the majority was a kind of unpleasant rubberiness. Ugh! I can see them now!" (DH 18–19). Eschewing the exact terms that Thurston applied to Cthulhu in his sculpted form for more suggestive images, Thurber defines these creatures primarily through their occupations, of which he says "don't ask me to be too precise" (DH 19). In fact, he manages to be just precise enough about the nature of his friend's art, which ranges from "frightful pictures that turned colonial New England into a kind of annex of hell" to "modern studies" (DH 20).

Pickman's paintings display a sardonic humor worthy of Ambrose Bierce. Prime examples include "a study called 'Subway Accident,' in which a flock of the vile things were clambering up from some un-known catacomb through a crack in the floor of the Boylston Street subway and attacking a crowd of people on the platform," and another, in which scores of the beasts, their faces seemingly "distorted with

epileptic and reverberant laughter," "crowded about one who held a
well-known Boston guide-book and was evidently reading aloud" (DH
20), entitled "Holmes, Lowell, and Longfellow Lie Buried in Mount
Auburn." Like Joseph Curwen, the ghouls violate the tombs of the
great, though evidently for no higher, cosmic purpose. Given their
underground habitat and link to humankind, they would appear to
represent the triumph of the unconscious over the conscious, the irratio-
nal mocking the rational. As Barton St. Armand has pointed out,
Pickman belongs to the same symbolic tradition as Goya, Fuseli, and
the other artists of the fantastic with whom he is compared throughout
the tale.[8]

Near the end of his tour the narrator twice screams, rousing a menace
in a covered well that Pickman, who disappears into the next room
from which shortly comes the sound of a "deafening discharge with all
six chambers of a revolver, fired spectacularly as a lion-tamer might fire
in the air for effect" (DH 23), attributes to "rats." Thurber, of course,
accepts this explanation until he gets home and looks at the curled-up
photograph he absentmindedly picked off Pickman's easel and stuck in
his pocket and sees that it shows a ghoul posing against the background
of the studio wall. "But by God, Eliot, it was *a photograph from life*"
(DH 25), he exclaims in the confirmatory last sentence. However contrived this resolution, it does not undermine the power of the horrific
vision of the tale, achieved by an attention to realism that parallels
Pickman's own literal technique. The ghouls have access to the studio
not through some well of Democritus but a circular brick well, "five
feet across, with walls a good foot thick and some six inches above the
ground level—solid work of the seventeenth century" (DH 21). In
"Pickman's Model" Lovecraft constructed a story as solid as this well.[9]

The Case of Charles Dexter Ward

The Case of Charles Dexter Ward (1927) stands as Lovecraft's paean to
Providence, a celebration of the eighteenth-century city and especially
of the College Hill neighborhood within whose precincts he had been
living since his return from New York the previous spring. As in
"Pickman's Model," references to actual streets, buildings, and historical events and personages serve to recreate the colonial atmosphere in
which his horrors seem naturally to thrive. Extracts from books, journals, newspapers, diaries, and letters, each in the peculiar period style
of its author, vary the omniscient, third-person narrative, efficiently

substituting for the dialogue of conventional fiction. Little more than a hundred pages encompasses a Faustian drama as richly realized as any epic in the genre.

The longest and most accessible of Lovecraft's three short novels, *The Case of Charles Dexter Ward* has aspects of both a generational saga and a bildungsroman, even though its tragic young hero experiences none of the customary coming-of-age trials. Here, the tale is told as a retrospective case study of an apparent aberration grown "from a mere eccentricity to a dark mania." In an urbane, understated voice that might belong to one of Lovecraft's cultivated physicians, the omniscient narrator recalls that he who "bore the name of Charles Dexter Ward" was "an exceedingly singular person" (MM 107). In many respects he resembles his creator. Like that other major autobiographical character of the period, his Boston neighbor Randolph Carter, Ward as a baby is wheeled out in his carriage by his nurse to a spot blessed with spectacular sunsets: "The nurse used to stop and sit on the benches of Prospect Terrace to chat with policemen; and one of the child's first memories was of the great westward sea of hazy roofs and domes and steeples and far hills which he saw one winter afternoon from that great railed embankment, all violet and mystic against a fevered, apocalyptic sunset of reds and golds and purples and curious greens" (MM 113). In effect, he feels the same ecstasy as Randolph Carter gazing down upon his sunset city at the start of *The Dream-Quest of Unknown Kadath* or Lovecraft first viewing Marblehead on that late winter's afternoon. As a young man in May 1926, after two years of arcane study in Europe, he returns triumphantly at sunset to Providence—"It was twilight, and Charles Dexter Ward had come home" (MM 166)—just as Lovecraft had the previous month. [10]

Predictably the main formative influence is not the family: "Charles Ward was an antiquarian from infancy, no doubt gaining his taste from the venerable town around him, and from the relics of the past which filled every corner of his parents' old mansion in Prospect Street on the crest of the hill. With the years his devotion to ancient things increased; so that history, genealogy, and the study of colonial architecture, furniture and craftsmanship at length crowded everything else from his sphere of interests" (MM 109–10). Here Lovecraft paints an exaggerated and idealized picture of himself. Ward, "tall, slim, and blond" (MM 112), has the fair features that Lovecraft liked to boast he had possessed as a child before his hair and eyes darkened. Ward attends Moses Brown, an exclusive boys' school, and while he declines to matriculate at Brown at least he has the choice. His family occupies "a great Georgian mansion" (MM 113) on Prospect Street, around the corner from Lovecraft's Victorian roominghouse on Barnes Street. If Ward's father and mother prove ineffectual in dissuading their willfull only child from pursuing his morbid studies, they appear to be free of the serious mental and physical ills that afflicted Lovecraft's own parents.

The novel's epigraph, the incantation attributed to "Borellus," likely derived at second-hand from a passage in Cotton Mather's *Magnalia Christi Americana,* as Barton St. Armand has shown,[11] sets the supernatural premise on alchemical grounds. Where Herbert West had required fairly fresh, whole specimens, Joseph Curwen, Ward's eighteenth-century ancestor, needs merely "the essential Saltes of humane Dust" (MM 107), along with the appropriate spell, to raise up the dead. In that highly synoptic flashback that dramatizes eighty or so years of Rhode Island history, Curwen practices this grim art on a scale and for a purpose beyond anything conceived by West, while maintaining a veneer of respectability as one of Providence's wealthiest merchants. In his guise of model citizen in 1761, for example, he helps "rebuild the Great Bridge after the October gale" and replaces "many of the books of the public library consumed in the Colony House fire" (MM 123).

Like Dorian Gray, Curwen excites attention when he fails visibly to age. Following his extirpation on Good Friday 1771 by the raiding party approved by nearly every eminent man in the colony from the four Brown brothers to Governor Stephen Hopkins, the suppression of his memory "can be compared in spirit only to the hush that lay on Oscar Wilde's name for a decade after his disgrace" (MM 147). A century-and-a-half later Ward uncovers an oil portrait, hidden behind an overmantel in an old Providence house, that confronts him "with his own living features in the countenance of his horrible great-great-great-grandfather" (MM 155). Here Ward faces his personal equivalent of the picture of Dorian Gray. In another, less subtle association, Ward resurrects his ancestor—"J. C."—on Good Friday 1927, while in the novel's final scene his malign double ends up "scattered on the floor as a thin coating of fine-bluish-grey dust" (MM 234) on Good Friday 1928. Like the being in "The Shunned House," he behaves like a vampire—"must have it red for three months" (MM 175) Mrs. Ward overhears outside her son's door—yet one clichéd attribute may be granted to a character who otherwise distinguishes himself as arguably Lovecraft's most compelling supernatural villain.

Like Lovecraft, Curwen in his isolation cares deeply about books. In

1746 he reputedly owns "the best library in Providence" (MM 120), while in 1763 he helps "Daniel Jenckes found his bookshop" and is "thereafter his best customer" (MM 128), though he is not content with book learning alone. With "the calm calculativeness of schoolboys swapping books," Curwen and his cohorts traffic in the remains of "the world's wisest and greatest men, in the hope of recovering from the bygone ashes some vestige of the consciousness and lore which had once animated and informed them" (MM 199). Fittingly enough the written word, coupled with a naive faith in the sanctity of the mails, contributes to Curwen's downfall in both centuries. Rather as Lovecraft bared his soul in those racist letters to his aunts with no thought to the damage they might do his posthumous reputation, so Curwen and fellow fiends like Simon Orne of Salem—"In this Community a Man may not live too long, and you knowe my Plan by which I came back as my Son" (MM 138)—unwittingly confide their darkest secrets to letters subject to interception by their enemies. At the secondary climax below Curwen's Pawtuxet bungalow, a message from a most uncanny source scrawled in "the pointed Saxon minuscules of the eighth or ninth century A.D." and "in such Latin as a barbarous age might remember" (MM 220) provides Dr. Marinus Bicknell Willett,[12] the Ward family physician, with instructions for Curwen's extermination.

As Barton St. Armand has observed, "The simple moral of *The Case of Charles Dexter Ward* is that it is dangerous to know too much, especially about one's own ancestors."[13] Writing to Dr. Willett at the eleventh hour, Ward confesses: "I have brought to light a frightful abnormality, but I did it for the sake of knowledge" (MM 182). If this "eager, studious, and curious boy" is undone by a "love of mystery and of the past" (MM 230), as Dr. Willett asserts to Mr. Ward in a letter, so too does he fall prey to an overly romantic sense of family. Curwen acts entirely selfishly, marrying and leaving behind that set of papers inscribed "*To Him Who Shal Come After, & How He May Gett Beyonde Time & ye Spheres*" (MM 157) only to ensure his own revival. Without a qualm he murders his descendant and assumes his identity when the boy becomes too squeamish. Not interested like Ward in the pursuit of knowledge as an aesthetic pastime, Curwen uses the information gleaned from "half the titan thinkers of all the ages" (MM 213) toward a terrible end, of which his colleague Edward Hutchinson gives a hint in his letter dated 7 March 1928: "It will be ripe in a yeare's time to have up ye Legions from Underneath, and then there are no Boundes to what shal be oures" (MM 197). No doubt Ward does not overstate the case in his letter dated 8 February 1928 when he warns Dr. Willett: "Upon us depends more than can be put into words—all civilisation, all natural law, perhaps even the fate of the solar system and the universe" (MM 181–82). This, together with passing allusions to such things as the *Necronomicon* and a new deity, Yog-Sothoth, lends to the novel a cosmic dimension ultimately as chilling as that in "The Call of Cthulhu."

Left unpublished in Lovecraft's lifetime largely because as a two-finger typist he found the prospect of preparing a typed copy too daunting, *The Case of Charles Dexter Ward* suffers from a certain obviousness and a few logical flaws. After his encounter below the Pawtuxet bungalow Dr. Willett realizes that supernatural mischief is afoot, yet he is slow to conclude that Ward has resurrected Curwen, who transparently has been posing as "Dr. Allen." Both Ward and the writer of the Saxon minuscules urge Dr. Willett to dissolve Curwen's body in acid, the method used to dispose of the creature in "The Shunned House," but at the climax the proper incantation suffices to put the old wizard down. In the final paragraph, in a throwback to the pat ending of "The Shunned House," the narrative voice confidently declares that "that man of unholy centuries and forbidden secrets never troubled the world again" (MM 234). Such consolation will be rare in Lovecraft's fictional world in the future.

Chapter Seven
New England Dream-Quests

In that productive year following his return to Providence in April 1926, Lovecraft wrote three final dreamland fantasies, openly philosophical works more intimately related to his own experience than previous tales in the Dunsanian mode. His renewed New England sensibility pervades them all.

"The Silver Key"

Lovecraft's Randolph Carter persona in "The Silver Key" (1926) delights in Dunsanian visions of "strange and ancient cities beyond space, and lovely, unbelievable garden lands across ethereal seas" (MM 408), but the ennui of ordinary existence keeps him earthbound. Since he is not an inhabitant of dreamland, Carter must first seek aesthetic satisfaction in the mundane human world. His progressive disillusionment with life, on a grand scale, reflects his creator's own feelings at their bitterest.

The beliefs that Lovecraft rejected in youth, such as "the gentle churchly faith endeared to him by the naive trust of his fathers," as well as the alternatives of those who "had traded the false gods of fear and blind piety for those of licence and anarchy" (MM 410), Carter pursues from age thirty to well over forty, as chronicled in the philosophical manifesto that makes up the first half of the tale. Possessed of seemingly unlimited wealth, Carter carries his self-indulgent search to a level impossible for Lovecraft, as illustrated by his studying seven years with a man in the South "till horror overtook them one midnight in an unknown and archaic graveyard, and only one emerged where two had entered" (MM 413), a passing nod to "The Statement of Randolph Carter." Carter, too, is the successful novelist that Lovecraft never dared dream of becoming. At one point he gives up his friends, having grown "weary of the crudeness of their emotions, and the sameness and earthiness of their visions" (MM 411), an extreme act that Lovecraft, who so depended on friendship, could only have contemplated in the depths of his New York exile. Again, as Lovecraft would never have done even if he could have afforded to, Carter dallies with decadence: "He decided to live on a rarer plane, and furnished his Boston home to suit his changing moods; one room for each, hung in appropriate colours, furnished with befitting books and objects, and provided with sources of the proper sensations of light, heat, sound, taste, and odour" (MM 412). By maintaining his distance from Carter, however much he might sympathize with him, Lovecraft saves the story from degenerating into an exercise in self-pity.

Finally, just as Lovecraft may have done in New York, Carter considers suicide: "He thought it rather silly that he bothered to keep on living at all, and got from a South American acquaintance a very curious liquid to take him to oblivion without suffering. Inertia and force of habit, however, caused him to defer action; and he lingered indecisively among thoughts of old times, taking down the strange hangings from his walls and refitting the house as it was in his early boyhood—purple panes, Victorian furniture, and all" (MM 413). As if mindful, on a romantic if not moral level, of Jesus' injunction to become as a little child in order to enter the kingdom of God, Carter realizes that he must return to the past to gain his equivalent of heaven. Through the aid of the silver key, of which his long-dead grandfather reminds him in a dream, Carter literally recovers his childhood, thus fulfilling one of Lovecraft's own most cherished fantasies.

In order to make this transition Carter must also return home to Arkham and at sunset ascend the slope leading to the old family homestead:

Afternoon was far gone when he reached the foot, and at the bend half way up he paused to scan the outspread countryside golden and glorified in the slanting floods of magic poured out by a western sun. All the strangeness and expectancy of his recent dreams seemed present in this hushed and unearthly landscape, and he thought of the unknown solitudes of other planets as his eyes traced out the velvet and deserted lawns shining undulant between their tumbled walls, the clumps of faery forest setting off far lines of purple hills beyond hills, and the spectral wooded valley dipping down in shadow to dank hollows where trickling waters crooned and gurgled among swollen and distorted roots. (MM 415)

This vision of a lovely patch of New England terrain in the sunset glow, with its intimations of the cosmic, serves merely as the route by which

Carter returns to the Dunsanian world where his galleys can "sail up the river Oukranos past the gilded spires of Thran, or his elephant caravans tramp through perfumed jungles in Kled" (MM 408), and where, according to the narrator who curiously obtrudes at story's end, he might now be king "on the opal throne in Ilek-Vad" (MM 420). Although the action takes place after events in *The Dream-Quest of Unknown Kadath,* which Lovecraft was probably already at work on, "The Silver Key" paradoxically depicts Carter at an earlier stage of development, for he has yet to recognize that New England, not the dreamworld, is his goal. More somber than the *Dream-Quest,* "The Silver Key" expresses more stridently the same longing—to retreat to the happier, more innocent days of boyhood. In so doing Randolph Carter, like some middle-aged Peter Pan, escapes the adult responsibilities that Lovecraft had recently found so burdensome as an unsuccessful husband and breadwinner in New York. Tellingly enough, in the course of all his experimentation, Carter never once in "The Silver Key" seeks romantic love.

"The Strange High House in the Mist"

After the straight exposition of "The Silver Key," adorned only at beginning and end with the tropes of dreamland, "The Strange High House in the Mist" (1926) returns to the mannered style of earlier Dunsanian efforts: "When tales fly thick in the grottoes of tritons, and conches in seaweed cities blow wild tunes learned from the Elder Ones, then great eager mists flock to heaven laden with lore, and oceanward eyes on the rocks see only a mystic whiteness, as if the cliff's rim were the rim of the earth, and the solemn bells of buoys tolled free in the aether of faery" (D 277). Evidently blinded by the fog of his own high-flown prose, Lovecraft remarked to August Derleth in late 1926 that "The Strange High House" "is by all odds my own favourite among my recent yarns" (2:94). Compared unsentimentally to other tales of that prolific year, however, it is a slight piece.

In this story drenched with sea imagery, Lovecraft turns the Kingsport of "The Terrible Old Man" and "The Festival" into a coastal version of one of his dream cities. That philosopher Thomas Olney, who teaches "ponderous things in a college by Narragansett Bay" and comes to Kingsport with "stout wife and romping children" (D 278), has the job and family alien to Randolph Carter's experience does not save him from a similar malaise. But where Carter takes years to explore

the enticements of religion, occultism, and decadence, Olney has simply to make a single visit to a mysterious house, perched atop the local
Kingsport equivalent of Mount Olympus, to find a cure for his discontent: "And ever since that hour, through dull dragging years of
greyness and weariness, the philosopher has laboured and eaten and
slept and done uncomplaining the suitable deeds of a citizen. Not any
more does he long for the magic of farther hills, or sigh for secrets that
peer like green reefs from a bottomless sea. The sameness of his days no
longer gives him sorrow, and well-disciplined thoughts have grown
enough for his imagination (D 284). Even if Lovecraft's protagonist has
resigned himself to prosaic reality, the authorial voice suggests, as in
"The Silver Key," that the life of a dreamer is preferable.

Being a dreamer, however, has its risks. The strange high house holds
out the promise of horror as well as beauty. The black-bearded man
whom Olney meets at this gateway to the gods of dreamland tells him,
among other dire tales, of "how the Kings of Atlantis fought with the
slippery blasphemies that wriggled out of rifts in the ocean's floor" (D
282). At the end the patriarchs of Kingsport worry that the "olden
gods. . . . may come out of the deep and from unknown Kadath in the
cold waste and make their dwelling on that evilly appropriate crag so
close to the gentle hills and valleys of quiet simple fisherfolk" (D 285). In
this ambivalent mix of fear and wonder, "The Strange High House in the
Mist" anticipates more immediately than does "The Silver Key" the
concerns of Lovecraft's last and most ambitious dreamland narrative.

The Dream-Quest of Unknown Kadath

More than any other fictional work of Lovecraft's, *The Dream-Quest of
Unknown Kadath* (1926–27), "a picaresque chronicle of impossible adventure in dreamland, composed under no illusion of professional publication" (2:95), requires an understanding of his life and thought to be
appreciated. Combining sly humor with dark fantasy, he wrote it as an
extended experiment in symbolic autobiography, with just one audience in mind—himself. "There is nothing of popular or bestseller
psychology in it," he admitted at the time, seeing it as "useful practice
for later and more authentic attempts in the novel form" (2:95). As I
have shown elsewhere,[1] the *Dream-Quest* owes much of its "Oriental"
tone and imagery to "the celebrated *History of the Caliph Vathek* by the
wealthy dilettante William Beckford" (D 383), which Lovecraft treats
at length in *Supernatural Horror in Literature,* while S. T. Joshi has made

a case for "the influence of classical antiquity,"[2] citing parallels to the *Odyssey,* the *Aeneid,* and Greek and Roman mythology.

Randolph Carter, here at his most Lovecraft-like, descends into dreamland resolved "to find the gods on unknown Kadath in the cold waste, wherever that may be, and to win from them the sight and remembrance and shelter of the marvellous sunset city" (MM 308), of which he has dreamed three times before being "snatched away while still he paused on the high terrace above it" (MM 306). Despite the episodic, rapidly shifting nature of Carter's quest, as befits an actual dream, the plot progresses in a coherent, linear fashion. Written "continuously like *Vathek* without any subdivision into chapters" (2:94) (nor any breaks from the third-person narrative flow until Nyarlathotep's speech near the end), the *Dream-Quest* yet manages to sustain interest over a span of more than a hundred pages by means of lively incident and colorful detail. Regarded by some as no more than a rough draft, it survives in truth in nearly as polished a form as *The Case of Charles Dexter Ward,* the novel composed immediately afterward that would likewise languish unpublished in handwritten manuscript until after Lovecraft's death.

In the course of his journey Carter encounters many peculiar creatures. Zoogs, gugs, and ghasts—names that lend "a juvenile flavor"[3] to the action, as L. Sprague de Camp has pointed out—all viciously prey and feed upon one another and, in the case of the primitive ghasts, themselves. Allying himself variously with friendly cats, obliging ghouls, and cooperative night-gaunts, Carter does battle with the more repellent dreamland dwellers like the toad-like moon-beasts, "great greyish-white slippery things," and their servants, the wide-mouthed merchants, who when seen "without turbans or shoes or clothing" seem not "so very human after all" (MM 320). Carter in fact meets few other human beings. Discounting the unfortunate black slaves of the moon-beasts, only Richard Upton Pickman, who has since "Pickman's Model" become a ghoul, and Kuranes, who died in "Celephaïs," could be considered to approach humanity. While the dreamworld appears to exist independently of any single dreamer like Carter, Pickman, or Kuranes, it essentially remains Lovecraft's private preserve. Through this boys' realm of danger and adventure his persona travels as a sort of disembodied consciousness, never at any real physical or mental risk, unencumbered by the emotional demands of others.

Kuranes, who has "formed a mighty longing for the English cliffs and downlands of his boyhood" (MM 354), supplies Carter with the key to his quest. Since he cannot return to the waking world like Carter, Kuranes must dream "himself a small tract of such countryside," though it can never match the real thing: "For though Kuranes was a monarch in the land of dream, with all imagined pomps and marvels, splendours and beauties, ecstasies and delights, novelties and excitements at his command, he would have gladly resigned forever the whole of his power and luxury and freedom for one blessed day as a simple boy in that pure and quiet England, that ancient, beloved England which had moulded his being and of which he must always be immutably a part" (MM 354–55). Similarly, Carter-Lovecraft, in a scene reminiscent of Vathek's confrontation with Eblis in the Halls of Eblis, realizes at the climax that he has always been inextricably a part of New England. "For know you, that your gold and marble city of wonder is only the sum of what you have seen and loved in youth," the angelic figure who turns out to be Nyarlathotep tells him in the castle atop Kadath in the cold waste. "It is the glory of Boston's hillside roofs and western windows aflame with sunset; of the flower-fragrant Common and the great dome on the hill and the tangle of gables and chimneys in the violet valley where the many-bridged Charles flows drowsily" (MM 400). Nyarlathotep continues in this lyrical vein, invoking "antique Salem with its brooding years, and spectral Marblehead scaling its rocky precipices into past centuries" among other actual places, together with Arkham "with its moss-grown gambrel roofs and rocky rolling meadows behind it," and "antediluvean Kingsport hoary with stacked chimneys and deserted quays and overhanging gables" (MM 400–401). By now Lovecraft's imaginary New England towns have taken on an architectural and scenic glow the equal of Providence or Boston or the old seaports along the Massachusetts North Shore.

"These, Randolph Carter, are your city; for they are yourself," Nyarlathotep reiterates, in a variation on Lovecraft's assertion, "I am Providence." "New-England bore you, and into your soul she poured a liquid loveliness which cannot die. This loveliness, moulded, crystallised, and polished by years of memory and dreaming, is your terraced wonder of elusive sunsets; and to find that marble parapet with curious urns and carven rail, and descend at last those endless balustraded steps to the city of broad squares and prismatic fountains, you need only to turn back to the thoughts and visions of your wistful boyhood" (MM 401). Here Lovecraft, at his most gushingly romantic, in effect expresses his joy at regaining if not the boyhood Carter literally recaptures in "The Silver Key" then the next best thing, his bachelorhood. In control of Carter's fate is not the grim, impersonal forces of the universe, as embodied in Nyarlathotep, *"the Crawling Chaos"* (MM 403), but the creative imagination of Lovecraft himself. Thus in this sunniest of Lovecraft fictions Carter prevails, despite Nyarlathotep's efforts to thwart him, returning in solitary triumph to: "Home—New England—Beacon Hill—the waking world" (MM 405).

Chapter Eight
Cosmic Backwaters

In a letter dated 21 November 1930 to August Derleth, Lovecraft explained why he was "less exclusively cosmic" than his fellow fantasists, Clark Ashton Smith and Donald Wandrei:

> I cannot think of any individual as existing except as part of a pattern—and the pattern's most visible and tangible areas are of course the individual's immediate environment; the soil and culture-stream from which he springs, and the milieu of ideas, impressions, traditions, landscapes, and architecture through which he must necessarily peer in order to reach the "outside." This explains the difference between my "Dunwich" and "Colour Out of Space" and Smith's "Satampra Zeiros" or Wandrei's "Red Brain". I begin with the individual and think outward—appreciating the sensation of spatial and temporal liberation only when I can scale it against the known terrestrial scene. . . . With me, the very quality of being cosmically sensitive breeds an exaggerated attachment to the familiar and the immediate—Old Providence, the woods and hills, the ancient ways and thoughts of New England. (3:220–21)

Shortly after paying tribute to "Old Providence" in *The Case of Charles Dexter Ward,* Lovecraft wrote "The Colour Out of Space," the first of several long stories to feature more remote parts of New England, isolated regions that had undergone economic decline and depopulation in the nineteenth century with the rise of industrialization and the general migration westward.

While "The Colour Out of Space" has the by now generic Arkham setting, Lovecraft's travels would supply him with the backgrounds for his next three New England tales. In a letter dated 19 June 1931 to J. Vernon Shea, he said of "The Dunwich Horror": "I used considerable realism in developing the locale of that thing—the prototype being the decaying agricultural region N.E. of Springfield, Mass.—especially the township of Wilbraham, where I visited for a fortnight—in 1928." He continued: "My 'Whisperer in Darkness' will reflect a Vermont visit made in the same year" (3:379–80). As Donald R. Burleson has shown,[1] Lovecraft derived many of the character and place names for both "The Dunwich Horror" and "The Whisperer in Darkness" from the extended trip that he took that summer through southern Vermont and western Massachusetts. An expedition to Newburyport, Massachusetts, in the fall of 1931, as he reported soon afterward in a letter to Clark Ashton Smith, inspired "The Shadow over Innsmouth": "I certainly hope you can get to see Newburyport sooner or later, for its antiquity and desolation make it one of the most spectrally fascinating spots I have ever seen. It has started me off on a new story idea—not very novel in relation to other things of mine, but born of the imaginative overtones of such a place" (3: 435).

These tales of the late twenties and early thirties display Lovecraft at the peak of his form. Here, writing at that nebulous length between the short story and the novel, he could most effectively scale his cosmic horrors against "the known terrestrial scene," such as Townshend, Vermont, which so deeply affects the narrator of "The Whisperer in Darkness" upon his arrival there:

The town seemed very attractive in the afternoon sunlight as we swept up an incline and turned to the right into the main street. It drowsed like the older New England cities which one remembers from boyhood, and something in the collocation of roofs and steeples and chimneys and brick walls formed contours touching deep viol-strings of ancestral emotion. I could tell that I was at the gateway of a region half-bewitched through the piling-up of unbroken time-accumulations; a region where old, strange things have had a chance to grow and linger because they have never been stirred up. (DH 246)

This passage with its wholly unforced combination of archetypal elements—the memories of childhood, the architectural vista, the sense of continuity of the past—epitomizes the mature Lovecraft manner.

"The Colour Out of Space"

"The Colour Out of Space" (1927), like "The Picture in the House," begins with a description of the woods beyond Arkham, which appears to lie up the Miskatonic river valley, far from the sea. Where the earlier tale had relied on a philosophical preamble and staring, eyelike windows of a Gothic cast to generate atmosphere, here a naturalistic account of the landscape suffices: "West of Arkham the hills rise wild, and there are valleys with deep woods that no axe has ever cut. There are dark narrow glens where the trees slope fantastically, and where thin brooklets trickle without ever having caught the glint of sunlight. On the gentler slopes there are farms, ancient and rocky, with squat, moss-coated cottages brooding eternally over old New England secrets in the lee of great ledges; but these are all vacant now, the wide chimneys crumbling and the shingled sides bulging perilously beneath low gambrel roofs" (DH 53). After further description of the country-side in decline comes the first intimation of cosmic dread: "I vaguely wished some clouds would gather, for an odd timidity about the deep skyey voids above had crept into my soul" (DH 55). Of this opening passage, as fine as any in his fiction, Lovecraft might well have been thinking when he replied to a correspondent in June 1927: "Yes—my New England is a dream New England—the familiar scene with certain lights and shadows heightened (or meant to be heightened) just enough to merge it with things beyond the world" (2:130).

Again, as in "The Picture in the House," ordinary business brings the nameless narrator into the woods. Surveying for a new reservoir, an echo of the Quabbin Reservoir that Lovecraft surely knew was soon to flood a remote area of central Massachusetts, he stops at the "ancient tottering cottage" (DH 55) of one Ammi Pierce: "Only with persistent knocking could I rouse the aged man, and when he shuffled timidly to the door I could tell he was not glad to see me. He was not so feeble as I had expected; but his eyes drooped in a curious way, and his unkempt clothing and white beard made him seem very worn and dismal" (DH 56). Unlike the uncouth old man of the earlier tale whom he superfi-cially resembles, this elderly individual proves to be a sympathetic character, who by acting as another layer of perception between the narrator and the central story lends credibility to otherwise incredible events.

Contributing also to the realism of "The Colour Out of Space" is its air of scientific authenticity. Apparently as well versed an amateur astronomer and chemist as Lovecraft, the narrator can reconstruct from Ammi's account the sequence of acids and solvents to which the savants at Miskatonic University more than forty years earlier must have sub-jected the specimens of meteorite recovered from Nahum Gardner's farm. Of course, that the meteorite should register in the visible spec-trum an unclassifiable "colour"—"it was only by analogy that they called it colour at all" (DH 59)—is strictly impossible, a contradiction rather than an extension of natural law, though only a pedant would quarrel with such an imaginative leap.

As John Taylor Gatto has observed, " 'The Colour Out of Space' is

H. P. Lovecraft's *Book of Job.*"[2] In the months following the meteorite's fall, Nahum Gardner, his wife, and three sons, two of whom possess the Old Testament names Zenas and Thaddeus, stoically suffer one misfortune after another. With the onset of Mrs. Gardner's madness, Nahum locks her up in the attic, per rural New England custom.[3] After the contamination of the well water, "He and the boys continued to use the tainted supply, drinking it as listlessly and mechanically as they ate their meagre and ill-cooked meals and did their thankless and monotonous chores through the aimless days. There was something of stolid resignation about them all, as if they walked half in another world between lines of nameless guards to a certain and familiar doom" (DH 66). Unaware that no just God exists in the Lovecraft universe, Nahum can only speculate: "It must be all a judgment of some sort; though he could not fancy what for, since he had always walked uprightly in the Lord's ways so far as he knew" (DH 68).

The Gardner farm becomes a kind of travesty of the Garden of Eden, where one by one the bounties of the earth give out on their masters. A woodchuck's body proportions seem "slightly altered in a queer way impossible to describe" and its face has taken on "an expression which no one ever saw in a woodchuck before" (DH 61), while the skunk cabbages are "odd in shape and odour and hue" (DH 62). Such understatement represents an advance, for example, over the "detestable parodies of toadstools" (MM 238) that grow up under parallel circumstances in "The Shunned House."[4] Powerless to leave their place of torment, the innocents are condemned to witness the beasts of the field and the fruits of the earth—and ultimately themselves—decay and finally crumble into a greyish dust, a result that Edmund Wilson was charitable enough to note "more or less predicts the effects of the atomic bomb."[5]

Despite the emphasis on externals, images of dream arise, challenging the rational basis of the tale. Shortly before his final interview with Nahum, Ammi wonders: "What eldritch dream-world was this into which he had blundered?" (DH 70). In their flight from the farm the next day, Ammi and the other men in the investigating party "walked and stumbled as in a dream." When they look back at the farm, all "shining with the hideous unknown blend of colour," it resembles "a scene from a vision of Fuseli" (DH 78). At the very end, ruminating on a fate that threatens to engulf not only the old man but ultimately himself, the narrator admits: "I would hate to think of him as the grey, twisted, brittle monstrosity which persists more and more in troubling my sleep" (DH 82). Thus the story concludes, not in screaming italics of confirmation, but on a sad note of human concern.

Prompted in part by the pride he took in "the abnormally chromatic entity" (2:316) whose amorphousness stands in such contrast to the concreteness of his usual monsters, Lovecraft in later years regarded "The Colour Out of Space" as his best tale. At the very least it makes a solid capstone to that intensely creative phase from the summer of 1926 to the spring of 1927 that includes "The Call of Cthulhu," " Pickman's Model," "The Silver Key," *The Dream-Quest of Unknown Kadath,* and *The Case of Charles Dexter Ward.* In the purity and elegance of the cosmic intrusion (Cthulhu and his minions do not crop up even in passing), as well as in the story's overall austerity and control, Lovecraft had good reason to feel that he had nearly attained his ideal of the ineffable.

"The Dunwich Horror"

Like "The Colour Out of Space," "The Dunwich Horror" (1928) opens with a naturalistic description of a sinister country landscape— one lying well beyond Arkham up the Miskatonic river valley. Like its namesake, the ancient former capital of East Anglia eroded over the centuries by the sea, Dunwich has long been in decline.[6] One reason people shun the township "is that the natives are now repellently decadent, having gone far along that path of retrogression so common in many New England backwaters. They have come to form a race by themselves, with the well-defined mental and physical stigmata of degeneracy and inbreeding. The average of their intelligence is woe-fully low, whilst their annals reek of overt viciousness, and of half-hidden murders, incests, and deeds of almost unnamable violence and perversity" (DH 157). Amidst such a community the birth on the second of February, 1913, of a "dark, goatish-looking infant" to the husbandless Lavinia Whateley, "a somewhat deformed, unattractive albino woman, living with an aged and half-insane father about whom the most frightful tales of wizardry had been whispered in his youth" (DH 159), is scarcely matter for comment.

As in "The Colour Out of Space," the narrative follows the travails of a single family, but while the Gardners had passively fallen victim to a terror beyond their understanding, Wizard Whateley and his grandson Wilbur plot "to wipe out the human race and drag the earth off to some nameless place for some nameless purpose" (DH 198). The Dunwich horror poses such an immediate, dire threat to mankind that the erudite Henry Armitage, "A.M. Miskatonic, Ph.D. Princeton, Litt.D. Johns Hopkins" (DH 169), who much like Dr. Willett in *The Case of Charles Dexter Ward* arrives mid-way through the story to lead the opposition, has little time to ponder the philosophical implications. Skilled "in the mystical formulae of antiquity and the Middle Ages" (DH 182), Armitage like Willett arms himself with the appropriate spell in order to fight a menace likewise linked to "the dreadful name of *Yog-Sothoth*" (DH 162).

If "The Dunwich Horror" on the surface amounts to a "good versus evil" struggle, the tale's "villains" possess attributes that make this conflict far from black and white. James Egan has pointed out that the birth of Wilbur and his brother "satirically parallels the Immaculate Conception of Christ in the womb of a human mother, Lavinia being the perfect antithesis of the Virgin Mary,"[7] while Donald R. Burleson has suggested that the Whateley twins together "can be seen closely to fit the archetypal pattern of the hero in myth."[8] With the same sort of sardonic inversion Lovecraft mocks his own youth and upbringing in the portrait of the Whateley family, whose three members may be viewed as grotesque parodies of his grandfather, his mother, and himself. Under the tutelage of the Old Whateley, who arranges his library of "rotting ancient books and parts of books" (DH 163) for his grandson's benefit, the precocious Wilbur grows up to be "a scholar of really tremendous erudition" (DH 167). Physically ugly, as Mrs. Lovecraft felt her son to be, Wilbur hides a terrible secret under his clothes. That after Lavinia's disappearance he should appear "under a cloud of probable matricide" (DH 170) may well reflect Lovecraft's resentment of his own mother. While such connections can be carried too far, they do not seem out of place in what in other respects stands out as Lovecraft's least inhibited tale.

Sexual imagery surrounds the secondary climax, the death of "the monstrous being known to the human world as Wilbur Whateley" (DH 172), torn apart by the savage campus watchdog in his bungled attempt to steal the *Necronomicon*. The prefatory sentence smoothly avoids the clumsiness of the disclaimers of earlier stories over the difficulty of describing the indescribable:

It would be trite and not wholly accurate to say that no human pen could describe it, but one may properly say that it could not be vividly visualised by anyone whose ideas of aspect and contour are too closely bound up with the common life-forms of this planet and of the three known dimensions. It was partly human, beyond a doubt, with very man-like hands and head, and the goatish, chinless face had the stamp of the Whateleys upon it. But the torso and lower parts of the body were teratologically fabulous, so that only generous clothing could ever have enabled it to walk on earth unchallenged or uneradicated.

Above the waist it was semi-anthropomorphic; though its chest, where the dog's paws still rested watchfully, had the leathery, reticulated hide of a crocodile or an alligator. The back was piebald with yellow and black, and dimly suggested the squamous covering of certain snakes. Below the waist, though, it was the worst; for here all human resemblance left off and sheer phantasy began. The skin was thickly covered with coarse black fur, and from the abdomen a score of long greenish-grey tentacles with red sucking mouths protruded limply. (DH 174)

Here Lovecraft would seem almost deliberately to be baiting the Freudians. The passage continues in the same vivid vein, constituting perhaps his most successful attempt at direct alien description, made all the more shocking for the slow build-up over the five preceding sections.

At the primary climax the Dunwich horror itself appears more obliquely, through the eyes of one of the local rustics, who watches its progress up Sentinel Hill through binoculars: "Bigger'n a barn . . . all made o' squirmin' ropes . . . hull thing sort o' shaped like a hen's egg bigger'n anything, with dozens o' legs like hogsheads that haff shut up when they step" (DH 194). Here the humble language of the farm succinctly conveys the terror of the beast. While this sort of literal rendering of speech, once common in both popular and serious fiction, may be out of fashion, the extreme dialect of the Dunwich natives does serve to thicken the narrative texture, especially in those dramatic phone calls over the party lines during the week the horror roams at large. Quotations from assorted documents also enliven the third-person narration, from the Reverend Abijah Hoadley's "memorable sermon on the close presence of Satan and his imps" (DH 158) in 1747 to the quasi-biblical passage from the *Necronomicon* that so neatly summarizes the Old Ones' gestalt: "The Old Ones were, the Old Ones are, and the Old Ones shall be. Not in the spaces we know, but *between* them, They walk serene and primal, undimensioned and to us unseen" (DH 170).

As in the final scene of *The Case of Charles Dexter Ward,* an exchange takes place that approaches actual dialogue in the aftermath of the horror's destruction. Rather like the archetypal fictional detective at mystery's end, Dr. Armitage explains the fine points of the case for the less astute, though he cannot resist moralizing: "We have no business calling in such things from outside, and only very wicked people and very wicked cults ever try to" (DH 197). Such heavy-handedness, however, is consistent with the overall tone of the tale. Armitage, for instance, during Wilbur Whateley's first visit to the Miskatonic University library, feels uneasy in the presence of "the bent, goatish giant before him" who "seemed like the spawn of another planet or dimension; like something only partly of mankind, and linked to black gulfs of essence and entity that stretch like titan phantasms beyond all spheres of force and matter, space and time" (DH 170–71). As exceptionally intuitive as he might be, he could hardly at this stage have such accurate insight into Wilbur's nature. Even such a passing phrase as "anaemic, bloodless-looking cows" (DH 161) would seem to contain one adjective too many. When in the wake of *Weird Tales'* rejection of *At the Mountains of Madness* in 1931, Lovecraft grumbled, "That ass Wright got me into the habit of obvious writing with his never-ending complaints about the indefiniteness of my early stuff" (3:395), he could well have been thinking of "The Dunwich Horror."

If Lovecraft made concessions to popular taste, the tale yet ranks among his strongest, by virtue of its high level of excitement and suspense. While the horror's defeat may be a foregone conclusion, the final revelation—"*It was his twin brother, but it looked more like the father than he did*" (DH 198)—comes for many as a genuine surprise rather than simply as confirmation. Indeed, in every suggestive incident and weird detail, from the Whateleys' cattle buying to the business of the legend of the whippoorwills, "psychopomps lying in wait for the souls of the dying" (DH 158), "The Dunwich Horror" exhibits the master's touch.

"The Whisperer in Darkness"

As in "The Colour Out of Space," the action in "The Whisperer in Darkness" (1930) centers on a lone farm under extraterrestrial siege. But where in the earlier story an impersonal cosmic blight had inexorably subverted a family of simple rustics, here a large force of cunning, crab-like creatures toy with their prey, an isolated scholar. Variously referred to as the Winged Ones, the Outer Ones, and the fungi from Yuggoth, they seek nothing so mundane as his death but, both literally and figuratively, to capture his mind.

Some of the "run-down farmers" (DH 236) of the Vermont hill country like the "surly" (DH 224) Walter Brown—clearly kin to the ignorant folk who populate the area west of Arkham and Dunwich— serve as allies of the Outer Ones, but their role is minor. Given the intellectual struggle that is at the heart of the tale, the dramatic focus falls naturally on two men of learning, the narrator Albert N. Wilmarth, "an instructor of literature at Miskatonic University in Arkham, Massachusetts, and an enthusiastic amateur student of New England folklore" (DH 209), and Henry Wentworth Akeley, "a man of character, education, and intelligence, albeit a recluse with very little worldly sophistication" (DH 215). Between them they debate the existence of the Winged Ones through that most Lovecraftian and civilized of means, correspondence. To a degree Akeley is a hapless victim like the Gardners, his only mistake to inhabit a region of alien infestation. Yet because like Charles Dexter Ward, whose epistolary cry for help also arrives too late, he learns more than is humanly healthy, he must suffer a fate perhaps worse than death, one with a peculiar cosmic twist.

Even more than in "The Dunwich Horror," the myths regarding intelligent pre-human races appear to be a matter of fairly common knowledge among certain cognoscenti. Appreciative of "the magnificent horror fiction of Arthur Machen" (DH 214),[9] Wilmarth has read "the monstrous and abhored *Necronomicon* of the mad Arab Abdul Alhazred" (DH 222) before hearing of the fungi from Yuggoth from Akeley. From his correspondent he also learns of a host of other things: "I found myself faced by names and terms that I had heard elsewhere in the most hideous of connexions—Yuggoth, Great Cthulhu, Tsathoggua, Yog-Sothoth, R'lyeh, Nyarlathotep, Azathoth, Hastur, Yian, Leng, the Lake of Hali, Bethmoora, the Yellow Sign, L'mur-Kathulos, Bran, and the Magnum Innominandum—and was drawn back through nameless aeons and inconceivable dimensions to worlds of elder, outer entity at which the crazed author of the *Necronomicon* had only guessed at in the vaguest way" (DH 223). In invoking not only the gods of his own pantheon but those of such earlier authors as Ambrose Bierce and Robert W. Chambers, together with those of such contemporary writer-friends as Clark Ashton Smith and Robert E. Howard, Lovecraft would seem to be pushing the limit for such literary cross-references. As Will Murray notes, "these asides are distracting even when they are amusing,"[10] tending to undercut, however slightly, the seriousness Lovecraft was always insisting was essential to the best weird fiction.

A physical description of the Outer Ones occurs quite early in the story, in connection with the bodies seen to be floating in the rivers following the "unprecedented Vermont floods of November 3, 1927" (DH 209): "They were pinkish things about five feet long; with crustaceous bodies bearing vast pairs of dorsal fins of membraneous wings and several sets of articulated limbs, and with a sort of convoluted ellipsoid, covered with multitudes of very short antennae, where a head ordinarily would be" (DH 210). Free of the usual loaded adjectives, this clinical description anticipates Lake's minutely scientific account of the Old Ones' morphology in *At the Mountains of Madness.* While Wilmarth will later deplore their smell and particularly their buzzing voices, "like the drone of some loathsome, gigantic insect ponderously shaped into the articulate speech of an alien species" (DH 227), this almost neutral presentation of their aspect, preceded by no foreshadowing, shows Lovecraft moving toward a more sympathetic view of his monsters. According to the Pennacook myths, they inhabit the region for economic reasons, the Winged Ones having "mines in our earthly hills whence they took a kind of stone they could not get on any other world" (DH 212).

The tension in "The Whisperer in Darkness" lies not in whether these beings exist, nor in whether they plan to destroy all terrestrial life, for as Akeley asserts in his first letter, "They could easily conquer the earth, but have not tried so far because they have not needed to. They would rather leave things as they are to save bother." As do the men of Tsath in "The Mound," written the year before, the Outer Ones like "to keep informed on the state of things in the human world" (DH 218). Like Joseph Curwen they seek knowledge from a wide assortment of individuals, but more tidily than he they can remove a living brain "by fissions so adroit that it would be crude to call the operation surgery" (DH 260) and preserve it in an "ether-tight cylinder" (DH 257), an adaptation of sorts of the "Tulu-metal" cylinder that holds Zamacona's narrative in "The Mound."

That Lovecraft did not intend the fungi to appear as entirely "evil" is reflected in the range of Wilmarth's responses throughout his ordeal. After he receives the phony Akeley letter and weighs its import, he reacts with enthusiasm: "My own zeal for the unknown flared up to meet his, and I felt myself touched by the contagion of the morbid barrier-breaking. To shake off the maddening and wearying limitations of space and time and natural law—to be linked with the vast outside—to come close to the nighted and abysmal secrets of the infinite and the ultimate—surely such a thing was worth the risk of one's life, soul, and sanity!" (DH 243). Lovecraft often expressed this same sentiment in his letters. Wilmarth later waivers as he travels from Arkham to Vermont, saying, "I do not know whether dread or adventurous expectancy was uppermost in me as I changed trains at Boston" (DH 244), and, once into the hills themselves, "The purpose of my visit, and the frightful abnormalities it postulated, struck at me all at once with a chill sensation that nearly overbalanced my ardour for strange delvings" (DH 247). Of course, by the end his "scientific zeal had vanished amidst fear and loathing" (DH 262). While this may represent Wilmarth's final judgment, a fundamental ambivalence remains.

Critics have complained that Wilmarth's naive behavior exceeds all credible bounds. In contrast to Dr. Willett, who is hoodwinked for a time by an imposter who is at least outwardly human, he seems too easily fooled, for example, by the Outer One in disguise, wearing "the face and hands of Henry Wentworth Akeley" (DH 271). John Taylor Gatto provides the key to such obtuseness when he calls "The Whisperer in Darkness" "Lovecraft's 'dirty' story."[11] In effect Wilmarth plays the role of ingenuous virgin while the beings who try to entice him into their cosmic harem act the part of seducer. He may start in horror at the prospect of flying to Yuggoth and beyond as a disembodied consciousness, yet Wilmarth flees the Akeley farmhouse only after a lengthy flirtation. Since the price of immortality is to become as helpless as those unfortunates Joseph Curwen keeps in bottles as "essential saltes," he arguably makes the right choice. Still, initiation into the mysteries of the universe may be no worse than loss of sexual innocence. As the false Akeley informs Wilmarth, "To us, as to only a few men on this earth, there will be opened up gulfs of time and space and knowledge beyond anything within the conception of human science or philosophy" (DH 253). Such a proposition cannot be easily dismissed.

"The Shadow over Innsmouth"

Like the narrator of "The Festival," the unnamed narrator of "The Shadow over Innsmouth" (1931) uncovers some unpleasant truths about his ancestors in the course of a coastal excursion, here to "the ancient Massachusetts seaport of Innsmouth" (DH 303). The channel tides had played mockingly with the body of a tramp below the cliffs of an Innsmouth, England, in "Celephaïs," while the narrator of the *Fungi* sonnet "The Port" had hoped "that just at sunset" he could reach "The crest that looks on Innsmouth in the vale" (CP 113). Not, however, until he visited Newburyport, still decades away from the historic restoration and trendy tourist trade of our own era, did Lovecraft connect the name with an actual place, for the last of his grand narratives with a lush New England setting.

Like his contemporary John P. Marquand, he felt moved to mirror the decline of the once prosperous port in fiction, but while the residents of, say, Marquand's Wickford Point exhibit symptoms of genteel social decay, the denizens of Innsmouth suffer from "an exaggerated case of civic degeneration" (DH 310) originating in alien miscegenation. Yog-Sothoth's mating with Lavinia Whateley results in only two offspring in "The Dunwich Horror," but here the fishy features of the Deep Ones, manifested in what the narrator comes to call the "Innsmouth look" (DH 319), have for generations tainted almost the entire population of the town. Not just the appearance of the natives gives offense. "The odour of the fish was maddening" (D 16) on the upheaved sea bottom where the protagonist lands in "Dagon," but in Innsmouth the stink is far worse: "Pervading everything was the most nauseous fishy odour imaginable" (DH 317). Of all of Lovecraft's foul-smelling creatures, the Deep Ones take on an especial pungency stemming from his hatred of seafood.

The facts behind "that ill-rumoured and evilly shadowed seaport of death and blasphemous abnormality" emerge gradually. Celebrating his coming of age in typical Lovecraftian fashion with "a tour of New England—sightseeing, antiquarian, and genealogical," the narrator starts out in ignorance: "I never heard of Innsmouth till the day before I saw it for the first and—so far—last time." That lightly dropped "so far," together with his admission that the telling of the tale helps him to make up his mind "regarding a certain terrible step which lies ahead of me" (DH 305), subtly prepares for the sobering self-realization at story's end. Like de la Poer, he cannot avoid heredity catching up with him in the long run.

On a more immediate level, the narrator assumes interest as an autobiographical figure. Since the central action occurs over less than a full day and night (just as more than half of *At the Mountains of Madness*, written earlier in the year, concentrates on a period of only sixteen hours), ordinary personal details take on a particular prominence. Economy dictates the narrator's itinerary: "I had no car, but was travelling by train, trolley, and motor-coach, always seeking the cheapest possible route. In Newburyport they told me that the steam train was the thing to take to Arkham; and it was only at the station ticket-office, when I demurred at the high fare, that I learned about Innsmouth" (DH 305). For a dollar he receives forty cents in change from the driver of the Innsmouth bus, "a thin, stoop-shouldered man" with "a narrow head, bulging watery blue eyes that seemed never to wink, a flat nose, a receding forehead and chin, and singularly undeveloped ears" (DH 314), among other repellent physical traits. Such a character might be laughably absurd were he not presented in such a mundane context.

During his antiquarian tour of Innsmouth the narrator has to think about finding food: "Disliking the dinginess of the single restaurant I had seen, I bought a fair supply of cheese crackers and ginger wafers to serve as a lunch later on" (DH 323). As for dinner, "A bowl of vegetable soup with crackers was enough for me" (DH 352). His only extravagance is the quart bottle of bootleg whiskey "easily, though not cheaply, obtained in the rear of a dingy-looking variety store" (DH 327) that he buys for Zadok Allen, "the half-crazed, liquorish nonagenarian whose tales of old Innsmouth and its shadow were so hideous and incredible" (DH 326). In his frugality the narrator makes an ironic contrast to Captain Obed Marsh, his as yet unsuspected great-great-grandfather, who in driving his Faustian bargain with the Deep Ones in his voyages to Polynesia appears to have been motivated by commercial gain. As Zadok Allen suggests at one point in his monologue, hard times in Innsmouth spur Marsh to boast that he could "mebbe git a holt o' sarten paowers as ud bring plenty o' fish an' quite a bit of gold" (DH 333).

Like Wilmarth in "The Whisperer in Darkness," the narrator cuts short his overnight stay in a place whose other occupants make him uneasy, here the Gilman House, where for a dollar he has no choice but to put up after he learns that the eight o'clock bus to Arkham has suddenly developed engine trouble. Like Wilmarth, too, he is prone to be naive. Noticing that the bolt has been freshly removed from the connecting door in his dismal room, he observes: "No doubt it had become out of order, like so many other things in this decrepit edifice" (DH 343). Yet he has not been wholly fooled, as his reaction to hearing the connecting door being tried shows: "My sensations upon recognising this sign of actual peril were perhaps less rather than more tumultuous because of my previous vague fears. I had been, albeit without definite reason, instinctively on my guard" (DH 344). He adds, "The readiness with which I fell into a plan of action proves that I must have been subconsciously fearing some menace and considering possible avenues of escape for hours" (DH 345). This surfacing of subconscious fear constitutes another small step toward the irruption of the narrator's true nature, hidden like a time-bomb in his unconscious, that will form the story's final climax.

For the moment, however, he displays considerable presence of mind in his highly suspenseful flight through the streets of Innsmouth and out the abandoned branch railway line until, at the penultimate climax, he faces his pursuers: "I saw them in a limitless stream—flopping, hopping, croaking, bleating—surging inhumanly through the spectral moonlight in a grotesque, malignant saraband of fantastic nightmare" (DH 360). In another instant he faints, but not before he betrays a trace of equivocal feeling: "But for all their monstrousness they were not unfamiliar to me." While he may be specifically referring to the design on the tiara he had seen at the museum in Newburyport, in a larger sense he again lays the ground for his acceptance of the kinship between himself and these "blasphemous fish-frogs" (DH 361).

En route to Innsmouth the narrator alludes to Kingsport Head, "topped by the queer ancient house of which so many legends are told" (DH 316), and later uses the Poe-derived phrases "conqueror worm" (DH 324) and "imp of the perverse" (DH 326), yet basically he brings to his experience none of the kind of dark background lore known to Armitage and Wilmarth. While old Zadok mentions such things as Cthulhu, the Esoteric Order of Dagon, and shoggoths, the narrator is never subjected to a session of Akeley-esque cosmological name-dropping. Only at the very end, more than three years after his trip to Innsmouth, with the onset of "the dreams" (DH 366)—in particular, of his grandmother's grandmother, "Pth'thya-l'yi," who lives in the under-sea city of "Y'ha-nthlei" (DH 367)—and his acquiring the Innsmouth look, does he accept the supernatural reality. Again, as with de la Poer, his transformation is all the more affecting for the family background of madness and suicide, and for the great psychological distance he travels from normality to abnormality.

Yet a certain ambivalence, not present in "The Rats in the Walls," tempers the tragedy of the narrator's fate. Zadok recognizes the threat of the Deep Ones: "They'd ruther not start risin' an' wipin' aout human-kind, but ef they was gave away an' forced to, they cud do a lot toward jest that" (DH 337). Later he suggests that they are plotting to make a move soon—"it ain't what them fish devils *hez done*, but *what they're a-goin' to do!*" (DH 340)—while the narrator learns that they still intend to spread onto the land, after recovering from the setback of which he was the cause. Sinister though they may be, they hold out to him the promise of an immortality at least as appealing as that proffered to

Wilmarth in "The Whisperer in Darkness." Now one of them, he understandably welcomes the prospect, anticipating acting as decisively as he had in originally fleeing Innsmouth: "I shall plan my cousin's escape from that Canton madhouse, and together we shall go to marvel-shadowed Innsmouth. We shall swim out to that brooding reef in the sea and dive down through black abysses to Cyclopean and many-columned "Y'ha-nthlei, and in that lair of the Deep Ones we shall dwell amidst wonder and glory forever" (DH 367). With "this delectable parody of the ending of the 23rd Psalm,"[12] as Donald R. Burleson puts it, Lovecraft concludes with the narrator's mocking the Christian faith once spurned by his ancestor, Obed Marsh, in final affirmation of their bond.

Chapter Nine
Beyond New England

Three of Lovecraft's late, longer narratives focus on expeditions to earthly locales to which he journeyed only in his imagination: Oklahoma Indian country in "The Mound," the Antarctic in *At the Mountains of Madness,* and Western Australia in the latter part of "The Shadow Out of Time." In these "archaeological" works he chose to concentrate on laying out the ethnohistories of his monsters, in contrast to those other lengthy tales of the period, "The Whisperer in Darkness" and "The Shadow over Innsmouth," where measuring his horrors against the familiar New England scene left room for relatively little development of the Outer Ones' and the Deep Ones' backgrounds. A fourth story, "Through the Gates of the Silver Key," set in the New Orleans home of E. Hoffmann Price whom he visited in June 1932, features the more personal, if no less cosmic, voyagings of Randolph Carter.

In dwelling upon the political and economic organization of his alien races, their science, their art, their religion, Lovecraft fashioned utopias (or dystopias) that reflect the broadening of his outlook in the depression years, when he no longer blamed society for denying him the livelihood that he felt he deserved by virtue of birth and breeding but pondered how that society should best be changed to benefit all men. By the time he had conceived of the Great Race in "The Shadow Out of Time," as S. T. Joshi has remarked, "Lovecraft had ceased to want a *restoration* of the past, but now looks to *reform* for the future."[1] Indeed, toward the end of his life he had mellowed to the point where, as James Turner has observed, he "was re-forming the Mythos creatures in terms of his developing criteria for human excellence, his own idealized conception of man at his most humane and profound."[2]

"The Mound"

S. T. Joshi has properly called "The Mound" (1929–30) "a major Lovecraftian opus,"[3] though it has been neglected until recently on account of its status as a "revision." As Lovecraft indicated in a letter

dated 20 December 1929, his client, Zealia Bishop, supplied barely a
plot germ: "The alleged author intended to let the story go as a simple
tale of a haunted mound, with a couple of Indian ghosts around it; but I
decided at once that such a thing would be insufferably tame & flat.
Accordingly I am having the mound turn out to be the gateway of a
primordial & forgotten subterranean world—the home of a fearsomely
ancient & decadent race cut off from the outer earth since the prehistoric sinking of fabulous Atlantis & Lemuria" (3:97). Lovecraft had
earlier written a tale for Zealia Bishop with the same Oklahoma setting, "The Curse of Yig" (1928), which exhibits his usual careful
attention to local color in the snake legendry associated with the Aztec
god Quetzalcoatl, but it is at best no more than a competent piece.

"It is only within the last few years that most people have stopped
thinking of the West as a *new* land," declares the unnamed narrator, "an
American Indian ethnologist," who closes the opening paragraph by
quoting from " 'He Cometh and He Passeth By,' " a ghost story by
H. R. Wakefield: "Only a couple of years ago a British author spoke of
Arizona as a 'moon-dim region, very lovely in its way, and stark and
old—an ancient, lonely land' " (HM 96). The least revealing of
Lovecraft's later narrators because the most removed from the events he
relates, he conforms to the usual aristocratic type. "I am white and
Eastern enough myself" (HM 97), he admits, his forebears having been
"settled, homekeeping gentlemen of Somerset and Devon under Henry
the Eighth" (HM 115) at the time of the flashback that almost totally
subsumes the tale's present-day action, the paraphrase of the manuscript entitled "The Narrative of Pánfilo de Zamacona y Nuñez, gentleman, of Luarca in Astorias, *Concerning the Subterranean World of Xinaián,
A.D. 1545*" (HM 113). At the end, a mere confirmatory coda compared to the climax of, say, either "The Dunwich Horror" or "The
Whisperer in Darkness," he too braves the dangers of the mound, "for
as a Virginian I felt the blood of ancestral fighters and gentlemen-
adventurers pounding a protest against retreat from any peril known or
unknown" (HM 160).

In contrast to Lovecraft's New England narrators, whose scope is
limited to the first English settlers in the New World and vaguely the
Indians before them, he can hark back to the older civilizations of the
Southwest, both Spanish and Indian, in order to adumbrate more awesomely the antiquity of a still earlier civilization. After visiting the
mound and uncovering the cylinder containing Zamacona's manuscript, he muses:

I felt instinctively that the common problem of the Spaniard and myself was one of such abysmal timelessness, of such unholy and unearthly eternity, that the scant four hundred years between us bulked as nothing in comparison. It took no more than a single look at that monstrous and insidious cylinder to make me realise the dizzying gulfs that yawned between all men of the known earth and the primal mysteries it represented. Before that gulf Pánfilo de Zamacona and I stood side by side; just as Aristotle and I, or Cheops and I, might have stood. (HM 115)

Another fine example of this parallelism, so much more evocative than a string of strenuous adjectives, occurs soon after, in the description of Zamacona's entry into the underground world of "Xinaián," "which, from the writer's supplementary explanations and diacritical marks, could probably be best represented to Anglo-Saxon ears by the phonetic arrangement *K'n-yan*" (HM 131): "He had come to the unknown world at last, and from his manuscript it is clear that he viewed the formless landscape as proudly and exaltedly as ever his fellow-countryman Balboa viewed the new-found Pacific from that unforgettable peak in Darien" (HM 122).

If in "The Mound" Lovecraft begins to imagine the sweep of time on a geological scale, he does so without regard to geological accuracy. Bounded above by a "seething, impenetrable sky of bluish coruscations" (HM 122), K'n-yan in its openness resembles Randolph Carter's dreamland, a link made explicit in references to such places as the "red-litten world of Yoth" and "the vaults of Zin." Certainly those "morbid beasts of Tsath," the hybrid *"gyaa-yothn,"* who feed on the flesh of "a special slave-class which had for the most part ceased to be thoroughly human" (HM 139), would feel at home amid the unsettling menagerie of the *Dream-Quest,* at the same time they are akin in their manufactured origin and menial function to the shoggoths of *At the Mountains of Madness.* Not only in certain specifics but in its blend of fantasy and realism, "The Mound" can be seen as a transitional work between these two short novels.

Through telepathic communication with the Indian-like men of "the great, tall city of Tsath" (HM 133), wherein dwell all the inhabitants of K'n-yan, Zamacona learns a great deal about their decidedly decadent society: "Daily life was organised in ceremonial patterns; with games, intoxication, torture of slaves, day-dreaming, gastronomic and emotional orgies, religious exercises, exotic experiments, artistic and philosophical discussions, and the like, as the principal occupations." Furthermore, "Art and intellect, it appeared, had reached very high levels in Tsath; but had become listless and decadent. The dominance of machinery had at one time broken up the growth of normal aesthetics, introducing a lifelessly geometrical tradition fatal to sound expression" (HM 135). Here, airing one of his conservative crotchets, Lovecraft by extension blames technology for Western civilization's decline.

Tsath yet has its appealing features. Zamacona, "despite a growing sense of horror and alienage," upon his entry into the city finds himself "enthralled by its intimations of mystery and cosmic wonder. The dizzy giganticism of its overawing towers," "the odd vistas glimpsed from balustraded plazas and tiers of titan terraces," among other elements, all combine "to produce such a sense of adventurous expectancy as he had never known before" (HM 145). Scarcely a protagonist in Lovecraft, however dire his situation, fails to appreciate architectural beauty.

Though ultimately as doomed as Akeley in "The Whisperer in Darkness" to enslavement by his alien captors, Zamacona has within the confines of the mound world considerable freedom. His inviting living quarters include a library of "metal cylinders containing some of the manuscripts he was soon to read—standard classics which all urban apartments possessed." Indeed, his hosts have outfitted his abode with every amenity for a writer: "Desks with great stacks of membrane-paper and pots of prevailing green pigment were in every room—each with graded sets of pigment brushes and other odd bits of stationery. Mechanical writing devices stood on ornate golden tripods, while over all was shed a brilliant blue light from energy-globes set in the ceiling" (HM 146). For Zamacona, setting down his own history and leaving K'n-yan with it becomes the goal of his existence: "Of course he could not bear any gold, but mere escape was enough. He would, though, dematerialise and carry with him his manuscript in the Tulu-metal cylinder, even though it cost additional effort; for this record and proof must reach the outer world at all hazards" (HM 154). In this, the very act of composing his narrative, the intrepid Spaniard assumes his greatest nobility. On a symbolic level his poignant fate anticipates his creator's. Zamacona may die in his escape attempt, his corpse reanimated to serve as a ghostly sentinel, but his written words, more valuable than gold, do reach the "outer world," just as Lovecraft's prose would eventually gain him an audience of appreciative readers unimaginable in his lifetime.

Soon after completing "The Mound," Lovecraft wrote a third story for Zealia Bishop, "Medusa's Coil" (1930), a more lurid variation on the mythic snake theme of "The Curse of Yig" and his one excursion into the Southern Gothic, complete with a faded aristocratic family and a decayed mansion on the Mississippi River. In this tale of jealousy and murder, Denis de Russy's downfall begins when, like Edward Derby in "The Thing on the Doorstep," he begins to mix with the "aesthetes— the decadents. . . . Experimenters in life and sensation—the Baudelaire kind of chap" (HM 170). His painter friend, Frank Marsh, has taken "his pose of decadence pretty seriously, and set out to be as much of a Rimbaud, Baudelaire, or Lautréamont as he could" (HM 175). If decadence only masks far worse cosmic abnormalities, Lovecraft for once deals fairly frankly, as arguably he could only permit himself in a ghostwritten work, with the sexual, as embodied in the triangle consisting of Marsh, de Russy, and his bride of the "singular head of jet black hair" (HM 172), Marceline, who proves, in a final revelation perhaps worthy of Faulkner on an off-day, "in deceitfully slight proportion" to have been "a negress" (HM 200). While not up to the standard of "The Mound" and held in low esteem by Lovecraft himself, "Medusa's Coil" also merits more critical scrutiny than it has hitherto received.

At the Mountains of Madness

Since boyhood Lovecraft had been fascinated by Antarctica. "About 1900 I became a passionate devotee of geography & history, & an intense fanatic on the subject of Antarctic exploration" (1:37), he wrote in November 1916, while in November 1930 he confessed that the cold continent was "really paramount in my geographico-fantastic imagination" (3:218). As Jason C. Eckhardt has pointed out, the three years prior to his composition of *At the Mountains of Madness* (1931) saw four major south polar expeditions, notably Admiral Byrd's of 1928– 30, which no doubt supplied the most immediate inspiration for the novel, as reflected in the heavy reliance on radio communication and air travel by the Miskatonic University Expedition of 1930–31.[4]

For literary inspiration Lovecraft turned to "Poe's only long story— the disturbing and enigmatical *Arthur Gordon Pym,*" a work familiar to both the geologist narrator who leads the expedition (unnamed but identified as Dyer in "The Shadow Out of Time") and one of the graduate assistants, "a brilliant young fellow named Danforth," who is "a great reader of bizarre material" (MM 8). Lovecraft invokes Poe and *Pym* in particular throughout, from Danforth's remark as their ship approaches the Antarctic coast that the smoking cone of Mt. Erebus must have been Poe's source for the image in "Ulalume" of "the lavas that restlessly roll / Their sulphurous currents down Yaanek / In the ultimate climes of the pole" (MM 8) to Danforth's final cry of *"Tekeli-li! Tekeli-li!"* (MM 106) as their plane leaves the mountains of madness behind. When shortly before the climax Danforth hints "at queer notions about unsuspected and forbidden sources to which Poe may have had access when writing his *Arthur Gordon Pym* a century ago" (MM 97), Lovecraft suggests in effect that Poe had gotten only a glimmer of the horrible "reality" exposed in full by the Miskatonic explorers. Like Poe's Tsalal, Lovecraft's stupendous mountains—"Everest out of the running" (MM 14), their discoverer reports—lie just beyond the horizon of the known geography of his day.

Such links have led Marc A. Cerasini to call *At the Mountains of Madness* "surely a thematic sequel—with more than merely incidental tributes to the source novel."[5] Granted some thematic overlap between the two works, *Pym* remains at heart an inner journey toward self-knowledge while *Madness,* like Lovecraft's other longer tales of the period, is fundamentally an outward voyage toward knowledge of the universe and man's diminished place within it. The novel, however, does represent a philosophical advance in the value that Lovecraft now puts on man as a whole, a shift most touchingly displayed in the sympathy that Dyer evinces for the star-headed Old Ones when, after many hours spent below ground absorbing their history from bas-reliefs, he and Danforth find the bodies of several killed by shoggoths: ". . . poor Lake, poor Gedney . . . poor Old Ones! Scientists to the last—what had they done that we would not have done in their place? God, what intelligence and persistence! What a facing of the incredible, just as those carven kinsmen and forbears had faced things only a little less incredible! Radiates, vegetables, monstrosities, star-spawn—whatever they had been, they were men!" (MM 96). Written in February and March of 1931, *At the Mountains of Madness* anticipates if it does not actually coincide with Lovecraft's conversion to liberalism in the spring of that year.

One mark of the Old Ones' humanity, apart from the "abnormal-historic mindedness" (MM 57) that moved them to record their annals in bas-reliefs, is their interest in books, both their own, as evidenced by the "racks for the hinged sets of dotted surfaces forming their books" (MM 65), and others. Dyer and Danforth, during their investigation of the remains of Lake's ill-fated sub-expedition, note amidst the debris a "jumble of roughly handled illustrated books," while the missing materials from the camp include "illustrated technical and scientific books" (MM 38). Later in the mountains they find the sledges the revived Old Ones used to transport their specimens, among which are "tarpaulins obviously bulging with books" (MM 86). Such a mass of reading matter may not be so disproportionate for a party of twelve men, considering that Admiral Byrd had Little America, with a population of forty-two, outfitted with a library of 3,000 volumes.

In his close attention to geological and paleontological background, Lovecraft creates a sense of verisimilitude that certainly far surpasses that of Poe in the polar part of *Pym*. Dyer, for example, upon examining some fragments of the Old Ones' dwellings in those sublime mountains, observes: "Now and then we had a chance to study the petrified wood of a surviving shutter, and were impressed by the fabulous antiquity in the still discernible grain. These things had come from Mesozoic gymnosperms and conifers—especially Cretaceous cycads—and from fan-palms and early angiosperms of plainly Tertiary date. Nothing definitely later than the Pliocene could be discovered" (MM 53). Given such strong if selective detail, mundane environmental concerns—the severe cold, logistical difficulties, physical hardship—can remain undeveloped without loss of credibility. If Dyer and Danforth have no more use for oxygen masks during their extended ramble among those 40,000-foot high mountains than the original Old Ones needed spaceships or even protective clothing "to traverse the interstellar ether" (MM 61), they also find carven maps that "uphold in a striking way the theories of continental drift lately advanced by Taylor, Wegener, and Joly" (MM 66), fringe theories that would not in fact gain wide acceptance until years later. Propelled by scientific zeal, unlike the passive Pym, Dyer can claim that "above all my bewilderment and sense of menace there burned a dominant curiosity to fathom more of this age-old secret—to know what sort of beings had built and lived in this incalculably gigantic place, and what relation to the general world of its time or of other times so unique a concentration of life could have had" (MM 47).

Along with the scientific realism a subtle strain of traditional mythology helps to anchor the invented mythos of the novel. S. T. Joshi, viewing the Old Ones as "a type of *classic* civilization holding the same relation to mankind in general as the Greeks and Romans do to Western civilization,"[6] has cited Lovecraft's use of simile to liken the decline of the Old Ones to the decline of Rome. In "The Mound" had appeared

such Roman elements as the scroll-like books and gladitorial-like diver-
sions of the men of Tsath. In *Madness* images taken not only from
classical history but also from myth occur. Dyer and Danforth, as they
wander through the labyrinthine passages inside the mountains, leave
shreds of paper to mark their trail, rather as Theseus relied upon
Ariadne's thread in the palace of the Minotaur. Of their looking back at
the monster they chance to encounter, Dyer remarks: "Unhappy act!
Not Orpheus himself, or Lot's wife, paid much more dearly for a
backward glance" (MM 100). The "disturbing wind-piping" Dyer hears
as they escape in their plane prompts him to wish that he had "wax-
stopped ears like Ulysses' men off the Sirens' coast" (MM 104).

Danforth employs a more homely source to articulate his impressions.
" 'South Station Under—Washington Under—Park Street Under—
Kendall—Central—Harvard. . . .' The poor fellow was chanting the
familiar stations of the Boston-Cambridge tunnel that burrowed through
our peaceful native soil thousands of miles away in New England" (MM
100), Dyer says of his unstrung companion in their flight from the
creature whose "nearest comprehensible analogue is a vast, onrushing
subway train as one sees it from a station platform" (MM 101). With this
powerful metaphoric image the novel comes full circle, the expedition
having originally sailed from Boston. Like the men of Byrd's party, from
the admiral himself to Harvard student Freddy Crockett, Dyer and
Danforth on a cosmic scale face perils that test to the limit those traditional New England traits of hardiness and fortitude.

Like others at Miskatonic, they too have a solid grounding in "certain primordial and highly baffling myth-cycles" (MM 4). "At the
moment I felt sorry that I had ever read the abhorred *Necronomicon,* or
talked so much with that unpleasantly erudite folklorist Wilmarth at
the university" (MM 30), Dyer confesses after noting "how disturbingly
this lethal realm corresponded to the evilly famed plateau of Leng in the
primal writings" (MM 29). Danforth "is known to be among the few
who have ever dared go completely through that worm-riddled copy of
the *Necronomicon* kept under lock and key in the college library" (MM
106). The discovery of the bodies of the Old Ones serves to confirm
such lore for Dyer, who does not pretend that the mayhem at Lake's
camp can be accounted for purely on a "rational" basis: "For madness—
centring in Gedney as the only possible surviving agent—was the
explanation spontaneously adopted by everybody so far as spoken utterance was concerned; though I will not be so naive as to deny that each of
us may have harboured wild guesses which sanity forbade him to formu-

late completely" (MM 39). Arguably such findings, if made public, would constitute the most sensational news story of all time, yet Dyer, inhibited by fear of "the horrors of which even the horrors are afraid,"[7] aims for the most modest of audiences: "The full story, as far as deciphered, will shortly appear in an official bulletin of Miskatonic University" (MM 61). In order to preserve the proper sense of awe, man must keep such wonders at a distance, as the province of a sensitive few.

Lovecraft regarded *At the Mountains of Madness,* the only one of his three short novels that he made the enormous effort to type, as his "most ambitious story" (4:84). Its rejection by Farnsworth Wright seriously shook his confidence, as he reported to J. Vernon Shea in a letter dated 7 August 1931: "It is very possible that I am growing stale . . . but if so it merely signifies the end of my fictional attempts. There is no field other than the weird in which I have any aptitude or inclination for fictional composition. Life has never interested me so much as the escape from life" (3:395). Others since Wright have found the work problematic, overly long and confused in its intentions. As Darrell Schweitzer puts it, Lovecraft shoves "the square peg of science fiction into the round hole of the horror story."[8] But overriding any flaws, great or small, whether his straining too hard to capture ultimate horror in Danforth's final glimpse of those even higher mountains beyond or his choice as a leitmotif of the Asian mountain paintings of the obscure Nicholas Roerich, is the sheer power of the novel's imaginative vision. If stronger in conception than in execution, it yet stands in the front rank of the fiction.

Later in the year, still feeling sorry for himself, Lovecraft did not bother to submit "The Shadow over Innsmouth" to *Weird Tales.* Early in 1936 he would have the satisfaction of seeing both *Madness* and "The Shadow Out of Time" accepted through the intercession of an agent by *Astounding Stories,* which paid a total of $630 for the two stories, enough to relieve him of his immediate financial worries.

"Through the Gates of the Silver Key"

Taking the mathematical concepts if little actual prose from the draft of a tale entitled "The Lord of Illusion" foisted upon him as a collaboration by fellow fantasist E. Hoffmann Price, Lovecraft wrote "Through the Gates of the Silver Key" (1932–33), which explains what happened to Randolph Carter after his disappearance four years before in "The Silver Key." Employing the tableau format of "The Statement of Randolph Carter" and "The Unnamable," this sequel also concerns the debate of an issue, here the settlement of Carter's estate. Again, Lovecraft puts a friend and himself, this time as a character distinct from Carter, into the story.

Etienne-Laurent de Marigny, "the distinguished Creole student of mysteries and Eastern antiquities," who corresponds to Price, and Ward Phillips, "an elderly eccentric of Providence, Rhode Island" (MM 424), do not believe that the "great mystic, scholar, author, and dreamer" (MM 421) is dead.[9] Siding with them against the lawyer representing Carter's heirs is a man of indeterminate age, "with a dark, bearded, singularly immobile face of very regular contour, bound with the turban of a high-caste Brahmin," who has announced himself as "Swami Chandraputra, an adept from Benares with important information to give" (MM 425). These four engage in that rarest form of communication in Lovecraft, a group conversation, though a paraphrase of the swami's account occupies the bulk of the omniscient narrative.

As he had in dreamland, Carter in his wandering among space and time passes through certain prescribed stages on his way to a new self-understanding, which in the event proves more horrifying than that in the *Dream-Quest:* "No death, no doom, no anguish can arouse the surpassing despair which flows from a loss of *identity*. Merging with nothingness is peaceful oblivion; but to be aware of existence and yet to know that one is no longer a definite being distinguished from other beings—that one no longer has a *self*—that is the nameless summit of agony and dread" (MM 438). Monsters had assumed human disguise in *The Case of Charles Dexter Ward,* "The Dunwich Horror," and "The Whisperer in Darkness," but here occurs the first major instance of alien personality exchange or displacement, a conceit that will also underlie "The Thing on the Doorstep" and "The Shadow Out of Time." Like Peaslee in that latter tale, Carter eventually finds himself trapped in a foreign body, "rugose, partly squamous, and curiously articulated in a fashion mainly insect-like yet not without a caricaturish resemblance to the human form" (MM 447). He retains his handwriting, though as the swami asserts it is "almost illegible," since he "now has no hands well adapted to forming human script" (MM 455). The handwritten word becomes for Lovecraft in his last stories the ultimate test of human identity.

During his sojourn on the planet Yaddith Carter acts as bravely as any Lovecraftian hero: "There was no time for fear. At all crises of his strange life, sheer cosmic curiosity triumphed over everything else." The "clawed, tapir-snouted denizens" of Yaddith also have their admirable qualities. Like the Old Ones in *At the Mountains of Madness,* they battle a shoggoth-like threat from "burrowing inner horrors" (MM 445), the "bleached, viscous bholes," besides being even more historically minded: "There were awed sessions in libraries amongst the massed lore of ten thousand worlds living and dead" (MM 448). Like Zamacona, Carter plots his escape, but unlike the Spaniard he succeeds, returning to earth, specifically to New England. As the swami puts it, with a passing reference to the exile of Ward Phillips/Lovecraft, "If any of you have been away from home long—and I know one of you has—I leave it to you how the sight of New England's rolling hills and great elms and gnarled orchards and ancient stone walls must have affected him" (MM 451). Just as Akeley could not readily leave his house in Vermont despite the growing menace of the Winged Ones, just as the Old Ones venerated the site of their first arrival in the Antarctic and chose to remain in the vicinity despite the increasing cold, just as Lovecraft returned to Providence from New York, so home feelings bring Carter back from the outer reaches of the universe.

At the climax the "swami," exposed as Carter himself, retreats into "that hieroglyphed, coffin-shaped clock" (MM 458) that had transported him to earth and that presumably sends him back to Yaddith, with the alien facet of his personality temporarily dominant. Thus his fate remains as open-ended as it had been in "The Silver Key," though in the fall of 1934 Lovecraft would beg off from collaborating with Price on a sequel that would provide further news of Carter: "The process is really wasteful—for with the same outlay of energy I could achieve infinitely better results if working alone and imaginatively unchecked. What I want to say is so infinitely different from anything that anybody else wants to say!" (5:45). Less awesomely cosmic than such longer works as *At the Mountains of Madness* and "The Shadow Out of Time," with their fully developed core narratives, "Through the Gates of the Silver Key" yet has more to recommend it as one of Lovecraft's more cleverly framed and plotted tales than he was willing to concede in his dissatisfaction over its artificial genesis.

"The Shadow Out of Time"

Like his colleague William Dyer four years before in *At the Mountains of Madness,* Professor Nathaniel Wingate Peaslee, the narrator of "The

Shadow Out of Time" (1934–35), takes part in an expedition to a remote corner of the globe, here the desert of Western Australia, where "on the night of July 17–18, 1935" he finds "a frightful confirmation of all I had sought to dismiss as myth and dream." Urging "a final abandonment of all the attempts at unearthing those fragments of unknown, primordial masonry which my expedition set out to investigate," Peaslee too writes his account "to warn such others as may read it seriously," though unlike Dyer he has a particular caretaker in mind for his manuscript, his son and fellow Miskatonic professor, Wingate, "the only member of my family who stuck to me after my queer amnesia of long ago, and the man best informed on the inner facts of my case" (DH 368–69). To this extent Lovecraft avoids the fuzziness regarding the audience and dissemination of that earlier grand geological romance.

Like de la Poer and the narrator of "The Shadow over Innsmouth," Peaslee has his family problems, though unlike them he is no victim of heredity. "It may be that centuries of dark brooding had given to crumbling, whisper-haunted Arkham a peculiar vulnerability as regards such shadows," he says of the strange affliction that hits him as he is conducting a class in political economy in 1908 and then almost as suddenly leaves him in 1913. "But the chief point is that my own ancestry and background are altogether normal. What came, came from *somewhere else*" (DH 370). Centuries of dark brooding have indeed made Arkham a dangerous place to reside, as the unfortunate Walter Gilman learned in 1928 in "The Dreams in the Witch House," but here the horror reaches out from such a vast remove of time and space that Peaslee could as well have stayed in his native Haverhill for all the difference his immediate surroundings make. In this last of Lovecraft's longer narratives, his only tale to project forward in time, local color is irrelevant.

Like Charles Dexter Ward, Peaslee forms a psychological case study, "lectured upon as a typical example of secondary personality," even though he now and then puzzles the lecturers "with some bizarre symptom or some queer trace of carefully veiled mockery" (DH 372). If external horrors rather than inner demons continue to plague his protagonists, Lovecraft by the end of his career was respectful enough of psychology to use it as an important plot basis. To gain an understanding of his condition, Peaslee, "aided by psychologists, historians, anthropologists, and mental specialists of wide experience," consults sources that include "all records of split personalities from the days of daemoniac-possession legends to the medically realistic present" (DH

377). Studying the discipline systematically, he changes fields in 1922, "accepting an instructorship in psychology at the university" (DH 391). In their emphasis on psychological authenticity, both "The Shadow Out of Time" and "The Thing on the Doorstep," written a year earlier, show how far Lovecraft had come from, say, "Beyond the Wall of the Sleep" and "From Beyond" with their anti-Freudian sneers.[10]

For Peaslee, dreams afford a glimpse not into the soul but into the past. He feels he must be "in the earth's southern hemisphere, near the Tropic of Capricorn" (DH 382), at a period "somewhat less than 150,000,000 years ago, when the Palaeozoic age was giving place to the Mesozoic" (DH 398). "Primal myth and modern delusion" have joined to assume "that mankind is only one—perhaps the least—of the highly evolved and dominant races of this planet's long and largely unknown career." Far surpassing man is the Great Race, "the greatest race of all because it alone had conquered the secret of time" (DH 385), whose members resemble "immense rugose cones" (DH 386), as Peaslee's dreams will later corroborate: "They seemed to be enormous, iridescent cones, about ten feet high and ten feet wide at the base, and made up of some ridgy, scaly, semi-elastic matter. From their apexes projected four flexible, cylindrical members, each a foot thick, and of a ridgy substance like that of the cones themselves" (DH 392). Peaslee's account of his visions almost matches Lake's description of the Old Ones in its detachment, until he finds himself in such a body: "That was when I waked half of Arkham with my screaming as I plunged madly up from the abyss of sleep" (DH 394).[11]

With time, however, he grows half-reconciled to his monstrous form, for even though he has, like Akeley's brain canned in its cylinder, "but two of the senses which we recognise—sight and hearing" (DH 398), he is able to "talk, in some odd language of claw clickings, with exiled intellects from every corner of the solar system" (DH 395). Furthermore, captive minds are allowed "to delve freely into the libraries containing the records of the planet's past and future," which reconciles many of them to their lot, "since none were other than keen, and to such minds the unveiling of hidden mysteries of earth—closed chapters of inconceivable pasts and dizzying vortices of future time which include the years ahead of their own natural ages—forms always, despite the abysmal horrors often unveiled, the supreme experience of life" (DH 387). Among the hidden mysteries is "a horrible elder race of half-polypous, utterly alien entities" (DH 400), which pose a subterranean, shoggoth-like threat that verges on the formulaic, though their presence does function to prompt the Great Race's mass migration to the future and to frighten Peaslee during his climactic trek through the ruined city beneath the desert.

In the first of his "dream-glimpses" Peaslee sees "an enormous vaulted chamber" with high pedestals and wall shelves "holding what seemed to be volumes of immense size with strange hieroglyphs on their backs. . . . There were no chairs, but the tops of the vast pedestals were littered with books, papers, and what seemed to be writing materials—oddly figured jars of a purplish metal, and rods with stained tips" (DH 379–80). Later he discovers that these books contain "the whole of earth's annals—histories and descriptions of every species that had ever been or would be, with full records of their arts, their achievements, their languages, and their psychologies" (DH 386). Lovecraft can scarcely be faulted for not anticipating the computer era, yet the Great Race set down their data with no more efficiency than medieval monks. Of course, the ending would have lost much of its poignancy had Peaslee gazed upon a printed page instead of "the letters of our familiar alphabet, spelling out the words of the English language in my own handwriting" (DH 433). But beyond plot exigencies, lending the tale extra conviction, this final image captures the essence of the man who, never having had his work collected in book form,[12] daily delighted in putting fountain pen to paper, typically either to record his peculiar personal vision in letters or to transform it in fiction, in his distinctive, spidery script. For Lovecraft, such an exercise, coupled with the pure acquisition of knowledge, was among the highest of human endeavors.

In conflict with this assertion is the cosmic indifferentism that pervades the tale. "What was hinted in the speech of post-human entities of the fate of mankind produced such an effect on me that I will not set it down here" (DH 396), says Peaslee, who also remarks, "If that abyss and what it held were real, there is no hope" (DH 433). Yet to the degree that the members of the Great Race embody the best of what it means to be human there is hope. Their society may have its elitist aspects, but in contrast, say, to the selfishness of Joseph Curwen or the Outer Ones they respect other intelligent beings enough to restore the minds they borrow, however imperfect their methods of memory suppression. In this regard as in others they, like the Old Ones, are men.

While *At the Mountains of Madness* and "The Shadow Out of Time" border on science fiction, "In the Walls of Eryx" (1936) is Lovecraft's only tale to fall solidly into that genre.[13] The Venusian setting was the idea of his friend and collaborator Kenneth Sterling, who like E. Hoffmann Price supplied him with a story draft from which Lovecraft prepared a final text in prose almost entirely his own. Sterling also contributed the concept of the invisible maze, an image of which his older mentor must have surely approved.[14] In "Through the Gates of the Silver Key," for example, Phillips mentions "that fabulous town of turrets atop the hollow cliffs of glass overlooking the twilight sea wherein the bearded and finny Gnorri built their singular labyrinths" (MM 424), while in "The Shadow Out of Time" Peaslee refers to the ruins he explores as "this labyrinth of primordial stone" (DH 417). Lovecraft's direct hand can be detected in such particulars as the earthlings' economic motivation and the shining crystal, whose mystical significance calls to mind the cube in "The Challenge from Beyond" and the trapezohedron in "The Haunter of the Dark," and especially at the climax, where the dying explorer-narrator, like some extraterrestrial Scott of the Antarctic, writes entries in his diary to the end.

Chapter Ten

Sunset

In the thirties Lovecraft set a number of tales in New England that are on a more intimate, less ambitious scale than those lengthy narratives of the same period that extend far beyond his native region. In these shorter stories supernatural horror irrupts, not in remote and decadent towns like Dunwich and Innsmouth, but within the relatively civilized urban confines of Providence, Boston, and Arkham in its most Salem-like incarnation.

"The Dreams in the Witch House"

Like Randolph Carter in the *Dream-Quest,* Miskatonic student Walter Gilman in "The Dreams in the Witch House" (1932) wanders in his dreams in some alternative dimension, here a realm consistent with modern theories of physics and mathematics. Through his encounters with the witch Keziah Mason and her rat-like familiar, "Brown Jenkin,"[1] he comes to understand the Salem witchcraft episode of 1692–93 in terms of Einsteinian space-time, an experience he finds severely taxing: "Non-Euclidean calculus and quantum physics are enough to stretch any brain; and when one mixes them with folklore, and tries to trace a strange background of multi-dimensional reality behind the ghoulish hints of the Gothic tales and the wild whispers of the chimney-corner, one can hardly expect to be wholly free from mental tension" (MM 263). Typically, both Gilman's environment and his own abstruse researches bring about his doom.

Within "the mouldy, unhallowed garret gable" of Arkham's equivalent of Salem's "Witch House," he grows as sensitive to sounds, including "the sinister scurrying of rats in the wormy partitions" (MM 262), as does that other, more traditional student of the arcane, the narrator of "The Music of Erich Zann," to the violin playing of his fellow lodger. Yet Gilman, compared to protagonists of other mature tales, remains in his supernatural plight too much at an emotional remove. The omniscient viewpoint that had served Lovecraft well in such wide-ranging tales as *The Case of Charles Dexter Ward* and "The Dunwich Horror," is not so controlled here, as shown by the comment that May-Eve, "Walpurgis-Night," "was always a very bad time in Arkham" (MM 271). Had such a phrase come from the mouth of one of the many superstitious ethnics that dread the season, as it does indirectly later—"It was, he added, a very bad time of year for Arkham" (MM 288)—it would not have seemed quite so banal. If plot contingencies made it too awkward for Gilman to tell his own story, surely Lovecraft could have developed the Frank Elwood character, "the one fellow-student whose poverty forced him to room in this squalid and unpopular house" (MM 271), to fill the narrator role and thus provide the appropriate focus.

In other respects too the master nods or coasts. At one point Gilman knows that "the evil old woman" in his dreams "was the one who had frightened him in the slums" (MM 272), a reference with no antecedent. Lapsing into conventional occultism, Lovecraft has his hero arm himself with a crucifix: "At the sight of the device the witch seemed struck with panic, and her grip relaxed long enough to give Gilman a chance to break it entirely" (MM 292). Even the elements drawn out of his own repetoire—"the changeless, legend-haunted city of Arkham, with its clustering gambrel roofs" (MM 262), the *Necronomicon*, Azathoth and Nyarlathotep—have an air of staleness in the context of a middling story.[2]

If the tale in execution fails to match the orginality of its conception, it yet contains stretches of strong prose, notably the accounts of what Gilman sees in his otherworldly flights: "All the objects—organic and inorganic alike—were totally beyond description or even comprehension. Gilman sometimes compared the inorganic masses to prisms, labyrinths, clusters of cubes and planes, and Cyclopean buildings; and the organic things struck him variously as groups of bubbles, octopi, centipedes, living Hindoo idols, and intricate Arabesques roused into a kind of ophidian animation" (MM 267). Certainly this concrete imagery represents an improvement over the fuzziness of, say, the analogous passage in "Hypnos."

Nearly as long as "Through the Gates of the Silver Key," "The Dreams in the Witch House" forms a single, running narrative, unbroken by either the quoted speech or the document extracts that periodically punctuate all the post–New York fiction, except the anomalous *Dream-Quest*. Despite its cosmic scope, it seems a narrow tale, on a par with such shorter pieces of the period as "The Thing on the Doorstep" and "The Haunter of the Dark." In a letter dated 27 February 1933,

Lovecraft confessed that "it most emphatically fails to satisfy me" (4: 156), an assessment tempered by the pessimism he continued to feel in the wake of the rejection of *At the Mountains of Madness* in 1931. If "The Dreams in the Witch House" stands as the weakest of his later tales under his own name, he believed enough in its integrity to forbid the sale of radio rights to prevent its debasement in a popular medium.

"Out of the Aeons"

Of the five tales that Lovecraft ghostwrote for Hazel Heald, two fit solidly into the mainstream of his own fiction. Like Richard Upton Pickman, George Rogers in "The Horror in the Museum" (1932) has a hideous creature at his disposal with the photographs to prove it, though the naive narrator, Stephen Jones, assumes it is just another waxen image in his friend's Madame Tussaud–like London museum. Unearthed from Cyclopean ruins three million years old in Alaska, "Rhan-Tegoth" possesses a familiar physiognomy: "Most of the body was covered with what at first appeared to be fur, but which on closer examination proved to be a dense growth of dark, slender tentacles or sucking filaments, each tipped with a mouth suggesting the head of an asp. On the head and below the proboscis the tentacles tended to be longer and thicker, and marked with spiral stripes—suggesting the traditional serpent-locks of Medusa" (HM 224–25). That the museum should hold an entire gallery of such beings, from "a lean, rubbery night-gaunt" to great Cthulhu with his "long, facial tentacles" (HM 230), points to Lovecraft's less than serious approach to this, his version of a "horror of the wax museum" tale, in which at the end the mad curator predictably falls victim to his own monster.

Another, more cleverly crafted museum story followed soon after, "Out of the Aeons" (1933), which like "The Call of Cthulhu" opens with a headnote identifying it as a posthumous document: "(Ms. found among the effects of the late Richard H. Johnson, Ph.D., curator of the Cabot Museum of Archaeology, Boston, Mass.)" (HM 264). Like Cthulhu, the Cabot Museum mummy that comes to create such a sensation has a watery source, having been picked up by a passing freighter in 1878 "from a crypt of unknown origin and fabulous antiquity on a bit of land suddenly upheaved from the Pacific's floor" (HM 265). Unlike Cthulhu, however, it portends no potentially imminent global threat.

Though the Cabot Museum "stands in the heart of Boston's exclusive

Beacon Hill district" (HM 266), the setting has none of the rich historical or architectural atmosphere of the Boston of "Pickman's Model." Lending the only New England flavor are the narrator's comments on the various reactions to the mummy, which mark him as a class-conscious snob of the late George Apley stripe: "The gruesome object had a local celebrity among cultivated Bostonians, but no more than that" (HM 269), until a news story in the Boston *Pillar,* which caters to a "vast and mentally immature clientele," pulls in the crowds. "Full of inaccuracies, exaggerations, and sensationalism, it was precisely the sort of thing to stir the brainless and fickle interest of the herd—and as a result the once quiet museum began to be swarmed with chattering and vacuously staring throngs such as its stately corridors had never known before." Furthermore, he pompously notes that "we are a scientific institution without sympathy for fantastic dreamers" (HM 270). Here Lovecraft would seem to be not condoning his character's prejudices but gently mocking them, rather as Marquand does Apley's.

A less plebeian visitor to the museum is "a dark, turbaned, and bushily bearded man with a laboured, unnatural voice, curiously expressionless face, clumsy hands covered with absurd white mittens, who gave a squalid West End address and called himself 'Swami Chandraputra,' " while "the famous New Orleans mystic Etienne-Laurent de Marigny" has "a highly learned article in *The Occult Review*" (HM 270) on the mummy. The cameo appearance of two of the principals from "Through the Gates of the Silver Key" can be regarded as simply another one of Lovecraft's in-jokes, yet they help underline how widespread is the publicity that such a phenomenon would realistically attract: "Apparently the mummy and its origin formed—for imaginative people—a close rival to the depression as chief topic of 1931 and 1932" (HM 271). Here, as S. T. Joshi has observed, in "the only direct reference to the Great Depression"[3] in the fiction, Lovecraft indirectly acknowledges that even "imaginative people" (like himself and his fellow weird tale writers) need pay attention to economic reality.

"Out of the Aeons" has its cosmic aspects, but any philosophical implications remain subordinate to plot, to the unraveling of the mystery of the mummy, with the aid of such occult tomes as "von Junzt's horrible *Nameless Cults*" (HM 268–69). In "the year of the Red Moon (estimated as B.C. 173,148 by von Junzt)," in "a province called K'naa" in a vanished land "to which legend has given the name of Mu" (HM 271), the priest T'yog sets out to deliver his people from the brooding menace of the "Dark God" Ghatanothoa, elsewhere described as "gigantic—tentacled—proboscidian—octopus-eyed—semi-amorphous—plastic—partly squamous and partly rugose—ugh!" (HM 286). Medusa-like, Ghatanothoa can turn a victim "to stone and leather on the outside, while the brain within remained perpetually alive" (HM 272). If in his revision work Lovecraft draws more obviously on the same devices over and over, he does so here with enough imaginative variation to keep the story fresh.

Like one of those presumptuous heroes of dreamland, T'yog climbs "the bleak basalt cliffs of Mount Yaddith-Gho" (HM 272), to "confront the shocking devil-entity in its lair" (HM 274), with the blessing of more benign gods and a charm, a protective formula on a scroll enclosed in a carven metal cylinder, "which he believed would keep the possessor immune from the Dark God's petrifying power" (HM 273). Ensuring the failure of T'yog's mission by secretly substituting a similar but useless scroll is "Imash-Mo, High Priest" of the "hundred priests of the Dark God," who have a stake in maintaining the worship of Ghatanathoa: "Each priest had a marble house, a chest of gold, two hundred slaves, and an hundred concubines, besides immunity from civil law and the power of life and death over all in K'naa save the priests of the King" (HM 273). Within this compact flashback deriving from the dross of dreary theosophical tracts by the likes of "Colonel Churchward and Lewis Spence concerning lost continents and primal forgotten civilisations" (HM 269), Lovecraft creates a miniature satire on the folly of the idealist and the cynicism of the rich that calls to mind the comic fiction of his British contemporary, Evelyn Waugh.[4]

At the climax, after the bungled burglary reminiscent of Wilbur Whateley's thwarted theft of the *Necronomicon,* T'yog's brain proves, like Akeley's, to have survived the death of its body, though without the consolation of sight and hearing or any cosmic travel. After eons in limbo it is exposed only to die. In this, his most sardonic of late tales, Lovecraft ends by mocking the Christian hope of resurrection and everlasting life.

"The Thing on the Doorstep"

"What lay behind our joint love of shadows and marvels," says Daniel Upton, the narrator of "The Thing on the Doorstep" (1933), of himself and his precocious younger friend, Edward Pickman Derby, "was, no doubt, the ancient, mouldering, and subtly fearsome town in

which we lived—witch-cursed, legend-haunted Arkham, whose huddled, sagging gambrel roofs and crumbling Georgian balustrades brood
out the centuries beside the darkly muttering Miskatonic" (DH 277).
Like his fellow Arkham resident Walter Gilman, Derby falls prey to
the supernatural in female form, but, unlike in "The Dreams in the
Witch House," his nemesis is no old crone from another dimension but
a young woman he meets at Miskatonic, where she "was taking a
special course in mediaeval metaphysics." Physically "dark, smallish,
and very good-looking except for overprotruberant eyes," Asenath "was
one of the Innsmouth Waites, and dark legends have clustered for
generations about crumbling, half-deserted Innsmouth and its people"
(DH 280), though here mention of that sinister town up the coast
serves merely as background coloring.

Lovecraft's most prominent female character, the predatory Asenath
can be regarded as a composite caricature of his wife and mother, for both
of whom he probably still felt lingering resentment. The fact that she
proves to be possessed by the consciousness of her late father, who appears
to have been a victim in his turn of whatever parasitic demon has been
hopping from body to body down through the ages, muddles the gender
issue, though which sex it is more preferable to be is never in doubt.
According to Derby, Asenath quite literally desires his body because, in
large part, "She wanted to be a man—to be fully human" (DH 288).

Lovecraft's sympathies clearly lie mainly with his male protagonist,
whose family history he outlines with considerable psychological sophistication. By age twenty-five a "prodigiously learned man and a fairly
well-known poet and fantaisiste" (DH 279), Derby is otherwise lacking
in his development. "In self-reliance and practical affairs, however,
Derby was greatly retarded because of his coddled existence. His health
had improved, but his habits of childish dependence were fostered by
overcareful parents; so that he never travelled alone, made independent
decisions, or assumed responsibilities" (DH 278). Defects in his personality, rather than any compulsion to explore the unknown, lead to his
downfall. When Derby's father asks Upton to use his influence to get
his son to break off his engagement, Upton pronounces on the futility
of trying to change his friend's mind in suitably psychoanalytic language: "This time it was not a question of Edward's weak will but of
the woman's strong will. The perennial child had transferred his dependence from the parental image to a new and stronger image, and
nothing could be done about it" (DH 282).

Derby reflects his creator's awareness of his own problems growing up, but more generally he fits an aesthetic type that Lovecraft had come to know well in the person of such early amateur associates of his as Samuel Loveman, Alfred Galpin, and perhaps most especially Frank Belknap Long, his closest friend in later years.[5] Upton's comment that Derby's "attempts to raise a moustache were discernible only with difficulty" (DH 278) echoes Lovecraft's description of the twenty-year-old Long after their first meeting in New York in the spring of 1922: "I think he likes the tiny collection of lip-hairs—about six on one side and five on the other—which may with assiduous care some day help to enhance his genuine resemblance to his chief idol—Edgar Allan Poe" (1:180). Against the sentimentalism of, say, "The Silver Key," Derby's fate serves as a warning to the "Kid" Longs of the world who would prolong their childhoods far beyond the normal span.

Upton, in contrast, though he once had "leanings toward art of a somewhat grotesque cast" and found in Derby "a rare kindred spirit" (DH 277), follows the conventional path: "I had been through Harvard, had studied in a Boston architect's office, had married, and had finally returned to Arkham to practice my profession" (DH 278). In his role of the staid family man who seemingly takes more interest in the career of his eccentric friend than in his own affairs, he in effect plays Dr. Watson to Derby's Sherlock Holmes.[6] He may dismiss the "superficially 'smart' language and meaninglessly ironic pose" of "the 'daring' or 'Bohemian' set" (DH 278–79) that Derby looks enviously at then later joins, but Upton is no fool. When his weak-willed friend after his marriage to Asenath becomes involved in studies that "shocked even the most callous of the other decadents" (DH 284) in the college set and starts mumbling about the *Necronomicon,* Upton is to some degree prepared: "He repeated names which I recognised from bygone browsings in forbidden volumes" (DH 289). A skeptic, he at first seeks rational explanations for Derby's split personality, but in the face of the overwhelming evidence at the climax comes to accept that Asenath can swap minds with her husband: "As for me, *I now believe all that Edward Derby ever told me*" (DH 300). Like Dr. Willett, he acts to destroy an asylum-bound imposter, as revealed in the paradoxical opening sentence of the story: "It is true that I have sent six bullets through the head of my best friend, and yet I hope to shew by this statement that I am not his murderer" (DH 276). But unlike Willett at the end of *The Case of Charles Dexter Ward,* he can take no comfort in the outcome: "I may be next. But my will is not weak—and I shall not let it be undermined by the terrors I know are seething around it" (DH 300).

Upton's claim of having "purged the earth of a horror whose survival might have loosed untold terrors on all mankind" (DH 277) has a grandiose ring in the context of what amounts to a sordid domestic tragedy. Too, Derby's hysterical accounts of Asenath's doings lack subtlety, though the action builds to a powerful climax, where again the assertion of identity through the handwritten word is crucial. His mind trapped in the rotting corpse of the wife he has murdered, Derby at first tries to telephone his friend but in the end scrawls a note, rather as does the author of the Saxon minuscules in *Ward,* to warn and advise. "I'm too far gone to talk—I couldn't manage to telephone—but I can still write" (DH 302), he declares in his extremity on paper. In "The Thing on the Doorstep," as elsewhere in the later Lovecraft, the act of writing assumes heroic proportions, constituting the true road to immortality.

"The Haunter of the Dark"

Early in 1935 one of Lovecraft's correspondents, Robert Bloch, se-cured his permission to use him as a character in a weird tale. Chiefly notable as a spoofing tribute by the teenage Bloch to his mentor, "The Shambler from the Stars" moved Lovecraft to return the favor by put-ting his young friend as a character into "The Haunter of the Dark" (1935), his last story solely his own work. "Robert Blake," however, bears little resemblance to Bloch. As "a writer and painter wholly devoted to the field of myth, dream, terror, and superstition, and avid in his quest for scenes and effects of a bizarre, spectral sort," he gener-ally fits the familiar aesthetic mold. Only a reference to an earlier stay in Providence, "a visit to a strange old man as deeply given to occult and forbidden lore as he" that "had ended amidst death and flame" (DH 93), marks the tale as in any way a sequel. As in *The Case of Charles Dexter Ward,* an elevated, third-person voice soberly presents the data, derived from entries in Blake's diary.

Like Walter Gilman, Blake takes up residence in an old house, but one free of supernatural affliction:

Young Blake returned to Providence in the winter of 1934–5, taking the upper floor of a venerable dwelling in a grassy court off College Street—on the crest of the great eastward hill near the Brown University campus and behind the marble John Hay Library. It was a cosy and fascinating place, in a little garden oasis of village-like antiquity where huge, friendly cats sunned themselves atop a convenient shed. The square Georgian house had a monitor roof, classic doorway with fan carving, small-paned windows, and all the other earmarks of early nineteenth-century workmanship. Inside were six-panelled doors, wide floor-boards, a curving colonial staircase, white Adam-period mantels, and a rear set of rooms three steps below the general level. (DH 93–94)

Here Lovecraft is describing his last home on College Hill, his bachelor paradise of cats and colonial architecture, free of interferring women and even of male companions.[7]

Indeed, the solitary Blake can be regarded as the most Lovecraft-like of later protagonists, especially as measured by his ecstatic response to the westward view from his window:

Blake's study, a large southwest chamber, overlooked the garden on one side, while its west windows—before one of which he had his desk—faced off from the brow of the hill and commanded a splendid view of the lower town's outspread roofs and of the mystical sunsets that flamed behind them. On the far horizon were the open countryside's purple slopes. Against these, some two miles away, rose the spectral hump of Federal Hill, bristling with huddled roofs and steeples whose remote outlines wavered mysteriously, taking fantastic forms as the smoke of the city swirled up and enmeshed them. Blake had a curious sense that he was looking upon some unknown, ethereal world which might or might not vanish in dream if ever he tried to seek it out and enter it in person. (DH 94)

In the spring, "just before the aeon-shadowed Walpurgis time," Blake in his restlessness does try to seek that world out, "crossing the city and climbing bodily up that fabulous slope into the smoke-wreathed world of dream" (DH 96). He focuses his search, however, on a solid, earthly object, "a certain huge, dark church" that "stood out with especial distinctness at certain hours of the day, and at sunset the great tower and tapering steeple loomed blackly against the flaming sky" (DH 95). Significantly, he enters the old Free-Will Church in the late afternoon, and flees it at twilight.

In contrast to his refuge of light and reason on College Street, Blake finds this dark, Gothic revival edifice, suitably enough, a repository of hidden horror. In the tower chamber he discovers the skeleton of a newspaper reporter, "Edwin M. Lillibridge," whose pocketbook holds "a paper covered with pencilled memoranda," which, despite the "disjointed text," conveys all the essential events in the transformation of the congregation into the "Starry Wisdom" cult in the mid-nineteenth century by one Dr. Enoch Bowen, who like Obed Marsh returns from foreign parts (here Egypt) with an alternative to conventional worship. Just as the leaders of Providence had convened to deal with Joseph Curwen, so a century later "a secret committee call on Mayor Doyle" and act to suppress the menace of the "Haunter of the Dark" (DH 103). So too with great economy does Lovecraft evoke the history of the gem-like "Shining Trapezohedron," that "window on all time and space" into which Blake has the misfortune to peer, from "the days it was fashioned on dark Yuggoth" up through the human era until its removal from a "windowless crypt" (DH 106) in Egypt.

Blake is not alone in dreading the church. "There had been a bad sect there in the ould days," a police officer, "a great wholesome Irishman" (DH 97), tells him, while after his visit the neighborhood Italians whisper of "unaccustomed stirrings and bumpings and scrapings in the dark windowless steeple," of something "constantly watching at a door to see if it were dark enough to venture forth" (DH 106–7). As in "The Dreams in the Witch House," superstitious ethnics act as a chorus, in their naive faith instinctively shunning the horror that stirs a more complicated response in the story's protagonist: "In writing of these things in his diary, Blake expresses a curious kind of remorse, and talks of the duty of burying the Shining Trapezohedron and of banishing what he evoked by letting daylight into the hideous jutting spire. At the same time, however, he displays the dangerous extent of his fascination, and admits a morbid longing—pervading even his dreams—to visit the accursed tower and gaze again into the cosmic secrets of the glowing stone" (DH 107). Caught between repulsion and attraction, Blake feels the same cosmic ambivalence that gives dramatic tension to such longer tales as "The Whisperer in Darkness" and "The Shadow over Innsmouth."

Like Derby, Blake cannot escape—"He seemed to feel a constant tugging at his will" (DH 109)—but he too can write to the bitter end, as he does the night of the summer thunderstorm that causes the power failure that sends the Haunter of the Dark hurtling the distance from Federal Hill to College Hill: "Blake had prolonged his frenzied jottings to the last, and the broken-pointed pencil was found clutched in his spasmodically contracted right hand" (DH 114). Like Lillibridge, whose fate has anticipated his own, his greatest legacy is the written record discovered in his possession at the scene of his death.[8] The final vision of Blake/Lovecraft at his window shows him a rigid corpse, Erich Zann-like with "glassy, bulging eyes" (DH 113), but a truer autobiographical tableau occurs earlier: "At sunset he would often sit at his desk and gaze dreamily off at the outspread west—the dark towers of Memorial Hall just below, the Georgian court-house belfry, the lofty pinnacles of the downtown section, and that shimmering, spire-crowned mound in the distance whose unknown streets and labyrinthine gables so potently provoked his fancy" (DH 94). Here, in this final self-portrait of the artist, Lovecraft adopts his most poignant pose, lost in dream in the sunset glow of the old town he loved so well.

Chapter Eleven
Critical Reputation

"The trouble with most of my stuff is that it falls between two stools," Lovecraft once lamented. "My tales are not bad enough for cheap editors, nor good enough for standard acceptance and recognition" (3: 436). Today, more than fifty years after his death and nearly one hundred after his birth, he remains on the fringe of literary respectability in his own country. (He has received more attention abroad, especially in France, Italy, Germany, and Japan, owing in part to their lack of prejudice against imaginative fiction.) Distinguished American critics, when they have deigned to comment at all, have often been severe. In his notorious *New Yorker* notice of the forties, Edmund Wilson grumped that "the only horror here is the horror of bad taste and bad art,"[1] while more recently Jacques Barzun has snorted, "How the frequently portentous but unintelligible H. P. Lovecraft has acquired a reputation as a notable performer is explained only by the willingness of some to take the intention for the deed and by a touching faith that words put together with confidence must have a meaning."[2]

Poe authority T. O. Mabbott, three years after Lovecraft's death, ventured cautious praise in his review of *The Outsider:* "Time will tell if his place be very high in our literary history; that he has a place seems certain."[3] In the academic world that place would still seem to be uncertain, if Stephen A. Black's remarks in a review article in the fall 1979 issue of the *Canadian Review of American Studies* can be taken as representative. Black observes that "despite the protestations of his enthusiasts, Lovecraft is likely to be almost entirely unknown to academic readers of this journal. (In the past twenty-two years of my academic life I have heard his name mentioned only once and never heard a conversation about his work. Until several months ago . . . I had not read any of Lovecraft's sixty-odd 'weird' stories and novelettes. Most of my colleagues, I learn upon enquiring, are nearly as ignorant as I was with regard to Lovecraft.)"[4] The decade since 1979 has witnessed an explosion in Lovecraft studies, but the fact is that the vast majority of work has been published in journals devoted to the horror-fantasy genre. Few articles have appeared in the academic mainstream.

Lovecraft's keenest advocates, myself among them, are essentially "amateurs," rather in the spirit of HPL himself. We preach mainly to and among ourselves. As Gary Crawford has noted, "One of the most interesting aspects of Lovecraft is that, although much has been written about him, most scholarship is by 'fan' scholars. S. T. Joshi's journal *Lovecraft Studies* is largely written by nonacademics."[5] No department of English sponsors *Lovecraft Studies* or *Crypt of Cthulhu,* the other chief critical outlet for the field. While S. T. Joshi has persuaded the Modern Language Association to index *Lovecraft Studies* in its annual bibliography as of 1984, only a handful of American university libraries carry the leading Lovecraft journal. Arkham House, founded in the late thirties by Lovecraft's friend August Derleth and based in his hometown of Sauk City, Wisconsin, publishes his fiction in hardcover, not one of the name New York houses.[6] The paperback editions of his stories bear the imprints of science fiction lines, not Signet Classic or Penguin. His lesser works have been issued by Necronomicon Press, not by an academic publisher.

Since the mid-seventies, of course, several important books have come out from both trade and university presses. These include L. Sprague de Camp's controversial *Lovecraft: A Biography* (1975), which some felt did for Lovecraft without the malice what Rufus Griswold had done for Poe; *H. P. Lovecraft: Four Decades of Criticism* (1980), edited by S. T. Joshi; Joshi's definitive *H. P. Lovecraft: An Annotated Bibliography* (1981); and Maurice Lévy's *Lovecraft: A Study in the Fantastic* (1988), the first full-length critical treatment, originally published in 1972 in Paris. As with Poe, the French can claim the honor of having been first to appreciate Lovecraft's worth.

Then again, to be classed with Poe is no guarantee of a place in the pantheon. Poe historically has been belittled by some of our most eminent critics and authors, from Henry James to T. S. Eliot. As Harold Bloom observes in a review dating to 1984, "Poe's survival raises perpetually the issue whether literary merit and canonical status necessarily go together. I can think of no other American writer, down to this moment, at once so inescapable and so dubious."[7] By Bloom's standards Lovecraft would seem both escapable and dubious. If Henry James could think that to take Poe with more than a certain degree of seriousness is to lack seriousness oneself, then no doubt he would have regarded an enthusiasm for the master of *Weird Tales* as the mark of a stage of reflection so decidedly primitive as to be beneath notice. For many Lovecraft's is essentially an adolescent sensibility that appeals to other adolescents. When John Updike says that "I read Lovecraft with suitable chills and rapture when I was about fifteen and haven't much looked at him since,"[8] he in effect speaks for the majority of mature adults, for whom in literature as in life "ordinary events and feelings," as Lovecraft concedes in *Supernatural Horror in Literature*, "will always take first place" (D 366).

Granted its "juvenile" quality, Lovecraft's fiction yet bears comparison with the best of such literature, in particular the Sherlock Holmes stories of Arthur Conan Doyle, a connection Edmund Wilson makes explicit at the conclusion of his attack: "But the Lovecraft cult, I fear, is on even a more infantile level than the Baker Street Irregulars and the cult of Sherlock Holmes."[9] On a far more modest scale, Lovecraft has inspired the same sort of playful, affectionate response—the journals, the organizations, the rituals, the tongue-in-cheek quibbling over fine textual points—that characterizes the world of the greatest fictional detective. At this popular level he seems likely to continue to thrive.

As a subject of more serious critical consideration, Lovecraft can hold his own, as Brown University's Barton L. St. Armand has demonstrated, to single out one scholar who has placed him without apology in a larger literary context. Unlike his fellows in the *Weird Tales* triumvirate of the thirties, Clark Ashton Smith and Robert E. Howard, he has transcended his pulp origins. While the best work of M. R. James, Algernon Blackwood, and Arthur Machen may be technically superior to any one Lovecraft tale, theirs lacks the philosophical and psychological breadth that his possesses as a whole. In contrast to his successors, he stands as the last major figure in the field to have written exclusively in a literary tradition, uninfluenced by movies and television. While outside the genre he may be a pygmy beside such classical giants as Poe, Hawthorne, and Melville, Lovecraft in the darkness of his vision can be viewed as their spiritual heir. (The doctoral candidate who might otherwise select one of our standard authors for a dissertation topic may well find Lovecraft a rewarding and relatively wide-open alternative.) As for twentieth-century writers, he belongs in a broad sense, as Darrell Schweitzer has suggested, "on a level with Borges or Franz Kafka."[10]

Lovecraft needs to gain a wider audience outside the genre, however, before he can be said to have truly arrived. The prospect is not imminent. Until his work goes into the public domain, no trade publisher other than Arkham House is likely to issue the fiction in hardcover. A uniform critical edition of the fiction will almost certainly not appear until the next century. In the meantime, miscellaneous material continues to trickle forth from the fan presses, while in the next decade there may be hope for the publication of such books as an annotated volume of some of the better stories, a quality paperback compendium that would include letters and essays as well as tales, a collection of the scattered shorter reminiscences of his friends, and a new biography that examines him as both an artist and a thinker.

Critics can mellow. According to L. Sprague de Camp, for example, Edmund Wilson in his last years took delight in the first volume of the *Selected Letters*.[11] Colin Wilson, a few years after dealing harshly with Lovecraft in *The Strength to Dream,* wrote two Lovecraftian science-fiction novels, *The Mind Parasites* (1967) and *The Philosopher's Stone* (1969), which in their philosophical basis reveal an understanding of his work missing in the mass of Mythos fiction perpetrated by more worshipful imitators. The *Columbia Literary History of the United States* (1988) may contain no mention of him, but in the Columbia University Bookstore paperback copies of Lovecraft's tales are located on the literature shelf, flanked by such august neighbors as Jack London and Norman Mailer. A reviewer of the latter's Egyptian novel, *Ancient Evenings* (1983), reports, "Some years ago Gore Vidal cheekily remarked that Mailer was starting to sound like H. P. Lovecraft . . . In this book Mailer has larded Lovecraft's deep-purple, fungoid weirdness with slabs of James Michener Informative."[12] While hardly complimentary, such mention is another small indication that this peculiar New England gentleman, for so long the object of only an obscure "cult," is well on his way toward seeping, like one of his insidious horrors some might say, into the literary consciousness of America.

Notes and References

Chapter One

1. E. F. Bleiler, "Introduction to the Dover Edition" in H. P. Lovecraft, *Supernatural Horror in Literature* (New York: Dover, 1973), iii.

2. As Kenneth W. Faig, Jr., points out in "Lovecraft's Ancestors," *Crypt of Cthulhu* 7 (St. John's Eve 1988):19–25, Lovecraft tended to embroider both his paternal and maternal lines. Faig, for example, argues that he almost certainly did not descend from the Reverend George Phillips of *Arbella* fame.

3. Steven J. Mariconda, "Notes on the Prose Realism of H. P. Lovecraft," *Lovecraft Studies* 4 (Spring 1985):4. For another fine discussion of Lovecraft's style, see Mariconda's companion study, "H. P. Lovecraft: Consummate Prose Stylist," *Lovecraft Studies* 3 (Fall 1984):43–51.

4. H. P. Lovecraft, "The Brief Autobiography of an Inconsequential Scribbler" in *Uncollected Prose and Poetry 3*, ed. S. T. Joshi and Marc A. Michaud (West Warwick, R.I.: Necronomicon Press, 1982), 25.

5. Ibid.

6. S. T. Joshi, "Introduction" to H. P. Lovecraft, *Juvenilia: 1895–1905* (West Warwick, R.I.: Necronomicon Press, 1984), 4. This collection includes all the surviving stories and poems Lovecraft wrote as a child, together with reproductions of the drawings with which he illustrated them. The earliest piece actually dates to 1897.

7. For a discussion of the "frequently remarkable" parallels between the personalities of Hawthorne and Lovecraft, see J. Vernon Shea's *H. P. Lovecraft: The House and the Shadows* (West Warwick, R.I.: Necronomicon Press, 1982), 13.

8. See H. P. Lovecraft and J. F. Hartmann, *Science versus Charlantry: Essays on Astrology,* ed. S. T. Joshi and Scott Connors (Madison, Wis.: Strange Company, 1979).

9. T. E. D. Klein, "Foreword" to H. P. Lovecraft, *Writings in the United Amateur 1915–1925,* ed. Marc A. Michaud (West Warwick, R.I.: Necronomicon Press, 1976), iii. This foreword is an excellent introduction to Lovecraft's involvement in amateur journalism.

10. Of Derleth's dozen or so pastiches collected in *The Watchers Out of Time and Others* (Sauk City, Wis.: Arkham House, 1974), only *The Lurker at the Threshold* incorporates any Lovecraft prose—chiefly, the fragment "Of Evill Sorceries Done in New-England of Daemons in No Humane Shape."

11. S. T. Joshi, "Lovecraft's Revisions: How Much of Them Did He

Write?," in *Selected Papers on Lovecraft* (West Warwick, R.I.: Necronomicon Press, 1989), 56. This is an essential guide to the subject.

12. S. T. Joshi, "A Look at Lovecraft's Letters," in *Selected Papers on Lovecraft*, 70. This is the best discussion to date of the letters.

13. H. P. Lovecraft and Willis Conover, *Lovecraft at Last* (Alexandria, Va.: Carollton Clark, 1975), 226.

14. Vincent Starrett, "H. P. Lovecraft," in *Books and Bipeds* (New York: Argus Books, 1947), 120.

15. Winfield Townley Scott, "A Parenthesis on Lovecraft as a Poet," in *H. P. Lovecraft: Four Decades of Criticism*, ed. S. T. Joshi (Athens: Ohio University Press, 1980), 211. Like Vincent Starrett, Scott found Lovecraft's personality of far greater interest than his work.

16. Scott, "Parenthesis," in *Four Decades*, 212.

17. See Barton L. St. Armand and John H. Stanley, "H. P. Lovecraft's *Waste Paper*: A Facsimile and Transcript of the Original Draft," *Books at Brown* 26 (1978):31–52.

18. R. Boerem, "The Continuity of the *Fungi from Yuggoth*," in *Four Decades*, 224.

19. S. T. Joshi, "A Look at Lovecraft's Fantastic Poetry," *What Is Anything?* 2 (January 1988):12. This is the most penetrating treatment of the fantastic poetry to date.

20. Boerem, "Continuity," in *Four Decades*, 222.

Chapter Two

1. T. O. Mabbott, "H. P. Lovecraft: An Appreciation," in *Four Decades*, 43.

2. Lovecraft agreed to shorten the title to "Arthur Jermyn" for publication in *Weird Tales*, but was highly chagrined when he learned that it was finally to appear as "The White Ape." In a letter dated 3 February 1924 to editor Edwin Baird he wrote: "One thing—you may be sure that if I ever entitled a story 'The White Ape', *there would be no ape in it*. There would be something at first taken for an ape, which would not be an ape. But how can one ever get those subtleties across?" (1:294).

3. The African background may reflect the influence of the Tarzan stories, which Lovecraft read with enjoyment before his tastes became more sophisticated. In an exuberant letter printed in *All-Story Weekly* magazine for 7 March 1914 he said of Tarzan's creator: "At or near the head of your list of writers Edgar Rice Burroughs undoubtedly stands. I have read very few recent novels by others wherein is displayed an equal ingenuity in plot, and verisimilitude in treatment." Reprinted in H. P. Lovecraft, *Uncollected Letters*, ed. S.T. Joshi (West Warwick, R.I.: Necronomicon Press, 1986), 2.

4. Mabbott, "An Appreciation," in *Four Decades*, 44.

5. Ralph E. Vaughan, "The Old Man and the Sea: The Ocean and Life as Viewed by H. P. Lovecraft," *Lovecraft Studies* 2 (Fall 1982):3.

6. His first experience of the open sea, a boat trip from Boston to Provincetown, proved memorable. As he wrote Clark Ashton Smith in a letter dated 24 September 1930, it "was well worth the price of the excursion. To be on limitless water is to have the fantastic imagination stimulated in the most powerful way. The uniformly blank horizon evokes all sorts of speculations as to what may lie beyond, so that the sensations of Odysseus, Columbus, Madoc, Arthur Gordon Pym, the Ancient Mariner, & all the other voyagers of song & story are rolled into one & sharpened to expectant poignancy. Who knows what strange Lemurian or Saturnian or Sfanomöean port or weed-draped temple upheaved from the sea will loom suddenly ahead?" (3:169).

7. For a discussion of the Milton influence, see Thomas Quale's "The Blind Idiot God: Miltonic Echoes in the Cthulhu Mythos," *Crypt of Cthulhu* 6 (Lammas 1987):24–28.

8. S. T. Joshi, in "A Note on the Texts" in the corrected fifth printing of *Dagon,* states that the "correct" title derives from Lovecraft's advertisement in the *Providence Journal* for the lost typescript of the tale. Since he wrote it at the behest of *Weird Tales,* however, final choice of title may well have been left to the magazine.

9. In "The Shadow Out of Time" the narrator, a couple of years after the end of his amnesia episode in 1913, seems to be alluding to Slater in his observation on the infrequency with which nightmares of alien possession visited persons "largely of mediocre mind or less," one case occurring "only fifteen years before" (DH 378). Events in "Beyond the Wall of Sleep" occur during "the winter of 1900–1901" (D 26).

10. See S. T. Joshi, "The Sources for 'From Beyond,' " *Crypt of Cthulhu* 5 (Eastertide 1986):15–19.

11. For a perceptive discussion of Lovecraft's admiration for Dunsany and his work, see T. E. D. Klein's introduction to the corrected fifth printing of *Dagon,* "A Dreamer's Tales" (Sauk City, Wis.: Arkham House, 1986), xiii–lii.

12. Dirk W. Mosig, " 'The White Ship': A Psychological Odyssey," in *Four Decades,* 186.

13. Donald R. Burleson, *H. P. Lovecraft: A Critical Study* (Westport, Conn.: Greenwood Press, 1983), 28.

14. Darrell Schweitzer, "Lovecraft and Lord Dunsany," in *Discovering H. P. Lovecraft,* ed. Darrell Schweitzer (Mercer Island, Wash.: Starmont House, 1987), 98. This is an excellent general introduction to the Dunsanian influence.

15. Shea, *House* (West Warwick, R.I.: Necronomicon Press, 1982), 9.

16. S. T. Joshi, "The Dream World and the Real World in Lovecraft," *Crypt of Cthulhu* 2 (Lammas 1983):14. Joshi argues vigorously that all the early Dunsanian tales occur in the earth's distant past, but concedes that the later *Dream-Quest of Unknown Kadath* fits poorly into this scheme.

17. Barton L. St. Armand, *H. P. Lovecraft: New England Decadent* (Albuquerque, N. Mex.: Silver Scarab Press, 1979), 36, 7.

18. See Frank Belknap Long, *Howard Phillips Lovecraft: Dreamer on the Nightside* (Sauk City, Wis.: Arkham House, 1975), 237. The occasion prompted Long to produce his own tribute, a prose poem entitled "At the Home of Poe."

19. Steven J. Mariconda, " 'The Hound'—A Dead Dog?," *Crypt of Cthulhu* 5 (Eastertide 1986):5.

20. The nature of this "frightful carnivorous thing" is a matter of some debate, as Peter F. Jeffrey shows in "Who Killed St. John?," *Crypt of Cthulhu* 6 (St. John's Eve 1987):6–8.

Chapter Three

1. Will Murray, "In Search of Arkham Country," *Lovecraft Studies* 5 (Fall 1986):54–67.

2. In selecting this particular detail, Lovecraft may have had in mind the example of Timothy Dexter (1747–1806), "or Lord Timothy Dexter, as he lov'd to be call'd," a wealthy New England eccentric whom he described in 1923 as "still the principal topick of interest in Newburyport" (1:225). Dexter erected a collection of painted wooden statues of historical notables in the frontyard of his Newburyport mansion.

3. In a letter dated 4 October 1930 to Robert E. Howard, Lovecraft displayed his understanding of Puritan psychology:

It is the night-black Massachusetts legendry which packs the really macabre "kick". Here is material for a really profound study in group-neuroticism; for certainly, no one can deny the existence of a profoundly morbid streak in the Puritan imagination. What you say of the dark Saxon-Scandinavian heritage as a possible source of the atavistic impulses brought out by emotional repression, isolation, climatic rigour, and the nearness of the vast unknown forest with its coppery savages, is of vast interest to me; insomuch as I have often both said and written exactly the same thing! Have you seen my old story "The Picture in the House"? If not, I must send you a copy. The introductory paragraph virtually sums up the idea you advance. (3:174–75)

4. As S. T. Joshi shows in "Lovecraft and the *Regnum Congo*," *Crypt of Cthulhu* 4 (Yuletide 1984):13–17, Lovecraft derived his information for this tome, some of it inaccurate, from Thomas Henry Huxley's *Man's Place in Nature and Other Anthropological Essays*. Like his "God of fiction," Poe, Lovecraft was guilty at times of getting his knowledge secondhand.

5. What prompted Lovecraft's use of Bolton remains unknown. For speculation on the problem see Burleson, *Lovecraft,* 157.

6. Just as the character Harley Warren corresponds to his friend Sam Loveman in "The Statement of Randolph Carter," so Lovecraft may have had a friend in mind for Manton, possibly his amateur colleague, Maurice W. Moe, who was a school teacher.

7. In "The Unnamable" Lovecraft makes his only reference to the creator of Sherlock Holmes in the fiction, a veiled poke at the spiritualistic beliefs of "Sir Arthur Conan Doyle" (D 201).

8. For a discussion of the parallels between the two tales, see my "H. P. Lovecraft in Hawthornian Perspective," in *Four Decades,* 161–65.

9. In 1927 Lovecraft made a mock scholarly effort at systematizing the background of his mythic volume in "A History of the *Necronomicon.*" Robert M. Price has written two illuminating studies, "Higher Criticism and the *Necronomicon," Lovecraft Studies* 2 (Spring 1982):3–13, in which he treats the book and the "apocrypha" in terms of modern approaches to the Bible, and "Lovecraft's *Necronomicon:* An Introduction," *Crypt of Cthulhu* 3 (St. John's Eve 1984):25–29, in which he concludes that Lovecraft "seems to have had no one conception of the book save as a source of ancient arcana," 29.

Chapter Four

1. Colin Wilson, *The Strength to Dream* (Boston: Houghton Mifflin, 1962), 8.

2. L. Sprague de Camp, *Lovecraft: A Biography* (Garden City, N.Y.: Doubleday, 1975), 151.

3. See Dirk W. Mosig, "The Four Faces of the Outsider," in *Discovering H. P. Lovecraft,* 18–41, and Robert M. Price, "Homosexual Panic in 'The Outsider,' " *Crypt of Cthulhu* 1 (Michaelmas 1982):11–13. Mosig in turn views the tale as autobiography, a Jungian voyage of the human psyche, an anti-immortality tract, a comment on man's position in a mechanistic universe, and—in a fifth interpretation in a postscript—a critique of progress. Price's argument is nearly as ingenious.

4. William Fulwiler, "Reflections on 'The Outsider,' " *Lovecraft Studies* 1 (Spring 1980):3.

5. Price, "Homosexual Panic," 11.

6. Barton L. St. Armand, *The Roots of Horror in the Fiction of H. P. Lovecraft* (Elizabethtown, N.Y.: Dragon Press, 1977), 14.

7. Burleson, *Lovecraft,* 107.

Chapter Five

1. Vrest Orton, "Recollections of H. P. Lovecraft," *Whispers* 4 (March 1982):99. Of his prominent literary contemporaries, Lovecraft became acquainted only with the poet Hart Crane, a boyhood friend of Sam Loveman's.

2. One place he used the idea again is in the opening lines of the *Fungi* sonnet, "The Pigeon-Flyers":

> They took me slumming, where gaunt walls of brick
> Bulge outward with a viscous stored-up evil,
> And twisted faces, thronging foul and thick,
> Wink messages to alien god and devil
>
> (CP 115)

3. For an introduction to the Machen influence see Mark Valentine, "The Prophets of Pandemonium—Arthur Machen and H. P. Lovecraft," *Dagon* no. 17 (April–May 1987):19–23.

4. Robert M. Price makes a case for Suydam as a parodic self-portrait in "The Humor at Red Hook," *Crypt of Cthulhu* 4 (Yuletide 1984):6–8.

5. W. Paul Cook, *In Memoriam: Howard Phillips Lovecraft* (West Warwick, R.I.: Necronomicon Press, 1977), 15.

6. See Shea, "On the Literary Influences Which Shaped Lovecraft's Work," in *Four Decades*, 134, and Burleson, *Lovecraft*, 215, 226–27.

7. T. O. Mabbott, review of *The Outsider and Others*, *American Literature* 12 (1940):136. *The Outsider* (1939), the initial volume issued by Arkham House, the publishing company founded by Lovecraft's friend August Derleth to preserve his fiction in hardcover, is now a rare collector's item. In *Tales and Sketches 1831–1842* (Cambridge, Mass.: Belknap Press, 1978), volume 2 of the *Collected Works of Edgar Allan Poe*, Mabbott points out that the theme of "The Fall of the House of Usher" "is succinctly explained by Howard Phillips Lovecraft" (p. 393) and goes on to cite the relevant passage from *Supernatural Horror in Literature*.

8. Fred Lewis Pattee, review of *Supernatural Horror in Literature*, *American Literature* 18 (1946):175.

9. Bleiler, "Introduction," viii. For a penetrating recent assessment of the essay, see S. T. Joshi's "On *Supernatural Horror in Literature*," *Fantasy Commentator* 5 (1985):194–204.

10. For an able introduction to the Hawthorne influence in general and the connection between *The House of the Seven Gables* and *The Case of Charles Dexter Ward* (and "The Shunned House") in particular, see Donald R. Burleson's "H. P. Lovecraft: The Hawthorne Influence," *Extrapolation* 22 (1981):262–69.

11. In 1934 Lovecraft would pen what amount to two addendums to *Supernatural Horror in Literature*, "Notes on Writing Weird Fiction," an account of his personal method of composition, and "Some Notes on Interplanetary Fiction," a critique of the crude "scientifiction" of the day. Both provide advice still relevant to the aspiring writer of imaginative tales.

Chapter Six

1. David E. Schultz, "Lovecraft's New York Exile: Its Influence on His Life and Writings," *Crypt of Cthulhu* 4 (Eastertide 1987):9. This is an excellent assessment of the New York years. For more on Lovecraft's sources for the shunned house, see Steven J. Mariconda's "Lovecraft's 'Elizabethtown,' " *Twilit Grotto* 2 (August 1985):[3–6].

2. Other examples of giganticism in Lovecraft's fiction of this period include the eikon revealed by the receding waters in "What the Moon Brings"; the "curious mounds and hummocks in the weedy, fulgurite-pitted earth" that remind the narrator "of snakes and dead men's skulls swelled to gigantic proportions" (D 180) in "The Lurking Fear"; the gravestones that stick "ghoulishly through the snow like the decayed fingernails of a gigantic corpse" (D 209) in "The Festival"; and the five-headed beast that turns out to be a paw in "Under the Pyramids." There may be a certain irony in the fact that some of these images are no less ludicrous than the gigantic pieces of armor that keep cropping up in Horace Walpole's *The Castle of Otranto,* which Lovecraft described in *Supernatural Horror in Literature* as "a tale of the supernatural which, though thoroughly unconvincing and mediocre in itself, was destined to exert an almost unparalleled influence on the literature of the weird" (D 373).

3. As Steven J. Mariconda shows in his account of the genesis of the tale, "On the Emergence of 'Cthulhu,' " *Lovecraft Studies* 6 (Fall 1987):54–58, Lovecraft had conceived of much of it in New York but fortunately waited until returning to Providence to do the actual writing.

4. Important rebuttals to Derleth include Richard L. Tierney's "The Derleth Mythos," in *Discovering H. P. Lovecraft,* 65–67, and David E. Schultz's "Who Needs the Cthulhu Mythos?," *Lovecraft Studies* 5 (1986):43–53. As an alternative to the term "Cthulhu Mythos," Dirk W. Mosig has proposed "Yog-Sothoth Cycle of Myth," while Donald R. Burleson and S. T. Joshi have suggested "Lovecraft Mythos." Whatever its name its meaning remains a matter of debate, as shown in "What Is the Cthulhu Mythos?": A Panel Discussion with Donald R. Burleson, S. T. Joshi, Will Murray, Robert M. Price, and David E. Schultz, *Lovecraft Studies* 6 (Spring 1987):3–30.

5. Fritz Leiber, "A Literary Copernicus," in *Four Decades,* 50. This is still the finest general critical essay on Lovecraft.

6. In its convolutions the story both evokes and improves upon the "very clumsy" (D 380) framework of Charles Maturin's *Melmoth the Wanderer,* which Lovecraft praised at length in *Supernatural Horror in Literature,* feeling it represented "an enormous stride in the evolution of the horror-tale" (D 380). For an excellent discussion of structure, see S. T. Joshi, "The Structure of Lovecraft's Longer Narratives," in *Selected Papers,* 20–34.

7. For a discussion of the problematical pronunciation of "Cthulhu," see Robert M. Price's "Mythos Names and How to Say Them," *Lovecraft Studies* 6 (Fall 1987):47–53.

8. See St. Armand, *New England Decadent,* 46–49. St. Armand cites sources for Pickman's paintings in specific works of Goya and Fuseli.

9. The area of the North End where Pickman had his studio has proved less durable. When he visited the site in July of 1927, Lovecraft "found the whole scene torn down for two blocks around! I imagine the building inspectors must have found those ancient houses as sinister as I did, albeit with a different sort of perception. That is the perennial grief of an architectural antiquarian—in a city as large as Providence or Boston something quaint is always being demolished in the interest of alleged progress" (2:170).

10. For a discussion of this recurrent image, see my "Sunset Terrace Imagery in Lovecraft," in *Lovecraft Studies* 1 (Fall 1981):3–9. Like much else it has a childhood origin: "What has haunted my dreams for nearly forty years is *a strange sense of adventurous expectancy connected with landscape and architecture and sky-effects.* I can see myself as a child of 2½ on the railway bridge at Auburndale, Mass., looking across and downward at the business part of town, and feeling the imminence of some wonder which I could neither fully describe nor fully conceive—and there has never been a subsequent hour of my life when kindred sensations have been absent" (3:100).

11. See Barton L. St. Armand, "The Source for Lovecraft's Knowledge of Borellus in *The Case of Charles Dexter Ward,*" *Nyctalops* 2 (May 1977):16–17.

12. While Lovecraft makes no explicit family connection, Willett may have inherited some of the courage he displays in contending with Curwen from Lieutenant Colonel Marinus Willett, the radical firebrand who lead American forces in a daring raid in the battle for Fort Stanwix in 1777.

13. Barton L. St. Armand, "Facts in the Case of H. P. Lovecraft," in *Four Decades,* 178. In this splendid article, originally delivered as a lecture to the Rhode Island Historical Society, St. Armand stresses the importance of Providence, Rhode Island, to Lovecraft's fictional art. For an argument against St. Armand's view of knowledge in *Ward,* see S. T. Joshi, " 'Reality' and Knowledge: Some Notes on the Aesthetic Thought of H. P. Lovecraft," *Lovecraft Studies* 1 (Fall 1980):17–27.

Chapter Seven

1. See my "The Influence of *Vathek* on H. P. Lovecraft's *The Dream-Quest of Unknown Kadath,*" in *Four Decades,* 153–57.

2. S. T. Joshi, "H. P. Lovecraft and *The Dream-Quest of Unknown Kadath,*" *Crypt of Cthulhu* 5 (Candlemas 1986):30. This may be the best single discussion of the novel.

3. De Camp, *Lovecraft,* 278. Eating, drinking, and sleeping, appropriately enough for Lovecraft's most child-like story, figure prominently in the *Dream-Quest.* Such ordinary occupations are almost absent elsewhere in the fiction.

Chapter Eight

1. See Donald R. Burleson, "Humour Beneath Horror: Some Sources for 'The Dunwich Horror' and 'The Whisperer in Darkness,' " *Lovecraft Studies* 1 (Spring 1980):5–15. In this superb study Burleson identifies the town of Athol, Massachusetts, as an important source of names for "The Dunwich Horror."

2. John Taylor Gatto, *The Major Works of H. P. Lovecraft* (New York: Monarch Press, 1977), 53. In the one instance of biblical citation in the fiction, Lovecraft quotes a passage from the Book of Job in *The Case of Charles Dexter Ward* (MM 153), completed shortly before "The Colour Out of Space."

3. Lovecraft indicates the source for this detail in a letter from June 1927: "Living things—usually insane or idiotic members of the family—concealed in the garrets or secret rooms of old houses are or at least have been literal realities in rural New England—I was told by someone of how he stopped at a lone farmhouse on some errand years ago, and was nearly frightened out of his wits by the opening of a sliding panel in the kitchen wall, and the appearance at the aperture of the most horrible, dirt-caked, and matted-bearded face he had ever conceived possible to exist!" (2:139).

4. Will Murray, in "Sources for 'The Colour Out of Space,' " *Crypt of Cthulhu* 4 (Yuletide 1984):3–5, suggests that Lovecraft may have found a model for his tainted animals in Arthur Machen's *The Terror*. Murray also interestingly suggests that the anonymous gaseous entity in the story may be the same as the violet-colored gas in "Celephaïs" and the *Dream-Quest*, where it is named S'ngac.

5. Edmund Wilson, "Tales of the Marvellous and the Ridiculous," in *Four Decades*, 49. These effects also resemble those in William Hope Hodgson's "The Voice in the Night," though Lovecraft did not read Hodgson until 1934.

6. For speculation on Lovecraft's sources for the name "Dunwich," see Burleson, "Humour Beneath Horror," 7.

7. James Egan, "Dark Apocalyptic: Lovecraft's Cthulhu Mythos as a Parody of Traditional Christianity," *Extrapolation* 23 (1982):375. Granted certain correspondences with the gospel stories of Jesus, Wilbur's career more generally fits the pattern of classical mythology, a tie made explicit in Armitage's exclamation: "Shew them Arthur Machen's Great God Pan and they'll think it a common Dunwich scandal!" (DH 172).

8. Donald R. Burleson, "The Mythic Hero Archetype in 'The Dunwich Horror,' " *Lovecraft Studies* 1 (Spring 1981):9. Burleson makes an ingenious argument, yet seems unduly embarrassed by the story's "good versus evil" plot.

9. As S. T. Joshi notes in *H. P. Lovecraft* (Mercer Island, Wash.: Starmont House, 1982), the general concept of beings lurking in remote hills, together with the specific "black stone" with its strange hieroglyphs, owes much to Machen's "Novel of the Black Seal."

10. Will Murray, "An Uncompromising Look at the Cthulhu Mythos," *Lovecraft Studies* 5 (Spring 1986):29. In overstating the case that these inside jokes render all tales from "The Whisperer in Darkness" on corrupt, Murray makes some good points about Lovecraft's loss of control over his own material.
11. Gatto, *Major Works,* 61.
12. Burleson, *Lovecraft,* 176.

Chapter Nine

1. S. T. Joshi, "Lovecraft's Alien Civilisations: A Political Interpretation," in *Selected Papers,* 8. In this thorough examination of the subject, Joshi points to important links between Lovecraft's fiction and his political essays, "Some Repetitions on the Times" (1933) and "Heritage or Modernism: Common Sense in Art Forms" (1935).
2. James Turner, "A Mythos in His Own Image" in *Dagon* (1986), xvii.
3. S. T. Joshi, "Who Wrote 'The Mound'?," *Crypt of Cthulhu* 2 (Candlemas 1983), 27.
4. Jason C. Eckhardt, "Behind the Mountains of Madness: Lovecraft and the Antarctic in 1930," *Lovecraft Studies* 6 (Spring 1987):31–38. If Lovecraft did not read Byrd's popular book *Little America,* published in October 1930, he must surely have followed the newspaper accounts of the time.
5. Marc A. Cerasini, "Thematic Links in *Arthur Gordon Pym, At the Mountains of Madness,* and *Moby Dick,*" *Crypt of Cthulhu* 6 (Lammas 1987):17. In this major comparative study, Cerasini notes that the natives of Tsalal in *Pym* harvest a marine creature referred to as a *biche de mer,* commonly known as a sea cucumber, which strikingly resembles the description of Lovecraft's Old Ones. He also sees a significant parallel in the relationship between Pym and Peters and that between Dyer and Danforth.
6. S. T. Joshi, *H. P. Lovecraft,* 38.
7. Fritz Leiber, "A Literary Copernicus," in *Four Decades,* 57.
8. Darrell Schweitzer, *The Dream Quest of H. P. Lovecraft* (San Bernadino, Calif.: Borgo Press, 1978), 42.
9. As he had in the self-caricature in "A Reminiscence of Dr. Samuel Johnson," Lovecraft exaggerates his age and makes himself an object of humor. At one point Aspinwall, the lawyer, cries in exasperation: " 'Can't somebody shut that old fool up? We've had enough of his moonings. . . .' " (MM 427).
10. In his memoir "Caverns Measureless to Man," *Science-Fantasy Correspondent* 1 (1975):36–43, Kenneth Sterling, who as a Providence high school student met Lovecraft in 1934 and saw him frequently until his death, describes going to a Jewish cultural center with him to hear a talk by Alfred Adler, the Austrian psychiatrist and early Freud disciple: "Lovecraft was intensely interested in hearing Adler, calling him one of the greatest living contributors to our understanding of psychology and psychodynamics" (41).

11. In Lovecraft's section of "The Challenge from Beyond" (1935), the round-robin tale whose writers included C. L. Moore, A. Merritt, Robert E. Howard, and Frank Belknap Long, the protagonist likewise is shocked to find his mind transferred into the body of an alien creature. Lovecraft's portion of this curiosity of a tale, the most developed of the five, includes elements from other of his late stories such as "the disturbing and debatable Eltdown Shards" (DH 401) from "The Shadow Out of Time."

12. Several of Lovecraft's stories were selected for anthologies in his lifetime. His only real book, *The Shadow over Innsmouth,* issued in 1936 by a young fan named William Crawford, was a disappointment, "lousily misprinted and sloppily bound" (5:432). Had Lovecraft supervised an edition of his best tales, no doubt he would have corrected the choppy paragraphing of the text of "The Shadow Out of Time," which other than a single manuscript sheet survives only in its *Astounding* appearance.

13. The name "Eryx" derives from the Sicilian town of Erice, site of a major Greek temple devoted to the goddess Aphrodite (Venus).

14. Darrell Schweitzer notes that Sterling in turn borrowed this concept from an Edmond Hamilton story "about an explorer trapped in an invisible city" (*Dream Quest,* 49–50).

Chapter Ten

1. Will Murray, in "Was There a Real Brown Jenkin?," *Crypt of Cthulhu* 1 (Lammas 1982):24–26, suggests an interesting source for this creature with man-like face and hands in "Gef, the Talking Mongoose," a spook reported on the Isle of Man in the fall of 1931 shortly before Lovecraft wrote "The Dreams in the Witch House."

2. Once while sleeping, Gilman thinks that someone has "fumbled clumsily at the latch" (MM 286), a minor variation on a motif that crops up in several other late stories and that first appeared in the climactic couplet of the non-*Fungi* sonnet, "The Messenger": "Then at the door that cautious rattling came— / And the mad truth devoured me like a flame!" (CP 91). In "The Whisperer in Darkness" somebody tries to enter Wilmarth's room at night: "My first confused impression was of stealthily creaking floor-boards in the hall outside my door, and of a clumsy, muffled fumbling at the latch" (DH 265). In "The Shadow over Innsmouth" the narrator has an unwelcome nighttime visitor: "Without the least shadow of a doubt, the lock on my hall door was being tried—cautiously, furtively, tentatively—with a key. . . . After a time the cautious rattling ceased" (DH 344–45). In "The Haunter of the Dark," Blake engages in "a little fumbling" at the "ancient latch" (DH 99) of a closed door in the church he breaks into on Federal Hill. This image attains apotheosis as a metaphor in "The Shadow Out of Time," as Donald R. Burleson has noted (*Lovecraft,* 202), at the point where Peaslee plods on under an evil moon to his eldritch rendezvous: "Something was fumbling and rat-

tling at the latch of my recollection, while another unknown force sought to keep the portal barred" (DH 412).

3. S. T. Joshi, "Topical References in Lovecraft," *Extrapolation* 25 (1984):248. Joshi ably argues that Lovecraft's work reflects more of the contemporary world than has been commonly assumed.

4. Lovecraft probably never read Waugh, but he certainly knew the work of an earlier British writer of prominence, Rudyard Kipling. In Kipling's popular tale "At the End of the Passage," the image of the ghost that scared the protagonist to death is found on the retina of his eye, just as Ghatanathoa is visible on the retina of the mummy's eyes when they open near the end.

5. In "Autobiography in Lovecraft," *Lovecraft Studies* 1 (Fall 1979):7–19, S. T. Joshi detects in Derby a trace of Clark Ashton Smith as well.

6. For a discussion of the Sherlock Holmes influence on Lovecraft, see my "The Return of Sherlock Holmes and H. P. Lovecraft," *Baker Street Journal* 34 (1984):217–20.

7. In "The Shambler from the Stars," reprinted in *Mysteries of the Worm: All the Cthulhu Mythos Stories of Robert Bloch* (New York: Zebra Books, 1981), Bloch describes the same locale, understandably enough, with a less sure touch: "Providence is a lovely town. My friend's house was ancient, and quaintly Georgian. The first floor was a gem of Colonial atmosphere" (p. 43).

8. Such scribbling to the death in fiction can easily pass over into the absurd, as Robert M. Price shows in "Famous Last Words." *Crypt of Cthulhu* 1 (Michaelmas 1982):28–29. As a prime example, he cites the Lovecraft revision, written a month before "The Haunter of the Dark," "The Diary of Alonzo Typer" (1935), wherein the hero closes his account with the words "too late . . . cannot help self—black paws materialise—am dragged away toward the cellar . . ." (HM 322).

Chapter Eleven

1. Edmund Wilson, "Tales of the Marvellous and the Ridiculous," in *Four Decades*, 47.

2. Jacques Barzun, "The Art and Appeal of the Ghostly and Ghastly," in *The Penguin Encyclopedia of Horror and the Supernatural*, ed. Jack Sullivan (New York: Viking Penguin, 1986), xxvi.

3. Mabbott, review of *The Outsider and Others*, 136.

4. Stephen A. Black, "Literary Biography and Psychological Criticism: In the Matter of H. P. Lovecraft," *Canadian Review of American Studies* 10 (1979):244.

5. Gary Crawford, "Criticism," in *The Penguin Encyclopedia of Horror and the Supernatural*, ed. Jack Sullivan (New York: Viking Penguin, 1986), 103.

6. In the course of his lifetime Lovecraft was approached by a number of book publishers, including Morrow, Viking, Putnam's, and Knopf, but in

every instance negotiations for either a novel or short story collection fell through.

7. Harold Bloom, "Inescapable Poe," *New York Review of Books,* 11 October 1984, 23.

8. Note from John Updike to the author, 2 August 1986. Apparently Updike was remembering his teenage reading when he assigned the name of Lovecraft to an elderly couple in his "supernatural" novel set in Rhode Island, *The Witches of Eastwick* (1984).

9. Wilson, "Tales of the Marvellous and the Ridiculous," in *Four Decades,* 49.

10. Darrell Schweitzer, "H. P. Lovecraft: Still Eldritch After All These Years," *Amazing* 61 (March 1987):57. In this warm survey of Lovecraft's standing fifty years after his death, Schweitzer points out that Borges thought well enough of Lovecraft to dedicate a story to him, "There Are More Things." In his travel book *The Old Patagonian Express* (1979), Paul Theroux describes meeting Borges and discussing Lovecraft with him.

11. L. Sprague de Camp, "H. P. Lovecraft and Edmund Wilson," *Fantasy Mongers* 1 (March 1979):5. De Camp also sees a Lovecraft influence in Wilson's play, *The Little Blue Light* (1950).

12. Rhoda Koenig, review of *Ancient Evenings* by Norman Mailer, *New York Magazine,* 25 April 1983, 71.

Selected Bibliography

PRIMARY WORKS

Fiction

I have restricted this listing to the current Arkham House editions, those based on S. T. Joshi's corrected texts.

At the Mountains of Madness and Other Novels. Sauk City, Wis.: Arkham House, 1964. Corrected 5th printing, 1985. The three short novels plus shorter tales.

Dagon and Other Macabre Tales. Sauk City, Wis.: Arkham House, 1965. Corrected 5th printing, 1986. Minor tales, together with the definitive text of *Supernatural Horror in Literature* and chronology of the fiction.

The Dunwich Horror and Others. Sauk City, Wis: Arkham House, 1963. Corrected 6th printing, 1984. Major tales.

The Horror in the Museum and Other Revisions. Sauk City, Wis.: Arkham House, 1970. Corrected 3rd printing, 1989. Includes revisions identified since first printing.

Letters

H. P. Lovecraft in "The Eyrie." Edited by S. T. Joshi and Marc A. Michaud. West Warwick, R.I.: Necronomicon Press, 1979. Letters by and about Lovecraft from the letters column of *Weird Tales*.

Selected Letters. 5 vols. Edited by August Derleth and Donald Wandrei (vols. 1–3) and August Derleth and James Turner (vols. 4–5). Sauk City, Wis.: Arkham House, 1965–76. Index supplied by S. T. Joshi's *An Index to the Selected Letters of H. P. Lovecraft*, West Warwick, R.I.: Necronomicon Press, 1980.

Uncollected Letters. Edited by S. T. Joshi. West Warwick, R.I.: Necronomicon Press, 1986. Letters originally published in periodicals.

Poetry

Collected Poems. Sauk City, Wis.: Arkham House, 1963. Selected poems, including all the major horror verse. A more comprehensive volume, one that contains the bulk of Lovecraft's poetry, is forthcoming from Arkham House.

Medusa and Other Poems. Edited by S. T. Joshi. Mount Olive, N.C.: Cryptic Publications, 1986. Minor verse not collected elsewhere.

Saturnalia and Other Poems. Edited by S. T. Joshi. Bloomfield, N.J.: Cryptic Publications, 1984. Minor verse not collected elsewhere.

A Winter Wish. Edited by Tom Collins. [Brown Mills, N.J.]: Whispers Press, 1977. Substantial selection of poems not included in *Collected Poems.*

Miscellany

The Californian: 1934–1938. Edited by Marc A. Michaud. West Warwick, R.I.: Necronomicon Press, 1977. Amateur journalism from late in career.

Commonplace Book. 2 vols. Edited by David E. Schultz. West Warwick, R.I.: Necronomicon Press, 1987. Definitive text of Lovecraft's story idea notebooks, with extensive scholarly annotations.

The Conservative: Complete 1915–1923. Edited by Marc A. Michaud. West Warwick, R.I.: Necronomicon Press, 1977. Lovecraft's own amateur journal.

First Writings: Pawtuxet Valley Gleaner 1906. Edited by Marc A. Michaud. West Warwick, R.I.: Necronomicon Press, 1976. Astronomy columns.

Four Prose Poems. West Warwick, R.I.: Necronomicon Press, 1987. These are also included in the second Arkham House omnibus collection, *Beyond the Wall of Sleep* (1943).

In Defence of Dagon. Edited by S. T. Joshi. West Warwick, R.I.: Necronomicon Press, 1985. Literary philosophy.

The Lovecraft Collectors Library: Volume I–Volume VII. Edited by George T. Wetzel. Madison, Wis.: Strange Company, 1979. Reprint with supplementary materials of mimeographed booklets from the early 1950s containing amateur press poetry and prose.

To Quebec and the Stars. Edited by L. Sprague de Camp. West Kingston, R.I.: Donald M. Grant, 1976. First publication of the Quebec travelogue, along with representative selection of essays and "A Reminiscence of Dr. Samuel Johnson."

Uncollected Prose and Poetry. 3 vols. Edited by S. T. Joshi and Marc A. Michaud. West Warwick, R.I.: Necronomicon Press, 1978–1982. Major assortment of miscellany.

Writings in the Tryout. Edited by Marc A. Michaud. West Warwick, R.I.: Necronomicon Press, 1977. Amateur journalism and poetry.

Writings in the United Amateur: 1915–1925. Edited by Marc A. Michaud. West Warwick, R.I.: Necronomicon Press, 1976. Substantial selection of amateur journalism.

SECONDARY WORKS

Bibliographies

Joshi, S. T., ed. *H. P. Lovecraft and Lovecraft Criticism: An Annotated Bibliography.* Kent, Ohio: Kent State University Press, 1981. Massive and definitive.

————**and Leigh Blackmore, eds.** *H. P. Lovecraft and Lovecraft Criticism: An Annotated Bibliography: Supplement 1980–1984.* West Warwick, R.I.: Necronomicon Press, 1985.

————**and Marc A. Michaud.** *Lovecraft's Library: A Catalogue.* West Warwick, R.I.: Necronomicon Press, 1980. An annotated listing basic to the understanding of Lovecraft's intellectual development of roughly two-thirds of the books he owned. Second, expanded edition forthcoming.

Biographies and Memoirs

Note that the Arkham House collections of Lovecraft miscellany, *Marginalia* (1944), *Something About Cats* (1949), *The Shuttered Room* (1959), and *The Dark Brotherhood* (1966), also include insightful reminiscences by such friends as Rheinhart Kleiner, E. Hoffmann Price, Samuel Loveman, and Robert Barlow.

Cook, W. Paul. *In Memoriam: H. P. Lovecraft.* West Warwick, R.I.: Necronomicon Press, 1977. Random, anecdotal memoir, full of meaty detail, first published by Cook's Driftwind Press in 1941. The most substantial account by a friend who knew Lovecraft in the flesh.

Davis, Sonia H. *The Private Life of H. P. Lovecraft.* West Warwick, R.I.: Necronomicon Press, 1985. Unabridged, unedited version of memoir by former wife, first published in the *Providence Sunday Journal* 22 August 1948. Unique view of Lovecraft as husband and lover, highly revealing of both personalities.

de Camp, L. Sprague. *Lovecraft: A Biography.* Garden City, N.Y.: Doubleday, 1975. The standard biography, factually thorough, with emphasis on Lovecraft as impractical misfit and racist. Less than satisfying as a portrait of an artist, though provides an antidote to more saintly assessments.

Derleth, August. *H. P. L.: A Memoir.* New York: Ben Abramson, 1945. Appreciative sketch by the man responsible for preserving Lovecraft's work in hardcover. Dwells on such incidental topics as his tastes in music, and interprets the fiction from a perspective now outdated.

Everts, R. Alain. *The Death of a Gentleman: The Last Days of Howard Phillips Lovecraft.* Madison, Wis.: Strange Company, 1987. Detailed, clinical account of Lovecraft's final illness.

Faig, Kenneth W., Jr. *H. P. Lovecraft: His Life, His Work.* West Warwick,

R.I.: Necronomicon Press, 1979. Handy summary of the life with chronology and a list of Lovecraft's works.

———. "Howard Phillips Lovecraft: The Early Years, 1890–1914." *Nyctalops* 2 (April 1973):3–9 and 2 (July 1974):34–44. Detailed treatment of early life and writings.

Long, Frank Belknap. *Howard Phillips Lovecraft: Dreamer on the Nightside.* Sauk City, Wis.: Necronomicon Press, 1975. Thin, discursive memoir by Lovecraft's best friend. Includes some charming vignettes.

Lovecraft, H. P., and Willis Conover. *Lovecraft at Last.* Arlington, Va.: Carrollton Clark, 1975. Correspondence between Lovecraft and teenage admirer with connecting narrative by Conover. Moving portrait of Lovecraft in the final eight months of his life.

Orton, Vrest. "Recollections of H. P. Lovecraft." *Whispers* 4 (March 1982):95–101. Lovecraft from the unusual viewpoint of a fellow antiquarian and minor mainstream writer with no interest in horror fiction.

Scott, Winfield Townley. "His Own Most Fantastic Creation: Howard Phillips Lovecraft." In *Exiles and Fabrications.* Garden City, N.Y.: Doubleday, 1961, pp. 50–72. Sympathetic, psychological portrait by a poet and critic outside the Lovecraft circle. Originally printed in *Marginalia* (1944), but still the best single short biographical study.

Shea, J. Vernon. *H. P. Lovecraft: The House and the Shadows.* West Warwick: R.I.: Necronomicon Press, 1982. Reprint of article that first appeared in the *Magazine of Fantasy and Science Fiction* in 1966. One of the more perceptive and balanced memoirs by a correspondent friend.

Sterling, Kenneth. "Caverns Measureless to Man." *Science-Fantasy Correspondent* 1 (1975):36–43. Admiring memoir by a distinguished physician who as a student in Providence often met with Lovecraft from 1934 on. Argues from personal experience that Lovecraft was not an anti-Semite.

Talman, Wilfred B. *The Normal Lovecraft.* Saddle River, N.J.: Gerry de la Ree, 1973. In this, "A Memoir to Restore Balance to the Shade of a Man of Delightful Character," as the subtitle has it, Talman perhaps protests too much that Lovecraft was very little different from the average "me and thee," but in the process he relays some information of interest.

Criticism and Commentary

I have confined this listing to books, pamphlets, and journals, ranging from the popular to the scholarly. I have indicated the value of significant individual essays in the footnotes.

Beckwith, Henry L. P., Jr. *Lovecraft's Providence & Adjacent Parts.* 2d ed. West Kingston, R.I.: Donald M. Grant, 1986. First published in 1979, this short, anecdotal guide covers the major Rhode Island sites described in the fiction and the letters. Illustrated with maps and photographs.

Burleson, Donald R. *H. P. Lovecraft: A Critical Study.* Westport, Conn.:

Greenwood Press, 1983. First comprehensive survey of the fiction, strong on literary influences and general background. Too often, however, excessive plot summary substitutes for the cogent analysis to be expected throughout a study of this scope.

Cannon, Peter. *The Chronology Out of Time: Dates in the Fiction of H. P. Lovecraft.* West Warwick, R.I.: Necronomicon Press, 1986. An evaluation of the importance of dates in the fiction, followed by a chronology.

Carter, Lin. *Lovecraft: A Look Behind the "Cthulhu Mythos."* New York: Ballantine, 1972. A popular introduction, based largely on Derleth's misconceptions of the fiction. Unreliable.

Eckhardt, Jason C. *Off the Ancient Track: A Lovecraftian Guide to New-England and Adjacent New-York.* West Warwick, R.I.: Necronomicon Press, 1987. Heavily illustrated with maps and drawings, this slim volume while shorter than Beckwith (q.v.) is a more inclusive and practical field guide, though the text is restricted to quotations from Lovecraft's letters and tales.

Eisner, Steve, ed. *Fresco* 8 (Spring 1958). Memorial symposium issue of the *University of Detroit Quarterly* devoted to Lovecraft. Includes mostly items of minor interest today.

Frierson, Meade, and Penny Frierson, eds. *HPL.* Birmingham, Ala.: The Editors, 1971. A grab-bag of essays, Mythos fiction, and artwork.

Gatto, John Taylor. *The Major Works of H. P. Lovecraft: A Critical Commentary.* New York: Monarch Press, 1977. Notwithstanding its status as part of the Monarch Notes series and some careless factual errors, this selective study contains some fine insights, along with shrewd assessments of secondary works.

Joshi, S. T. *H. P. Lovecraft.* Mercer Island, Wash.: Starmont House, 1982. Concise and incisive survey, stressing the philosophical unity of the work. The best of the shorter general critical guides.

————, ed. *H. P. Lovecraft: Four Decades of Criticism.* Athens: Ohio University Press, 1980. Includes major essays by Fritz Leiber, Dirk Mosig, Barton St. Armand, Peter Penzoldt, Edmund Wilson, and others.

————, ed. *Lovecraft Studies.* The premier Lovecraft journal. Biannual since fall 1979 from Necronomicon Press.

————. *Selected Papers on Lovecraft.* West Warwick, R.I.: Necronomicon Press, 1989. Five indispensable essays by the leading scholar in the field.

Lévy, Maurice. *Lovecraft: A Study in the Fantastic.* Translated by S. T. Joshi. Detroit: Wayne State University Press, 1988. Penetrating study of the mythic and oneiric aspects of the fiction by a noted French academic, first published in 1972. Updated slightly by the translator, this study stands in the forefront of Lovecraft criticism.

Price, Robert M., ed. *Crypt of Cthulhu.* While less formally scholarly than *Lovecraft Studies,* this entertaining small press journal has published many excellent articles since its inception in 1981. Issued eight times a year, it is a testament to the vitality of the field today.

St. Armand, Barton L. *H. P. Lovecraft: New England Decadent.* Albuquerque, N.Mex.: Silver Scarab Press, 1979. Provocative and wide-ranging study placing Lovecraft in the decadent tradition of literature and painting. First-rate criticism.

————. *The Roots of Horror in the Fiction of H. P. Lovecraft.* Elizabethtown, N.J.: Dragon Press, 1977. Brilliant explication of "The Rats in the Walls" in Jungian terms.

Schweitzer, Darrell, ed. *Discovering H. P. Lovecraft.* Mercer Island, Wash.: Starmont House, 1987. Updated reissue of critical anthology published in 1976 under title *Essays Lovecraftian.* Includes worthy articles by the editor, Dirk Mosig, Richard Tierney, S. T. Joshi, and others.

————. *The Dream Quest of H. P. Lovecraft.* San Bernadino, Calif.: Borgo Press, 1978. A reader's guide, for the beginner, particularly good on the Dunsanian influence.

Shreffler, Philip A. *The H. P. Lovecraft Companion.* Westport, Conn.: Greenwood Press, 1977. Of chief critical interest is the first chapter relating Lovecraft to British and American literary traditions, both within the genre and without. Includes maps, photographs, plot summaries, and a listing of characters and monsters.

Wilson, Colin. *The Strength to Dream: Literature and the Imagination.* Boston: Houghton Mifflin, 1962. Dismissing him as a bad writer, Wilson focuses on Lovecraft as an interesting psychological case, in the company of Yeats, Wilde, and Strindberg. Uninformed, yet important as the first major study to place Lovecraft in a larger literary context.

Index

Abdul Alhazred, 2, 23, 24, 90; *see also* the *Necronomicon*
Abramson, Ben, 61
Adler, Alfred, 136n9.10
Akeley, Henry Wentworth, 90–92, 100, 107, 109, 116
Allen, Zadok, 94–95
Angell, Prof. George Gammell, 4, 65
Antarctica, 97, 101
Apley, George, 115
Argosy, the, 5
Arkham, Mass., 35, 37, 40, 41, 44, 63, 76, 83, 90, 92, 108, 112–13, 117–18
Arkham House, 11, 61, 124, 126, 132n7
Armitage, Dr. Henry, 87–89, 95
Aspinwall, 136n9
Astounding Stories, 105, 137n12
Athol, Mass., 135n1
Auburndale, Mass., 134n10
Australia (Western), 97, 108
Azathoth, 90, 113

Baird, Edwin, 10, 55, 128n2
Barker, Clive, 54
Barlow, Robert: "The Night Ocean," 9
Barry, Denys, 18, 28
Barzun, Jacques, 123
Baudelaire, Charles Pierre, 32, 101
Beacon Hill, 68, 81, 115; *see also* Boston, Mass.
Beckford, William: *History of the Caliph Vathek*, 78, 79
Bible, aspects of the (in the fiction), 28, 54, 76, 85, 87, 96, 116, 135n2
Bierce, Ambrose, 54, 69, 90
Birch, George, 53–54
Bishop, Zealia, 9, 98, 101
Black, Stephen A., 123
Blackwood, Algernon, 11, 125

Blake, Robert, 119–21, 137n2
Bleiler, E. F., 1, 61
Bloch, Robert, 119; "The Shambler from the Stars," 119, 138n7
Bloom, Harold, 124
Boerem, R., 13
Bolton, Mass., 40, 130n5
Borellus, 72
Borges, Jorge Luis, 125; "There Are More Things," 139n10
Boston, Mass., 7, 63, 68–70, 104, 112, 114–15, 134n9
Boswell, James, 17
Bowen, Dr. Enoch, 121
Brown, Walter, 90
Brown Jenkin, 112
Brown University, 3, 71, 119
Bulwer-Lytton, Edward, 20
Burleson, Donald R., 28, 54, 60, 82, 87, 96, 130n5, 132n10, 133n4, 135n6, 137n2
Burroughs, Edgar Rice, 128n3
Bush, David V., 8
Byrd, Adm. Richard E., 101, 103, 104; *Little America*, 136n4

Cabot Museum of Archaeology, the, 114–15
Californian, the, 9
Cannon, Peter, 131n8, 134n6.10, 134n7.1, 138n10.6
Carter, Randolph, 22–23, 30, 41–42, 67, 71, 75, 79–81, 97, 99, 105–7, 112
cats (in the fiction), 29, 51, 79
Cerasini, Marc A., 102
Chambers, Robert W., 90
Chandraputra, Swami, 106–7, 115
Chepachet, R.I., 56, 58
Christianity. *See* Bible, aspects of the (in the fiction)

College Hill, 2, 67, 70, 120–21; *see also* Providence, R.I.
Conover, Willis, 10–11; *Lovecraft at Last,* 11
Conservative, the, 6
Cook, W. Paul, 15, 58, 61
Crane, Hart, 23, 131n5.1
Crawford, Gary, 124
Crawford, William, 137n12
Crockett, Freddy, 104
Crofts, Anna Helen, 9
Crypt of Cthulhu, 124
Cthulhu, 66, 69, 86, 90, 95, 114
Cthulhu Mythos, 65, 133n4
Curwen, Joseph, 16, 17, 22, 54, 58, 60, 62, 70, 72–74, 91, 92, 110, 121, 134n12
Czanek, Joe, 36

Dagon, 21
Danforth, 22, 30, 101–4, 136n5
Davis, Dr., 54
deCamp, L. Sprague, 8, 46, 79, 126; *Lovecraft: A Biography,* 124
Deep Ones, the, 93–96, 97
de la Poer (Delapore), 51–53, 64, 93, 95, 108
de Marigny, Etienne-Laurent, 106, 115
Derby, Edward, 2, 15, 101, 116–19, 121
Derleth, August, 7, 9, 11, 65, 77, 82, 124, 132n7, 133n4; *The Lurker at the Threshold,* 127n10
de Russy, Denis, 101
Dexter, Timothy, 130n2
Doré, Gustave, 2, 20
Doyle, Sir Arthur Conan, 131n3.7; Sherlock Holmes, influence of, 2, 35, 42, 118, 125, 138n6
Dreiser, Theodore, 55
Driftwind Press, 61
Dudley, Jervas, 16, 17, 20
Dunsany, Lord, 11, 15, 24, 26–27, 35, 129n11; *A Dreamer's Tales,* 26; "Idle Days on the Yann," 28
Dunwich, Mass., 19, 86, 90, 112
Dunwich horror, the, 48, 86–89

Dyer, William, 22, 30, 101–5, 107–8, 136n5

Eckhardt, Jason C., 101
Eddy, Clifford M., 9
Egan, James, 87
Eliot, T. S., 36, 124; *The Waste Land,* 12
Elizabeth, New Jersey, 63
Elliot, Hugh: *Modern Science and Materialism,* 26
Eltdown Shards, the, 137n11
Elton, Basil, 27, 30
Elwood, Frank, 113
Esoteric Order of Dagon, 95
Essex County, Mass., 35, 41
Exham Priory, 51

face-hands, deception motif of, 44
Faig, Kenneth W., Jr., 127n2
Fantasy Fan, the, 61
Faulkner, William, 35, 101
Federal Hill, 120–21; *see also* Providence, R.I.
Fenner, Matt, 54
Finlay, Virgil, 14
Freud, Sigmund, 25, 26, 136n9.10; Freudian aspects (of the fiction), 53, 88, 109
Fulwiler, William, 47
fumbling latch, imagery of, 137n2
Fuseli, Henry, 70, 85

Galpin, Alfred, 118
Gardner, Nahum, 84–85; family of, 85, 90
Gatto, John Taylor, 84, 92
Gedney, 104
ghasts, 79
Ghatanothoa, 116, 138n10.4
ghouls, 43, 69–70, 79
giganticism, motif of, 133n2
Gilman, Walter, 108, 112–13, 117, 119
Goya, Francisco, 70
Great Race, the, 64, 97, 109–10
Greene, Sonia. *See* Sonia Lovecraft
gugs, 79

Haeckel, Ernst: *The Riddle of the Universe*, 40

Halsey, Dr. Allan, 39

Hamilton, Edmond, 137n14

handwriting, motif of, 106, 110, 111, 119, 138n8

Hart, Bertrand K., 13

Hartmann, J. F., 127n8

Haunter of the Dark, the, 121

Hawthorne, Nathaniel, 3, 35, 61–62, 125; *The Ancestral Footstep*, 50; "The Celestial Railroad," 28; "Fragments from the Journal of a Solitary Man," 47; *The House of the Seven Gables*, 62, 132n10; "P's Correspondence," 17; "Young Goodman Brown," 43

Heald, Hazel, 9, 114

Heinrich, Karl, 21

hereditary degeneracy, theme of, 1, 18, 51, 93

Hodgson, William Hope, 20; "The Voice in the Night," 135n5

Home Brew, 19, 39

Houdini, Harry, 9, 24–25

Houtain, George, 39

Howard, Robert E., 11, 39, 49, 90, 125, 130n3, 137n11

Hub Club, the, 7

Hutchinson, Edward, 73

Huxley, Thomas Henry, 130n4

Huysmans, Joris Karl: *A Rebours*, 33

Hyde, Sir Geoffrey, 16

Innsmouth, Mass., 28, 92–96, 112, 117

Iranon, 29–30, 32

Irving, Washington: "The Adventure of the German Student," 48–49

Jackson, Fred, 5

Jackson, Winifred V., 9

James, Henry, 124

James, M. R., 11, 125

Jeffrey, Peter F., 130n20

Jermyn, Arthur, 18

Jermyn, Sir Wade, 18

Johansen, 66

Johnson, Richard H., 114–15

Johnson, Samuel, 17

Jones, Stephen, 114

Joshi, S. T., 2, 10, 13, 26, 30, 78, 97, 115, 124, 129n8, 130n4, 132n9, 133n4, 133n6, 134n13, 135n9, 138n10.5

Jung, Carl, 51; Jungian aspects (of the fiction), 51, 53, 131n3

Kadath, 30, 79

Kafka, Franz, 125

Kalem Club, the, 55

Keats, John, 47

King, Stephen, 54

Kingsport, Mass., 35, 36, 42–44, 63, 77–78

Kipling, Rudyard: "At the End of the Passage," 138n10.4

Klein, T. E. D., 5, 129n11

Kleiner, Rheinhart, 3, 9, 43

K'n-yan, 99–100

Kuranes, 29, 30, 79–80

Lake, 91, 102, 104, 109

Legrasse, Inspector, 67

Leiber, Frank, 65

Lévy, Maurice: *Lovecraft: A Study in the Fantastic*, 124

Lillibridge, Edwin, 120–21

Long, Frank Belknap, 7, 11, 31, 40, 55, 118, 130n18, 137n11; "At the Home of Poe," 130n18; *Dreamer on the Nightside*, 32

LOVECRAFT, HOWARD PHILLIPS: as amateur journalist, 4–7; ancestry of, 1; astrology, opposition to, 4, 5; as astronomer, 4, 25, 84; cats and, 7, 10, 120; as chemist, 5, 84; childhood, 1–5; Christianity, rejection of, 5, 75; decadence and, 31; death of, 11; editors' acceptance of, 55, 105; editors' rejection of, 105, 138n11.6; as epistolarian, 9–11; as ghost-writer, 8–9; juvenilia of, 4, 20, 127n6; marriage of, 7, 55, 63; mother, feelings for, 4, 87, 117; philosophy of, 5; as poet, 12–14; politics of, 8, 10, 97, 102; racism of, 10, 36; reputation of, 123–26; Rome (ancient), love of, 2, 5, 10; the sea and, 20, 129n6; as traveler, 7–8; World War I and, 3, 6

WORKS—BOOKS
Outsider, The, 61, 123, 132n7
Selected Letters, 10
Shadow over Innsmouth, The, 137n12
Something About Cats, 7
To Quebec and the Stars, 8

WORKS—FICTION
"Alchemist, The," 15
"Arthur Jermyn." *See* "Facts Concerning the Late Arthur Jermyn and His Family"
At the Mountains of Madness, 21, 22, 24, 30, 42, 89, 91, 93, 97, 99, *101–5,* 107, 110, 114
"Beast in the Cave, The," 15
"Beyond the Wall of Sleep," 19, *25–26,* 32, 65, 109, 129n9
"Call of Cthulhu, The," 4, 13, 18, 20, 21, *64–68,* 74, 86, 114
Case of Charles Dexter Ward, The, 4, 54, 58, 60, *70–74,* 79, 82, 86, 87, 88, 106, 113, 118, 119, 132n10, 135n2
"Cats of Ulthar, The," *29,* 30
"Celephaïs," *29,* 30, 79, 92, 135n4
"Challenge from Beyond, The" (Moore, Merritt, Howard, Long), 111, 137n11
"Colour Out of Space, The," 22, 49, 82, *83–86,* 89, 135n2
"Cool Air," *59–60,* 68
"Curse of Yig, The," *98,* 101
"Dagon," 15, *20–21,* 67, 93
"Diary of Alonzo Typer, The" (Lumley), 138n8
"Doom That Came to Sarnath, The," 28
Dream-Quest of Unknown Kadath, The, 20, 29, 30, 71, 77, *78–81,* 86, 99, 106, 112, 113, 129n16, 135n4

"Dreams in the Witch House, The," 108, *112–14,* 117, 121
"Dunwich Horror, The," 15, 26, 34, 36, 44, 82–83, *86–89,* 90, 93, 98, 106, 113, 135n1
"Ex Oblivione," 31
"Facts Concerning the Late Arthur Jermyn and His Family," *18,* 50, 65, 128n2
"Festival, The," 23, 35, *42–44,* 77, 92, 133n2
"From Beyond," 26, 63, 109
"Haunter of the Dark, The," 111, 113, *119–22,* 137n2, 138n8
"He," 17, *57–59,* 60
"Herbert West—Reanimator," 19, 33, *39–41,* 44
"History of the *Necronomicon,* A," 131n9
"Horror at Red Hook, The," *56–57,* 58, 59, 60, 68
"Horror in the Museum, The" (Heald), 114
"Hound, The," 19, 23, *32–33,* 50
"Hypnos," *32,* 33, 113
"Imprisoned with the Pharaohs." *See* "Under the Pyramids"
"In the Vault," *53–54,* 68
"In the Walls of Eryx" (Sterling), 9, 28, *110–11*
"Little Glass Bottle, The," 20
"Lurking Fear, The," *19–20,* 21, 43, 133n2
"Medusa's Coil" (Bishop), 33, *101*
"Memory," 31
"Moon-Bog, The," *18–19,* 28
"Mound, The" (Bishop), 9, 91, *97–100,* 101, 103
"Music of Erich Zann, The," 46, *48–50,* 53, 58, 59–60, 68, 122
"Mysterious Ship, The," 20
"Nameless City, The," *23–24,* 25
"Nyarlathotep," 31
"Of Evil Sorceries Done in New England of Daemons in No Humane Shape," 127n10
"Other Gods, The," 30

"Out of the Aeons" (Heald), 9, 20, *114–16*
"Outsider, The," *46–48,* 49, 50, 52, 53, 54
"Pickman's Model," 22, 43, *68–70,* 79, 86, 115
"Picture in the House, The," 17, *37–39,* 40, 41, 42, 44, 48, 59, 65, 83, 84
"Polaris," *27,* 30, 58
"Quest of Iranon, The," 29–30
"Rats in the Walls, The," 18, 48, *50–53,* 60, 64, 95
"Reminiscence of Dr. Samuel Johnson, A," *17,* 136n9
"Shadow Out of Time, The," 24, 48, 64, 97, 101, 105, 106, *107–10,* 111, 129n9, 137n11, 137n9.12, 137n10.2
"Shadow over Innsmouth, The," 18, 19, 21, 22, 34, 83, *92–96,* 97, 105, 108, 121, 137n2
"Shunned House, The," *63–64,* 65, 72, 74, 85, 132n10
"Silver Key, The," *75–77,* 78, 80, 86, 105, 107, 118
"Statement of Randolph Carter, The," *22–23,* 30, 75, 105–6, 131n6
"Strange High House in the Mist, The," 77–78
"Street, The," *36–37,* 38, 48, 57
"Temple, The," *21–22,* 67
"Terrible Old Man, The," *36,* 37, 77
"Thing on the Doorstep, The," 2, 15, 33, 101, 106, 109, 113, *116–19*
"Through the Gates of the Silver Key" (Price), 9, 44, 97, *105–7,* 111, 113, 115
"Tomb, The," 15, *16,* 20, 21, 53, 63
"Transition of Juan Romero, The," 4, *22,* 23
"Tree, The," 28–29
"Under the Pyramids" (Houdini), 9, *24–25,* 64, 133n2
"Unnamable, The," 23, *41–42,* 106, 131n3.7
"What the Moon Brings," *31,* 133n2

"Whisperer in Darkness, The," 4, 19, 44, 82–83, *89–92,* 94, 96, 97, 98, 100, 106, 121, 137n2
"White Ape, The." *See "Facts Concerning the Late Arthur Jermyn and His Family"*
"White Ship, The," 20, *27–28,* 31

WORKS—NONFICTION
"Allowable Rhyme, The," 6
"Cats and Dogs," 7
"Charleston," 8
"Confession of Unfaith, A," 6
"Crime of the Century, The," 6
"Defence Remains Open!, The," 45–46
"Defence Reopens!, The," 45
"Descent to Auvernus, A," 8
Description of the Town of Quebeck, A, 8
"Final Words," 46
"Helene Hoffman Cole—Litterateur," 6
"Heritage or Modernism: Common Sense in Art Forms," 136n1
"Idealism and Materialism—A Reflection," 6
"Metrical Regularity," 6
"Mrs. Miniter—Estimates and Recollections," 6
"Notes on Writing Weird Fiction," 132n11
"Simple Spelling Mania, The," 6
"Some Notes on Interplanetary Fiction," 132n11
"Something About Cats." *See* "Cats and Dogs"
"Some Repetitions on the Times," 136n1
Supernatural Horror in Literature, 35, 45, *61–62,* 78, 125, 132n7, 132n11, 133n2, 133n6
"Unknown City in the Ocean, The," 8
"Vermont—A First Impression," 8
"Winifred Virginia Jackson: A 'Different' Poetess," 6

WORKS—POETRY
"Ancient Track, The," 12
"Despair," 12
"East India Brick Row," 13
"Eidolon, The," 12
Fungi from Yuggoth, 13–14; "Background," 13–14; "Expectancy," 14;
"Nyarlathotep," 31; "The Pigeon-Flyers," 132n2; "The Port," 92;
"Recapture," 13; "The Well," 22
"In a Sequester'd Providence Churchyard Where Once Poe Walk'd," 14
"Members of the Men's Club . . . to Its President, The," 12
"Messenger, The," 13, 137n2
"My Favourite Character," 12
"Nemesis," 12
"Outpost, The," 12–13
"Poem of Ulysses, The," 2
"Providence in 2000 A.D.," 12, 36
Psychopompos, 12
"To Templeton and Mount Monadnock," 12
Waste Paper: A Poem in Profound Insignificance, 12
"Wood, The," 13
"Year Off, A," 12

Lovecraft, Joseph, 1
Lovecraft, Sarah Susan Phillips, 2–4, 87, 117
Lovecraft, Sonia (Greene), 4, 7, 55, 117
Lovecraft, Winfield Scott, 1–2
Lovecraft Mythos. *See* Cthulhu Mythos
Lovecraft Studies, 124
Loveman, Samuel, 7, 23, 55, 118, 131n3.6, 131n5.1

Mabbott, T. O., 16, 19, 61, 123, 132n7
Machen, Arthur, 11, 56, 68, 90, 125; "The Great God Pan," 135n7; "The Novel of the Black Seal," 135n9; "The Novel of the White Powder," 60; *The Terror,* 135n4
Malone, Thomas F., 56–57, 68
Manton, Joel, 41, 131n3.6

Marblehead, Mass., 7, 35, 42, 71; *see also* Kingsport, Mass.
Marceline, 101
Mariconda, Steven J., 2, 33, 127n3, 133n1, 133n3
Marquand, John P., 93, 115
Marsh, Capt. Obed, 36, 94, 96, 121
Marsh, Frank, 101
Mason, Keziah, 112–13
Mather, Cotton: *Magnalia Christi Americana,* 38, 41, 69, 72
Maturin, Charles: *Melmoth the Wanderer,* 133n6
Melville, Herman, 125; *The Confidence Man,* 32; *Mardi,* 28; *Moby-Dick,* 40
Menes, 29
Merritt, A., 137n11
Millay, Edna St. Vincent, 55
Milton, John, 17, 129n7; *Paradise Lost,* 2, 17, 20
Miskatonic University, 40, 84, 101, 104, 105, 112, 117
Moe, Maurice W., 131n3.6
monologue, as narrative technique, 38
moon-beasts, 79
Moore, C. L., 137n11
Moore, Thomas, 24
Morton, James F., 68
Mosig, Dirk W., 28, 47, 131n3, 133n4
Muñoz, Dr. Hector, 60
Murray, Will, 35, 90, 133n4, 135n4, 137n1

Nantucket, Mass., 7, 8
Necronomicon, the, 2, 23, 44, 74, 87, 90, 104, 113, 116, 118, 131n9
Necronomicon Press, 124
Newburyport, Mass., 7, 83, 93, 95, 130n2; *see also* Innsmouth, Mass.
New England, as background, 10, 31, 35, 36, 37, 80–81, 82–83, 84, 93, 130n3, 135n3
New Orleans, La., 7, 66, 97
New York City, 2, 7, 10, 55–60, 76, 77
night-gaunts, 2, 79
Norris, Frank, 36

Norrys, Capt., 52
North End, the, 69, 134n9; see also Boston, Mass.
Nyarlathotep, 80–81, 90, 113

Oklahoma, 97, 98
Old Ones, the, 22, 67, 88, 91, 102–4, 107, 109, 110, 136n5
Old Whateley. See Wizard Whateley
Olney, Thomas, 77–78
O'Neill, Eugene, 34
Orne, Simon, 73
Orton, Vrest, 55
Outer Ones, the, 89–92, 97, 107, 110

Pattee, Fred Lewis, 61
Peaslee, Nathaniel Wingate, 106, 107–10, 111, 137n2
personality, displacement of (in the fiction), 106, 108–9, 117, 129n9
Phillips, Rev. George, 1, 127n2
Phillips, Ward, 106–7, 111
Phillips, Whipple V., 2–4
Pickman, Richard Upton, 68–70, 79, 114
Pierce, Ammi, 84–85
Pigafetta: Regnum Congo, 38
Pluto, discovery of, 4
Pnakotic Manuscripts, the, 30
Poe, Edgar Allan, 2–3, 6, 12, 20, 32, 42, 54, 61–62, 63, 95, 101–2, 118, 124, 125, 130n4; "The City in the Sea," 21; "A Descent into the Maelstrom," 22; "Facts in the Case of M. Valdemar," 60, 61; "The Fall of the House of Usher," 20, 44, 50, 51, 62, 132n7; "Ligeia," 62; "The Man of the Crowd," 57; "The Masque of the Red Death," 46; "Metzengerstein," 61; "MS. Found in a Bottle," 21, 61; The Narrative of Arthur Gordon Pym, 21, 28, 61, 101–3, 136n5; "The Philosophy of Composition," 62; "The Pit and the Pendulum," 24; "Ulalume," 102; "William Wilson," 46
Pope, Alexander, 6
Pound, Ezra, 12

Price, E. Hoffmann, 9, 97, 105–7, 111; "The Lord of Illusion," 105
Price, Robert M., 47, 131n3.9, 131n4.3, 132n4, 133n4, 133n7, 138n8
Providence, R.I., 2, 7, 9, 20, 55, 59, 63, 64, 66–67, 70, 112, 119–22, 134n13
Pth'thya-l'yi, 95

Quabbin Reservoir (Mass.), 84
Quale, Thomas, 129n7
Quebec, Canada, 7–8
Quetzalcoatl, 98

Re-Animator, 41
Recluse, the, 61
Red Hook (Brooklyn), 55
Rhan-Tegoth, 114
Ricci, Angelo, 36
R'lyeh, 67, 90
Roerich, Nicholas, 105
Rogers, George, 114
Rome (ancient), mythology of (in the fiction), 21, 66, 79, 103–4
Romero, Juan, 22

St. Armand, Barton, 12, 31, 50, 51, 70, 72, 73, 125, 134n13
St. John, 33
Salem, Mass., 3, 35, 41, 112; see also Arkham, Mass.
Sawyer, Asaph, 53–54
Schultz, David E., 63, 133n4
Schweitzer, Darrell, 28, 105, 125, 137n14
Scientific American, 4
Scott, Winfield Townley, 12
Shea, J. Vernon, 11, 29, 48, 60, 105, 127n7
Shelley, Mary: Frankenstein, 40
Sherlock Holmes, influence of. See Sir Arthur Conan Doyle
Shining Trapezohedron, the, 111, 121
shoggoths, 42, 95, 104
Silva, Manuel, 36
Slater, Joe, 19, 25–26, 129n9

Smith, C. W., 53
Smith, Clark Ashton, 11, 14, 46, 56, 68, 82, 83, 90, 125, 129n6, 138n10.5
S'ngac, 135n4
Stanley, John H., 12
Starrett, Vincent, 11
Starry Wisdom cult, the, 120–21
Sterling, Kenneth, 9, 136n9.10, 137n14
Stoker, Bram: *Dracula*, 50
Suydam, Robert, 56–57, 60
Swift, Jonathan, 5, 6

Terrible Old Man, the, 36, 37, 38
Theroux, Paul: *The Old Patagonian Express*, 139n10
Thornton, 52
Thurber, 68–70
Thurston, Francis Wayland, 65–68, 69
Tierney, Richard L., 133
Tillinghast, Crawford, 26, 63
Transatlantic Circulator, the, 45–46, 61
Tsath, 91, 99–100, 104
Turner, James, 97
T'yog, 115–16

United Amateur Press Association, 5–6
Updike, John, 125; *The Witches of Eastwick*, 139n8
Upton, Daniel, 2, 15, 116–19

Vaughan, Ralph E., 20
Vermont, 82, 83, 91–92, 107
Vidal, Gore, 126

Waite, Asenath, 117, 119
Wakefield, H. R.: " 'He Cometh and He Passeth By,' " 98
Walpole, Horace, 9, 11; *The Castle of Otranto*, 50, 133n2

Wandrei, Donald, 82
Ward, Charles Dexter, 4, 16, 57, 71–74, 90, 108
Warren, Harley, 22–23, 131n3.6
Waugh, Evelyn, 116, 138n10.4
Weird Tales, 1, 10, 11, 15, 24, 39, 55, 89, 105, 124, 125, 128n2, 129n8
wells, motif of, 22, 57, 70
West, Herbert, 22, 39–40, 60, 72
Whateley, Lavinia, 86–87, 93
Whateley, Wilbur, 44, 86–89, 116
Whateley, Wizard, 26, 36, 86–89
Whipple, Dr. Elihu, 63, 65
Whitman, Sarah Helen, 63
Wilcox, Henry, 66–68
Wilde, Oscar, 31; *The Picture of Dorian Gray*, 46, 72
Willett, Dr. Marinus Bicknell, 4, 73–74, 87, 92, 118, 134n12
Williams, Roger, 29
Wilmarth, Albert N., 19, 90–92, 94, 95, 96, 104, 137n2
Wilson, Colin, 46, 126
Wilson, Edmund, 85, 123, 125, 126; *The Little Blue Light*, 139n11
Winged Ones, the. *See* the Outer Ones
Wise, Rabbi Stephen, 10
Wright, Farnsworth, 18, 89, 105

Xinaián. *See* K'n-yan

Yaddith, 106–7
Y'ha-nthlei, 22, 95, 96
Yog-Sothoth, 36, 74, 87, 90, 93
Yog-Sothoth Cycle of Myth. *See* Cthulhu Mythos
Yuggoth, 89, 90, 92, 121

Zamacona, Pánfilo de, 91, 98–100, 107
Zann, Erich, 49–50
zoogs, 79